ALL'S WELL THAT ENDS WELL

Praise for All's Well That Ends Well

"With *All's Well That Ends Well,* Vivian Kasley offers a variety of strange tales that prick all the right nerves and tickle the funniest of bones. Frightfully disturbing, wickedly humorous, and possessing tremendous heart and wit, this debut collection signals the arrival of a unique and praiseworthy new storyteller!"

—Ronald Kelly, author of *Fear* and *Southern-Fried & Horrified*

ALL'S WELL THAT ENDS WELL

Vivian Kasley

All's Well That Ends Well

Copyright 2025 © Vivan Kasley

This book is a work of fiction. All of the characters, organizations, and events portrayed in these stories are either products of the author's imagination or are used fictitiously. Any resemblance to actual events or locales or persons, living or dead, is entirely coincidental.

All rights reserved. No part of this publication may be reproduced in any form or by any means without the express written permission of the publisher, except in the case of brief excerpts in critical reviews or articles. Nor can this publication be used in any manner for the purposes of AI data scraping and training.

No AI has been involved in the production of this book.

Edited by: Candace Nola

Formatted by: Stephanie Ellis

Cover illustration by: Ruth Anna Evans

First Edition: October 2025

ISBN (paperback): 978-1-963355-37-6

ISBN (ebook): 978-1-963355-36-9

Library of Congress Control Number:

BRIGIDS GATE PRESS
Overland Park, Kansas
www.brigidsgatepress.com
Printed in the United States of America

To Chip, who lights almost every fire that burns under my ass.

CONTENT WARNINGS

Boom Chicka Boom - violence, imprisonment, threats of torture

Canned Tuna - kidnapping, emotional abuse/manipulation

Dead Deception - graphic sex, violence

Heart-Shaped Box - cancer

Maternal Drive - hit and run, child injury/death

Roly-Poly - body dysmorphia, fat-shaming

Room For Change - voyeurism

Out of Her Gourd - infertility

Christmas Cookies - child abuse, domestic violence

Lake Sludge - child death

CONTENTS

Foreword ... 1

Boom Chicka Boom ... 3

Canned Tuna ... 15

Dead Deception ... 27

Heart-Shaped Box ... 39

Skin Tags ... 55

Catch and Release ... 65

Maternal Drive ... 79

Raggamuffin ... 89

Roly-Poly ... 99

Room For Change ... 111

Squid's Ink ... 123

Don't Give It Away ... 135

Porch Pirate ... 145

Out of Her Gourd ... 153

Christmas Cookies ... 161

Lake Sludge ... 173

Wild, Wild, West ... 179

All's Well That Ends Well ... 189

Acknowledgements ... 195

About the Author ... 197

More From Brigids Gate Press ... 199

FOREWORD

By Catherine McCarthy

We all have that one friend, right? The kind of friend with a heart of gold and the mind of a sewer. The kind of friend who makes you roar with laughter at their outrageous humor whilst at the same time you cannot help but shake your head and clench your toes—hard. That friend, for me, is Vivian Kasley.

We met on X (Twitter) a few years back, and hit it off despite the fact that our writing styles are quite different and our personalities even more so. I say that, but the fact is we also agree on an awful lot in our private conversations, where we frequently attempt to put the world to rights.

She champions my efforts and wins wholeheartedly, as I do hers. We cheer one another on with words of encouragement and simply by being a listening voice, and when either of us is down we know without reservation that a listening ear is only a few sentences away, even though the Atlantic Ocean separates us.

Over the past few years, Vivian has celebrated and supported my writing, and it is now my great pleasure to return the favor.

All's Well That Ends Well, is her debut collection, but she's no rookie when it comes to being published. As you will discover, several tales included within have been previously published by well-established markets, and those are not the sum of her successes. Trust me, there's more on the way.

Within these pages you will find tales of revenge and misfortune. Tragic tales of grief and longing, tales that will hold you captive as you yearn to discover the outcome, and with an imagination like Vivian Kasley's you can never be certain things will turn out the way you imagined they might.

The collection has a strong 1980s vibe with many of the stories feeling cinematic. One in particular, "Skin Tags," a grossly nauseating body horror tale, reminded me of those mad horror movies from the 1950s, even though it's not set in that era. It's just a vibe, if you know what I mean.

Two aspects stood out above all others for me as I read through the stories. One—the way in which Vivian's personality and voice shines throughout the whole collection. The no-holds-barred attitude, oozing with dark humor she is known for, and two—the depth of characterization, particularly when it comes to dialogue, is admirable. I was right there inside the heads of her characters. In the murk of "Lake Sludge" and the tattoo parlor of "Squid's Ink," the chaotic home of young Gunner in "Christmas Cookies," and the sleazy motel, not dissimilar to the one featured in Robert Bloch's *Psycho* in the story "Room For Change." And that is because she makes it easy for readers to enter the mindset of her characters, something not all writers manage to achieve.

I probably shouldn't share my favorite stories with you, but what the hell. I'm sure you'll discover your own, but "Catch and Release" (as published in *The Jewish Book of Horror*), "Roly-Poly," "Squid's Ink" and "Porch Pirate" are right up there, along with the titular tale, *"All's Well That Ends Well"* which features an anthropomorphic fridge no less, and is darkly comedic, something she definitely has a talent for.

As I said earlier, I'm sure you will have your own favorites.

Before I end, I would like to give a shout-out to cover artist Ruth Anna Evans for doing such a grand job of the artwork.

So there we have it. I shall raise a glass in celebration on publication day and hope that those who pick up this volume of tales will enjoy the hilarity and grossness between these pages as much as I did.

Cheers, my good friend! I wish you every success!

Catherine McCarthy
July 2025

BOOM CHICKA BOOM

The doors were locked. *You can never be too careful nowadays*, Hal Egerton thought. *You never know what kind of looney tunes are lurking around.* He checked one more time before he climbed the stairs and lay back in his bed. The blanket was pulled up to his chest and the pillow was fluffed. Florida's first seasonal weather had arrived. He was glad he'd cracked open the window to let in the crisp night air. His eyelids grew heavy as he watched the yellow curtains his wife picked out whirl in the breeze. The cadence of the crickets and cicadas soothed Hal. Soon he drifted to sleep. His eyes fluttered and his fingers twitched as he began to dream.

He was on his old boat, staring out at the calm turquoise water of the Gulf. His fingers curled around a tumbler of good bourbon in one hand and around a fishing pole in the other. He'd just thrown out his line when thunder began to roar. It was loud enough to vibrate the boat. Another loud crack caused the ice cubes in his drink to clink against the glass. Hal looked at the sky in confusion. The weather had been beautiful only moments before. Black clouds mushroomed above him and the roar continued to get louder and louder until it fused with his bones.

Hal opened his eyes and stared into the abyss of his bedroom. The glass in the windows rattled along with the walls. He sprang out of bed and looked out the curtains. A small red Honda rolled down the street and halted at the stop sign. He saw two people in the front seat bouncing around, smoke billowing out of the car's cracked windows. Hal's blood boiled and his pulse pounded in rhythm with the bass emanating from the car's speakers.

"Can't they go down another damn street?" he fumed. The car eventually turned the corner, but he could still hear it long afterward.

The Honda had been coming down the street for the past month, unapologetically disturbing Hal's slumber. The street was occupied by himself and two other couples, but they hadn't made it down from Ohio yet. Hal glanced at the clock.

"Two thirty in the goddamn morning. The nerve," he grumbled, ambling to the bathroom and forcing a pee. Then he tried to settle back into sleep, but his anger kept him awake far longer than he'd hoped.

It was after seven when Hal opened his eyes again. The early morning sun slid across the ceiling and baked his face. Groggy and still seething, he left his bed to go make coffee and grab the newspaper. While the coffee brewed, he slipped on his Crocs and walked outside. The chatter of squirrels greeted him as he went down the driveway. Tendrils of Spanish moss hung from the oak trees caressing the top of his balding head. Hal curled his lip in disgust when he noticed the soda bottles and ant-infested Wendy's bag that'd been flung into his yard, his peaceful oasis.

"Something's gotta be done," he muttered. Acorns popped under his feet as he walked back inside and pondered what that something was.

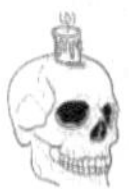

He waited for the new moon, when he knew the street would be its darkest. That morning, Hal began building a swing for the front deck. He hammered away in the driveway, smiling all the while.

Candy had always wanted him to build a swing, but he never got around to it. *She wanted a lot of fucking things.* Hal finished right before the sun went down, and he stood back and admired his handiwork. All it needed was some paint. "Not bad for a sixty-nine-year-old man," he said, then he went inside to clean up.

After dinner, Hal made a pot of coffee. He thought of Candy again and grimaced. *What would she'd've thought of my little idea? Oh, she'd probably tell me I was nuts, and to leave well enough alone. That's not an option though, honey pie, is it? At least I finally made your swing, and I also made a little something extra.* Three cups of black coffee later, Hal walked outside. It was well after nine o'clock and plenty dark. He grabbed the homemade contraption from underneath the swing and set it in the road in front of his house. He hoped no one else would run over it, but he was willing to take that chance.

With that done, he moved his car out of the garage and parked it in the driveway. Then he walked back out to the road one more time to inspect the placement of the wicked contraption. Earlier, while making the swing, he'd painted a fence post black and adhered several roofing nails onto it with Gorilla Glue. Hal grinned like the Grinch as he lit a cigar. He stared up at an owl in the tree and blew smoke rings. "This might be a night to celebrate, Mr. Owl. Revenge is sweet, after all."

Back inside, Hal settled into his La-Z-Boy and flipped mindlessly through the channels on the television. He hadn't meant to fall asleep, and it was after midnight when his eyes flung open. The sound of bass filled his living room and shook the pictures on the walls. He switched off the television and waited. After five minutes, he peered out the window and saw the red Honda parked on the road in front of his house. The music had been turned down and two men were standing outside of the car waving their hands around.

"Showtime," Hal said.

He slipped on his Crocs, turned the outside light on, and opened the front door. Holding his lower back, he shuffled down the driveway towards the two young men. One of them had their phone out, and the other—the driver, he presumed—was bent down by the back tires, cussing up a storm.

"Son of a bitch! Fucking, fuck! I just got these tires put on!"

"Looks like it messed your tires up real good, bro," the other man said.

"Are you fucking serious?" The driver stood up and used his phone's light to look over the rest of his tires. "How the hell'd this shit even happen? This's some straight up bullshit right here!" The driver wheeled around and saw Hal.

"There a problem?" Hal called out.

"Yeah, there's a problem! Someone put this fucking—whatever this thing is—in the road and it fucked up my tires! You know anything 'bout that, old man?"

"I … I don't know. Let me think? I was building a swing earlier today … I guess I maybe might've lost a post." Hal shrugged.

"Are you serious right now, old man? You think this shit's funny?"

"I'm truly sorry. Let me call someone. I'll pay for any damage I may've caused. Here, c'mon in and I'll call—"

"I got a fucking phone, numb nuts. And damn right you'll pay. I'll call my homie and then you're gonna give me cash."

"Ivan, bro, should we call the cops?"

"Hell no! I got shit in the car, idiot. I'm gonna call Pelly. His dad's got a huge-ass truck with a hitch."

"I can't give you cash unless I know how much it'll cost," Hal interrupted.

"'Scuse me? Did you fucking say something, old man?"

"I said, I won't give you any money unless I know how much it'll cost."

"Ivan, let's just call Pelly."

"Shut the fuck up, Marsh! This old-ass son of a bitch right here is gonna pay—look at my fucking tires! I think he did this shit on purpose—shit's painted black and everything!" Ivan walked toward Hal, but before he could reach him, Hal stood up straight and pulled a pistol from his pajama pants.

"That's right, numb nuts. Back up. I need you to throw your keys and phones my way and sit the hell down." Hal motioned toward the grass.

"Are you kiddin' me? You gonna shoot us, old man? For real?" Ivan chuckled, then shook his head and held his phone up to his ear.

"You make one more move and I'll blow your fucking brains out. Put your phone down, now. If you try and run, I'll shoot you in the back." Hal aimed the gun and cocked the hammer.

"Ivan, give it to him, bro!" Marsh cried, throwing his own phone over before he sat down.

Ivan gave up his phone and keys and cursed as he sat in the grass beside Marsh. Hal kept the gun trained on both men as he picked up their phones and keys, then he walked over to their car and turned it off. "That's better. Peace and quiet is nice, isn't it?" Hal asked.

A cold rain began falling, so Hal motioned for them to stand, directing them toward the house. He pushed the gun into the back of them and said, "Move faster. If I get wet in this cold weather, I could get sick. C'mon, move your asses inside. That's it."

Hal led the men into the garage and told them to sit. He pulled a bottle of whiskey down from a shelf and offered it to them. They both shook their heads.

"Take a fucking pull, ding dongs. A man offers you a drink, you take it," Hal muttered. "Here, I'll put some in a couple of glasses since you two ninnies can't slug it straight from the bottle like real men."

Ivan and Marsh took the glasses with shaky hands but were reluctant to take a sip. Hal pointed the gun and told them to drink.

"Why do you want us to drink this, old man? Gonna poison us?" Ivan asked.

Hal harrumphed. "Poison? What for? Just offering up a friendly drink to get your insides warm. It's chilly out there."

Ivan and Marsh both took a sip and winced as the alcohol bit the back of their throats.

Hal laughed, grabbed himself a chair, and sat down in front of them. "See? Good, isn't it? I just thought it'd be nice to have a drink before I teach you both a little lesson."

Ivan ground his teeth and sneered, then he stared up at a giant swordfish that hung on the wall. He couldn't take his eyes off it.

"You like him? Yeah, he was a biggun! Took me a good while to reel him in. Caught him with my best friend, Drew. What I mean is, I used Ol' Drew as bait. Worked like a charm too. You see, him and Candy—Candy was my wife—were diddling each other. I found out and took matters into my own hands."

"Pfft, bullshit, old man." Ivan rolled his eyes.

Hal sniggered, and darkness crept into his eyes. "No bullshit here, son. I think I still got a few of Drew's mummified fingers and toes round here somewheres if you'd like to see 'em—"

"I'm good, thanks." Ivan's face paled.

"Yeah, I took the no-good cocksucker out on my boat, forced him to strip down to his birthday suit, and then carved chunk after chunk outta him as I told him the tale of how I found out about the two of 'em. Ha! He cried like a molly in heat each time the blade neared. Can't count how many gobs of his pale doughy flesh I popped onto my hook as the sun baked his pussy-thieving blood to the deck of my boat. Caught a damn near record number of fish that day! Guess they like people meat better than rotten squid! Who knew?"

Hal slapped his knee and cackled when both men gagged.

"You should've seen Drew's face when I cut off his pecker though—it hung from my hook like a grub worm! I'll tell you what, no sooner had I cast that pathetic purple-headed grub out than I felt the tug of that monster up there. Ol' Drew was passed out by the time I reeled that sucker in, but he sure woke up as I was dragging what was left of him over the edge of the boat. You could say I chummed the water with my chum. Ha! Anyhow, Candy cooked some of the fish I brought home that evening with some lemon, butter, and those salty lil' green things … capers, I think they're called. Fantastic! She puked for a week after I told her how I'd caught the fish. But that swordfish, he was too pretty to eat, so I had him stuffed."

"Jesus Christ, bro," Marsh whined.

"You're a sick old fuck," Ivan said, tears welling in his eyes.

"Maybe. Anyway, Candy never did get over it. She drank rotgut whiskey all day and night. Ended up driving herself right over a bridge into the same body of water where her dickless beloved ended up. Had to sell my fishing boat to give her a proper send-off. I sure do miss her—my boat, that is. Hell, I miss Candy sometimes too, but mostly, I get horrible agita whenever I think of what they did behind my back. Never did forgive her, ah, but that's yesterday's news. I got new fish to fry." Hal winked and pointed at the two men as their eyes closed and their heads slumped over.

Ivan and Marsh were woken up by loud banging. They were tied to their chairs and could barely move.

Hal banged the lid of a metal pot next to their heads and shouted, "Wakey, wakey! You've been out for a couple hours. Wasn't sure how long it'd be, but looks like I dosed it right. I haven't used Rufinol since, well, since Drew. Wasn't even sure it'd still work after all these years. You two are trussed up like two Thanksgiving turkeys! Now, for the real fun. You ready?"

"Please, what do you want from us, old man?" Ivan wiggled in his chair.

"First, stop calling me 'old man.' Second, I want you to know how it feels."

"How what feels?" Ivan choked.

"This." Hal banged the pot and lid near their ears again. Then he dropped those and grabbed a leaf blower and turned it on. He swung it around their heads and blew it in their faces. He danced around the garage with it for a while before he turned it off. Then he picked up a chainsaw and began to tug on it.

"Please, mister, what'd we do? I just wanna go home! Please!" Marsh begged.

"Old ma—look, sir, whatever we did, we're sorry. Just let us go. My car's on the road. Someone'll notice eventually," Ivan said.

"Not many cars come down this road at night, but you're right. Let me go move it. But before I do …" Hal grabbed duct tape and placed it over their mouths. It wasn't easy moving the car with the post still stuck in the wheel, but he managed and got the car into the end of the driveway. When he returned, both men had fallen over and struggled to free themselves.

"Oh, look at you Silly Sallys!" Hal tipped them upright and waved his finger at them. "Technically, no one'll probably hear us, but still can't be too careful." He ripped the tape from their mouths and they cried out in pain.

"I bought this house over twenty years ago for the seclusion and peace and quiet. You spoiled that with your boom chicka boom at all hours of the night! I've gotta have my eight hours of sleep or else I can't function. I can get reeeeally crabby. Why, there's no telling what a man wouldn't do to get some motherfucking sleep!"

"We're sorry, mister! Right, Ivan? We won't come down this road anymore. We swear!"

"I only started coming down here because it's a shortcut to my girl's house. I won't no more! Please!" Ivan squirmed.

"I've lost loads of sleep, thanks to you. How many other people do you disturb? You drive around with that shit music in your car and all of a sudden this bothers you?" Hal tugged on the chainsaw again until it rumbled to life.

Both men howled as Hal held the running chainsaw by their heads, getting as close as he could to their ears without cutting them off. He shimmied between them, back and forth. When he tired, he turned the chainsaw off, then went to a utility cabinet and pulled out a bullhorn. Hal shook his head and sighed. "My wife used to use this. Yeah, Candy used to protest one thing or other years ago. Annoying habit of hers. Anyway, hopefully it still works!"

Hal turned it on, and a siren blared. "Well, would you look at that?" He put it up to Ivan's ear and began singing, then he switched to Marsh and did the same. Both men began to cry.

Hal mocked them. "Aw, poor babies! Is this hurting your wittle ears? Ooooh, do your ears hang low, do they wobble to and fro? Can you tie 'em in a knot, can you tie 'em in a bow? Can you throw 'em over your shoulders like a continental soldier? Do your ears hang looow!"

Marsh turned his head and threw up, and Ivan began to dry heave. Hal put down the bullhorn and grabbed some mulch. He covered the vomit, then scooted their chairs closer together. "Don't you go doing that again! Jesus, what'd you all eat? Cat turds covered in dumpster juice? It's awful!" Hal grimaced and pulled his pistol back out. "While I got you all here, someone's been throwing their trash from their car into my yard. You two road apples know anything 'bout that?"

"Please, sir! I'll never, ever, come down here again!" Ivan cried.

"Damn right you won't," Hal growled. Then he put two orange earplugs in and aimed the pistol.

"No! Sir, please! I have a little girl on the way," Ivan said.

"I can't die! I'm only nineteen years old and a virgin! It's not even my car ... it's his car!" Marsh nodded toward Ivan.

"What the fuck, Marsh? You fucking asshole!" Ivan strained against his binds.

Hal pointed to his ears, shook his head, and shrugged. Then he fired several shots. The bullets went through the space between the men and into several bags of mulch piled behind them. Hal choked on his laughter as the two young men peeled open their eyes. Both had red faces and snot dripped from their noses. A puddle had formed under Ivan's chair.

"Oh, look, you've gone and wet yourself." Hal snickered.

Neither of the men could hear Hal over the buzzing and ringing in their ears. Their heads felt like they might explode. They watched Hal laugh maniacally as he put the gun back into his waistband. When he lit the firecrackers in a pot beside them, they heard only the faintest of pops.

Hal sat down after the last firecracker screeched and popped. "Can you boys hear anything yet?"

When the men didn't answer, Hal got up and went inside the house. He returned with a notepad, wrote his question down, then held it up in front of them. Both men shook their heads. Hal wrote down that they'd probably regain some hearing, but it'd take a while. Then he went back inside and returned with a glass of water. He tipped the glass, and the men held their heads up like baby birds and let him pour some in. Hal asked again if they could hear.

"A little," Ivan croaked.

"I can barely hear myself talk," Marsh said.

Hal sat back down and scooted his chair close enough that his knees touched theirs. He pulled free a large hunting knife from what seemed like out of thin air and rested the tip on Ivan's fingers. The blade was dirtied by what looked like dried blood. He sliced into one of Ivan's fingers just enough to watch the young man squirm.

"Please … please stop," Ivan whispered.

"Listen carefully," Hal said, the pressure of the knife's blade still on Ivan's finger. "I'm gonna call a tow truck when it gets light, tell 'em you ran over something in the road. You're not going to breathe a word of this. I know a lot of people and a lot of people know me. It'd be a grave mistake, crossing me. Poor Mr. Egerton, the widowed, decorated Vietnam War vet. He was just defending his home against the two knuckleheads that tried to rob him when he offered to help with their car. You get my drift?"

Ivan and Marsh nodded.

"I'm no fool, boys. I've covered my bases, always do. You need to get your act together. Don't ever come down my street again with that shit. It's inconsiderate! And don't even think about coming back with any of your friends, because I got something for them too. I'm a cavalry all on my own."

Hal moved the two men further apart, checked their restraints for any weaknesses, and covered their mouths with more tape. Satisfied, he left them, climbed the stairs to his bedroom, and collapsed onto his bed, where he slept until the sunlight woke him. He brushed his teeth and put on some fresh clothes, then called for a tow truck. Before opening the door to the garage, Hal took a breath and stepped inside.

Both Ivan and Marsh had fallen asleep and were breathing noisily from their noses. Hal hollered their names, but they didn't stir. He walked over to them and ripped the tape from their mouths. Then he untied their hands and feet. The men stood up and wobbled when they tried to walk.

Hal shouted, "Take it easy. You got vertigo. Hopefully that goes away, but I can't guarantee it. Here's your keys. I called a guy I know with a tow truck, and he's on the way. I also wrote a check for the cost of the tow, but as far as your tires, you're on your own. Oh, and here's your phones. I won't hear from you again, will I?"

Both men shook their heads and squinted as the garage door began to go up. They staggered into the driveway and leaned against their hobbled car. Hal followed, making sure to push the button to close the door behind them. He waited until the truck arrived, handed the driver the check, and laughed with him as he explained what'd happened. He turned as the car was being attached.

"Well, this's it, boys. Oh, and I took the liberty of picking up some of your trash earlier. I put it in your car. Just remember what I said."

The men sulked but said nothing as they got into the tow truck. They pretended not to see Hal when he waved. An SUV pulled in next door just as the tow truck backed out of the driveway and a couple got out and rushed over to Hal.

"Everything alright, Hal?" they asked.

"Oh, Bea and Phil, you're back. How wonderful! Yeah, everything's fine. Just some young men that broke down. Looks like they ran over something in the road. I called my buddy to come out and tow their car. Even paid for it."

"Oh, goodness! Well, thank the good Lord that you were there to help. Helluva guy, you are!" Phil clapped Hal on the back. "Ain't he a helluva guy, Bea?"

"The best! Say, Hal, you wanna come over later for some cocktails, maybe play some cards? We need to catch up on everything we missed over the summer," Bea said.

"Trust me, you haven't missed much; you both know how quiet our street is. Also, no cards for me this time around. I didn't get much sleep last night, but maybe tomorrow. Something tells me I'll sleep just fine tonight." Hal winked and waved again at the tow truck halted at the stop sign. It honked three times before turning the corner, dragging the little red Honda behind it.

CANNED TUNA

Pearl was wheeled in on a pushcart dolly, same as always. He made a show of lifting her and then lowering her, tail first, into the heavily chlorinated water. His dark eyes never left hers, even as he accepted a glass of sweet tea and a plate of food. Pearl forced a smile and splayed her golden hair over her bronze shoulders. She pretended to enjoy the delighted squeals of the children as she flapped her shimmering tail in the water, soaking the faces of those who stood nearby. The adults chided the kids, telling them not to crowd her and to give everyone a turn to chat and take photos. For months, Pearl had answered the same questions over and over, but her eyes always begged for someone to rescue her.

It happened early on a Sunday morning. Pearl had been swimming in brackish water, a foolish act, but she had a penchant for the fiddler crabs and other marine life that hung out in the area. She was always careful to check for humans. To be seen was forbidden and could result in complications she didn't even want to ponder. Her belly was nearly full when she heard a man's voice call out to her.

Pearl turned to look, a mistake she wished she hadn't made. Her heart nearly stopped, and she almost dove under—except she didn't. The man had agreeable features for a human, with dark hair and eyes. Where he had come from or why he was there, she wasn't sure. She scanned further and spotted something long, thin, and yellow not far behind him.

"That's my kayak," the man said. "I dropped my phone in the water by accident."

Pearl stared at him, her mouth quivering. For some reason she couldn't move. Her tail was anchored, her limbs numb.

"Hey, it's alright. I'm not here to bother you. I was checking out the mangroves earlier and found this wide-open spot. You swim out here a lot? And topless? That's brazen." He chuckled. "Name's Grant." He lifted his hand from the water and stretched it toward her.

There was no way she was touching his hand, or telling him her name.

"Well, I'll leave ya to it. Guess I'll need to get a new phone. Doubt I'd find it anyhow."

The man swam away from her and headed back to his kayak. Pearl dove under the water, where she immediately saw the contraption he must've dropped and sped toward it. She picked it up. For some reason she felt the urge to return it to him. He didn't know she was what she was. He'd only seen her top half that she could tell. She raced toward the yellow vessel and watched from under water as the man struggled to get into it.

Pearl tapped the side of the kayak to get the man's attention, then reached out to give him what he called his phone. It was then she realized she'd flapped her tail and that it was visible. He smiled, showing all of his teeth, thanked her, and before she could blink, something came down onto her head so hard her ears rang. She was disoriented and couldn't see through the blood and white dots crowding in front of her eyes. The man got back into the water and she felt him lift her. If she could've struggled, she would've, but everything went as dark as the bottom of the sea.

She woke up in water, but it was not the sea. Her head throbbed, and she wondered why, but then she remembered. The man named Grant was sitting close by, watching her. Pearl shot up, sloshing water over the edge of the container he'd put her in. She tried to climb out and emitted an earsplitting noise when he grabbed her. He was smothering her mouth with his hand, which Pearl bit into. He rolled his hand into her bite until she was forced to let go, and then he threatened to shut her up the hard way if she didn't calm down. Pearl might not have spoken his language, but she understood enough about humans to know what he was getting at. Grant wiped his wounded hand on his shirt, sat back down, and began explaining where she was and what he intended to do with her.

"You're at my house, in my bathtub. Now, I know it's not very comfortable, but I got ideas for something that might be a better fit. For now, though, the bathtub'll have to do. Listen, I didn't bring you here to hurt or violate you. I just got laid off from my accounting job, and I brought you here with the hope you'd help make me some money. You see, we humans need money the way you need water. You follow? Can you speak English?"

Pearl didn't understand how to form the words he hoped she could. She shook her head and listened as he continued.

"You really are unbelievable. I wouldn't have thought in my wildest dreams that you existed. But seeing is believing! I didn't know what my first plan of action would be, you know, should I turn you in and maybe get some sort of reward? Should I sell you to some sort of weirdo collector on the black market? But who knows if any of that'd really be to my benefit? Plus, if everyone finds out what you really are, then they might try and find more of you and that would put a damper on my plans—I want you all for myself. Anyway, here's what I was thinking. You and me, we're gonna do kid's parties!"

Pearl quit looking directly at him and stared instead at the pattern of swirls on the tiled wall.

"Not right away, of course. I'll have to teach you some English and basic human interactions. We'll also have to find something for you to wear over those perky breasts of yours, but I think this could really work. Sure, you already got chicks that dress up like mermaids, but I got a real one! They won't know that, but just think of how word'll spread—about our attention to detail and all that! It's okay if you're kinda shy. It'll add to the charm."

Grant reached out to brush Pearl's cheek, and she flinched. He laughed at her reaction and told her she'd get used to things and would dislike him less when she understood he wasn't there to hurt her. Pearl hadn't cried since she was small, but she couldn't stop herself. Sadness overwhelmed her. Her body trembled all the way to her tail. She'd made a grave mistake; this was all her fault. The worst part was, no one would look for her because they couldn't and also, they wouldn't worry because they'd think she had decided to travel the vast ocean in search of something new. It happened often amongst their kind.

"Can you sing?" Grant asked. "If you could sing, that'd really be a bonus. I'm not great at it, but here, let me try." Grant started to sing, then he stopped and pointed at Pearl.

Pearl refused to acknowledge his request. She turned away from him and closed her eyes, hoping that maybe this was all a bad dream that she'd wake up from. But it wasn't, and she knew that.

"Your golden locks and emerald eyes are beautiful. And that tail of yours is remarkable! The colors in it are what I'd call metallic mint green or maybe it's more of a teal? Then there're shimmers of pink and purple—oh, man, this's gonna be great! I mean, you're a real live freakin' mermaid. I've hit the jackpot! I figure you eat, what, shrimp? Fish or squid maybe? We'll get it all squared away, just you watch. Oh, and don't think about trying to flop out of the tub again or trying to open the door. I've seen to that. Anyhow, you'd have to drag yourself at least fifteen miles before you found any suitable water. The road would be rough on your tail, and shoot, someone would see you and they wouldn't treat you the way I'm gonna treat you, believe me. Who knows what they'd do?"

Grant left the bathroom and shut the door behind him. Pearl thought about screaming again or attempting escape, but she didn't know how far water was and she was afraid. Besides, who'd help her? Wouldn't another human also hurt her or maybe do something worse? Humans were not to be trusted. Merpeople had always stressed that. Never engage with them, not ever. Though they had similar features up top, their differences extended far beyond legs and tails. They were not cut from the same cloth.

Long ago they'd coexisted with humans and even helped one another, but over time, humans became consumed by their own traits, traits which merpeople did not possess—vanity, arrogance, hate, jealousy, greed, and, worst of all, violence—and when that happened, the merpeople vowed to never interact with them again. Pearl hoped that the man wouldn't tell anyone about her true identity and spawn a hunt. They'd avoided humans for hundreds of years until her mistake, and it was a mistake she hoped would end with her.

Pearl wasn't sure how many days she'd spent in the man's bathtub being fed frozen shrimp and fish, but after what seemed an eternity, he burst through the door one afternoon and told her he was moving her to her new digs. He hummed as he carried her to another container filled with water. It was larger than the bathtub and soft on the sides. He called it a kiddie pool. Biggest one he could find, he'd said. Pearl stretched her limbs and flapped her tail about, something she hadn't really been able to do in the tub. Still, she didn't smile.

"Golly! Can I get a thank you, at least? I even put a load of aquarium salt in there—which wasn't cheap! Here I am putting a pool in my guest room and you've got nothing to say? I can put you back in the tub if you want?" He reached toward her, and she moved away and shook her head. "So, you like the pool?"

Pearl nodded.

"Good. Now I can teach you what you'll need to know to start our business. Oh, and hey"—he pointed to a box on the wall—"we can watch TV together. Won't that be fun? You'll pick up on speech then."

It wasn't long before she learned how to sound out human words. She'd spoken a few out loud when Grant wasn't around. Her voice was high-pitched and warbly, similar to when she spoke underwater. Impatient with her lack of speech, Grant began to withhold food from her. He'd ask if she could repeat after him as he wiggled an oily sardine above her, lowering it only if she spoke. If she smiled, he gave extra. Soon, she was able to hold short conversations, and he told her how proud he was of her progress. She never did tell him her name, but he decided he'd call her Gemma. Pearl downplayed her comprehension and smiled at him, but inside she was dying.

Grant bought Pearl an array of bikini tops and made her wear them. He combed her hair as he discussed his plans about what they'd be doing, and she pretended to be excited because she knew it pleased him. He told her he knew she had no use for money, but that he could buy her all the seafood she could ever dream of and that he'd even have a saltwater pool put in so that she'd be able to swim again. He told her not to worry, that he'd make sure there was a privacy fence, this way no one would see her. When he kissed the back of her neck, Pearl made a noise that could've broken glass.

"Hell, c'mon now, Gemma! I've been feeding you, brushing your hair, and scooping your rancid fish shit from the pool! It was just a kiss, a kiss to show that you mean everything to me. I just wanted to show affection. Don't tell me we're going back to square one?"

Pearl moved away from him. "N-n-no k-kiss," she stammered.

A storm cloud seemed to form in Grant's eyes. He snarled, threw the comb he'd been brushing her hair with into the water, then stood up. "Fine. If that's the way you want it. No goddamn kiss … for now, anyway." Then he left the room and slammed the door behind him. He didn't feed her that night or the three nights after that.

The next couple of weeks, Grant spent hours going over his plan again. He showed her the flyers he'd made, and the business cards he had printed. There was a pushcart he bought that he said he'd wheel her in on to give it a realistic effect. He said carrying her everywhere might not go over as well. Pearl nodded in agreement to everything he said.

He told her, "All you have to do is smile, answer yes or no, and hold very brief conversations. I know singing is off the table with that pitch of yours, but maybe you could do that pretty humming you do. That's right, I've heard you when you don't think I'm listening. And don't worry, I'll always be close by, so no one'll hurt you."

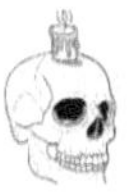

When their first party was booked, Grant was a bag of nerves. He made Pearl answer questions he felt kids and adults might ask. He ran through them multiple times.

"What's your tail made of?" he asked.

"S-s-silicone," Pearl answered.

"Where'd you get it from?"

"We had it s-s-specially made."

"Work on your s's Gemma, you're a mermaid, not a damn snake!"

"S-sorry."

"It's fine, just work on it. Where was I? Oh yeah. Is that your real hair?"

"Yes."

"Can I touch your tail?"

"Yes, but please be gentle and don't pull on it."

"Do you live in the ocean?"

Pearl looked down and didn't answer.

"Gemma? Do you live in the ocean?" Grant blew air from his nose in frustration. "You have to answer. Kids'll ask that!"

Pearl looked at him. "I used to, but now I live in my very own special pool," she said.

"Do you miss the ocean?"

"No," she lied.

"Good, you did good. Now, come closer, my love, and let me comb your hair. And will you hum for me? Hum me the song you'll hum at the party."

As Grant combed her hair, Pearl hummed a tune so beautiful you'd never know her soul was withering.

The first gig went well. Pearl was nervous, but she answered everyone's questions as best she could and hummed while the children splashed around her. Word spread quickly, and soon Grant was busy with bookings. Pearl's throat grew raw from all the talking and humming and the pool water burned and chapped her delicate skin and tail, but Grant made sure to never book too many parties in a row. *In order to give you a break*, he'd said. Everyone complimented her and told her how authentic she looked and Pearl thanked them. If they asked how she learned to swim with such a massive tail, she'd smile and shrug, aware that her captor was never too far away.

Grant was over the moon. He fed Pearl lobster and crab and he bought jeweled side combs for her hair. The pool, he promised, would come soon, as long as she continued to perform as well as she was. Pearl couldn't help but get caught up in his giddy enthusiasm, and she allowed herself to try and feel it too. When he kissed her neck again, she let him and this time she didn't make a sound. It wasn't that she forgot about where she was or what she was, but she didn't know what else to do. If she couldn't be who she really was, then she'd learn to adapt until she figured out a way to do so.

They had a party coming up that for some reason Grant was nervous about. He kept pacing as he spoke about it, running his hands through his hair and grinding his teeth. He told Pearl she had to be extra sweet and smiley to everyone. Pearl wondered what the fuss was all about, so she asked.

"It's just … I happen to know this couple personally and want them to be impressed."

"How do you know them?" Pearl asked.

"Don't get upset, but I used to be engaged to the mother of the little boy whose birthday it is." Grant searched Pearl's stoic face for a reaction.

"Engaged?" Pearl tilted her head.

"It means a promise to get married, become husband and wife, and to be together forever until death do you part … except Jill broke it off and I still don't know why. She said I was too controlling.

I always thought I was generous—too generous—but controlling? Do you think I'm controlling, Gemma?"

"No," Pearl told him.

"Yeah, well, we'll show her. She was rather nosy about how and why I chose to go into the children's entertainment business. I told her it was your idea, and that I was bored with accounting. Can you believe she ate it up? Ha! Oh, and I hope you don't mind, but I told her we're engaged. She seemed happy for me, but I could sense jealousy. And she should be jealous. She married a real asshole. And you're a knockout, even with that tail of yours. Jill's gonna flip!"

The morning of the party, Grant placed the jeweled side combs in Pearl's hair, and painted her lips with a pink sparkly gloss. He gave her a green bikini top to wear and told her how beautiful she looked. Then he told her something that made her briny blood run cold. He said he loved her and wanted to marry her for real.

"You mean like husband and wife … t-together forever … t-till death do us p-part?" Pearl's heart felt like a stone in her chest.

"Yes. Exactly that. Please Gemma, marry me? I love you more than anything," he said.

"But … what about … will I ever get to go back home?" As soon as she said it, she knew it was a mistake. Grant's face grew as red as the lobsters he fed to her.

"Home? Is this not your home? You've been living in my house for months! Eating extravagantly, getting groomed and pampered, among everything else I do for you! What more do you want, huh? You don't want to marry me? What, you want to go back and live in that disgusting fucking hellhole of a polluted ocean? Fine by me, sweetheart. Maybe you'll get captured again, but this time, instead of being pampered, you'll end up as nothing more than cheap canned tuna!"

"I'm s-sorry. You're right."

Grant sighed. "Look, I'm sorry too, I shouldn't have said that … but it's only because I care for you that I got so upset! Let's get through this party and revisit the conversation later. Agreed?"

"Yes," Pearl whispered.

Grant sipped his iced tea and made small talk. Pearl knew he was watching her, so whenever the husband of his ex-fiancée Jill flirted with her, she smiled really big and giggled too loud. The children had taken pictures and asked her enough questions to write a book, and now they were playing Marco Polo as she rested on the steps at the shallow end of the pool. Jill finally came over to where Pearl was. She was wearing a sarong over her bathing suit and she pulled it up before she sat down and dipped both feet into the pool.

Jill thanked Pearl for being great with the kids, commented on the detail of her tail, and gushed about how lovely her hair was. Pearl wanted to tell her how lovely her hair was, too, but she didn't. Then Jill asked how her and Grant met.

"In the sea," Pearl replied.

Jill laughed, but when she saw that Pearl didn't, she said, "You're not joking?"

"No. He was kayaking."

"Oh, that makes sense. He always did like to do that. I hated it! Thank God Jim is more into land activities. So, you and Grant are getting married? When's the big day?"

"I don't know."

"Yeah, planning a wedding can be a hassle. If you need any tips, let me know. You both have my number now, so feel free to call. Wouldn't it be grand if you had an under-the-sea-themed wedding?" She called over her shoulder then. "Jim? Don't you think if Grant and Gemma had an under-the-sea-themed wedding that it'd be so perfect?"

"Now that's an idea," Jim called back.

Grant overheard and had a look of contempt on his face. He walked over and stood at the edge of the pool, directly over Pearl. "Great party, Jill. I'm sure the birthday boy and your husband enjoyed the entertainment. It's almost time to wrap things up, though, I'm afraid. Gemma and I got an early day tomorrow—the mayor's granddaughter is turning five!"

"Of course, Grant. Let me just write the check out and send you home with some cupcakes. We ordered too many, and lord knows I don't need them in the house. Also, I told Gemma to call me if she needed any wedding tips. Ugh, trust me, it can become a thorn in your side!"

"Sure, yeah," Grant said.

Jill stood up and put her hand on Grant's forearm. Her eyes softened, and there was no malice when she spoke. "I'm really happy for you, Grant … for you both. She's a real doll. Truly. I mean it. Don't let her get away."

"I don't plan on it," Grant said. Then he lifted Pearl from the pool and waved goodbye to everyone as he carried her to the pushcart. The kids went nuts, and wanted to touch her tail all over again, so he let them. The sorrow that Pearl felt as he loaded her into the backseat of his SUV was more extreme than usual. She felt defeated. She'd missed her final chance to tell the truth. To ask Jill for her help. Tears trickled down her cheeks as she watched Grant walk back to the car, a plate of cupcakes in his hand.

Grant slammed the car door, and she knew right away he was angry. As he turned to look over his shoulder and back the car out of the driveway, he glared at her.

"What was your game back there?" he asked.

"I don't understand."

"The fuck you don't! You play dumb, but you understand perfectly well. I saw you with Jim. And I saw your eyes darting from him to me every time he made you laugh with his stupid jokes. And Jill? You're not her friend. We're not asking them for any wedding tips or anything else. Got it?" When Pearl didn't answer, he shouted. "I said, you got it?"

"Yes."

He was silent for some time before he spoke again, then he snorted. "These parties'll eventually stop, you know. When there's enough money saved, they'll stop and we'll get married and escape to a cabin in the woods where we can be alone. Not only will you have your own saltwater pool, but we'll get a saltwater hot tub. How about that?"

Pearl watched the trees whizz by through the window. She didn't care if there was a pool, a hot tub, or lobster and crab. All she wanted was to go home. Back to the ocean. Her eyes burned with more tears, and she didn't care if he saw them fall. A feeling she'd never known saturated every fiber of her being. It was rage, and it was ravenous. It consumed her. She thought about launching herself at Grant and biting into the cords of his neck where it pulsed. Never had she had such terrible thoughts about any living creature. She feared she was becoming more human by the day, and she'd rather be dead. She eyed the thing he'd called a Taser. He had it nearby, in case he ever had to use it, he'd said. He'd never used it on her, but he warned he would if she forced him to.

She noticed a bridge up ahead. The bridge looked like it went over a sizable river, and most rivers flowed to the sea. There were no other cars around, and Pearl knew she had to act fast. She opened her mouth and shrieked as loud as she could muster. Grant took his hands off the wheel and covered his ears. He was shouting at her, but she didn't stop. As soon as they neared the bridge, he hit the gas instead of the brake and lost control of the vehicle. It smashed into the guardrail. Grant flew through the windshield and went over the rail.

Other than some minor cuts and a bump on her head, Pearl was unscathed. She knew her doors were child-locked, so she pulled herself forward into the battered front seat. Shards of glass cut into her as she opened his door and dragged herself through the wreckage. She hit the road hard, but ignored the pain as she continued to drag herself toward freedom. It took all of her strength to pull herself up the barrier and lift her tail over. Once in midair, she quickly went into a perfect dive, ready to embrace whatever fate awaited head-on.

Once her tail slapped the cool water, she began to laugh. She'd done it; she was free! Pearl's elation simmered when she saw Grant bobbing nearby. She started to swim in the opposite direction, but then turned around. His body was broken and bloody, his mouth opening and closing in quick gasps for air. He was barely alive, and he was suffering. It was in this moment Pearl realized something that made her heart soar. Because she wasn't human, and because she was what she was, she decided to do Grant a kindness. She pushed his face down into the water until the bubbles ceased and she knew he was no more. She felt no joy in knowing that Grant was dead, no, instead she felt joy in knowing that she'd survived.

DEAD DECEPTION

Maribel seethed as she moved the shiny rock on her left finger up and down. She glared at her reflection in the mirror above the cold and empty fireplace and forced herself to smile. But even as she bared her fluorescent veneers, the fire in her eyes smoldered. Her dark, caramel-flecked hair was in a French twist, and she wore a crisp white Chanel pants suit that stood out against her tanned skin. One should always look their best one hundred percent of the time, even when that time was waiting for a private detective to bring video evidence that your husband was cheating. Hell, she knew Byron was a playboy born with a platinum spoon in his mouth, but she still loved him. She also loved his money and didn't want another skank moving in on the territory that she'd worked so hard to claim.

The cell buzzed in Maribel's hand and she could see that it was the detective, needing the gate to be opened. Her red-bottomed heels clicked on the marble tile as she made her way to the front door. With her hand on the doorknob, she took a few deep breaths, then stood tall and squared her shoulders. She peered down at her phone's screen and watched Dennis Foray park his clunker behind her Porsche, then make his way up the walkway. He was a pink glistening sausage of a man, his middle bursting out from the casing of his threadbare trench coat. The bags under his heavy-lidded eyes made it look as if he hadn't slept a wink in weeks. Before he could ring the doorbell, Maribel opened the door and greeted him.

"Good afternoon, Mr. Foray. Please, come in." Maribel stepped aside, her arm outstretched.

Dennis Foray shifted uncomfortably, but didn't step forward. He held a USB drive in his hand. "Good afternoon, Mrs. Wickhamp. I have the info you've requested."

"Mr. Foray, I think you know Byron isn't going to be home all weekend. It's quite alright for you to come in and have some coffee. Or would you prefer scotch? Byron stocks some of the best there is. I'll even open one of his investment bottles." Maribel chuckled and grinned like a mischievous cat.

"That's not necessary Mrs. Wick—"

"Call me Maribel, please."

"Mrs. Maribel, I'm swamped with other jobs, but thank you for the generous offer." Dennis held out the USB drive, sweat immediately beading on his forehead.

"I was right, wasn't I? He's fucking someone else? Just tell me. In case I can't bring myself to watch." Maribel reached for the tiny thing that contained the damning evidence.

"I think you should watch the video and see for yourself what you think is going on. He's definitely going to a motel and engaging with …" The detective averted his eyes from Maribel before he said the next part. "Well, with himself. Listen, Mrs.—"

"Maribel."

"Maribel, I just get the evidence my client pays me to get. Your husband's been using cash to get the same room at the same seedy motel for over a month, but what he's doing in there might surprise you—it did me, that's for sure."

"So, you're telling me there's no woman?" Maribel asked.

"Not that I'm aware of."

"A man then? Tell me, I can take it."

"I watched all the video and there was no woman or man that I ever saw."

"But I smelled the perfume on him … I know he's been with someone. He hasn't screwed me in months! And I mean, look at me, I'm pretty goddamn fuckable," Maribel cried.

Dennis Foray's face and neck turned the color of sunburn. He looked down at his feet but remained silent.

"I'm sorry. I didn't mean to embarrass you. Look, should I be concerned about anything? Anything at all?" Maribel frowned.

"I don't often give advice on personal matters, but, in my opinion, I'd say concern for his mental health might be in order. Well, if that's all you need from me, I better get going. Try to have a good day."

"Wait. Did my husband actually leave for Chicago this morning?"

"Yes, ma'am. He boarded a plane that was bound to Chicago."

"Thank you."

Dennis Foray nodded, then left Maribel with her own swirling thoughts. She felt exothermic, like every molecule in her body had overheated and she'd spontaneously combust at any moment. It took some time for her to catch her breath and cool down. She had to use the wall to help lead her to the kitchen, where her laptop was plugged in. The USB in her hand felt dangerous and powerful, a live grenade. She plugged the drive into her computer, then kicked off her heels. She decided she was going to open a bottle of Byron's good scotch after all.

Maribel carried her tumbler of scotch mixed with diet cola to the kitchen. Byron would be livid if he knew she'd opened one of his fancy investment bottles, *especially* the one she opened. It was a rare Japanese blend that came in a black lacquered box shaped like a miniature coffin. She almost broke a nail thanks to the blue wax seal around its top. And if he knew she mixed diet cola with it, he'd go ape shit. "Fuck that fucker," she mumbled to the empty room. She knew she wasn't crazy; she knew what she'd smelled on Byron when he came home: the scent of a jasmine forward perfume. The same scent that his ex-wife Angelica used to wear. Of course, she also knew the one thing the detective didn't know.

Maribel winced as she downed half of her potent concoction, then waited for it to soothe her nerves and settle her trembling hands. When it did, she sat down in front of the computer and brought up the footage that was taken of her husband.

She was amazed by the quality of the video on her computer screen. The detective didn't skimp on his camera, because she could see every angle of the filthy motel room. The comforter looked crusty and she could almost smell the nicotine-stained walls and mildewed carpet. Her breath caught and her heart jumped when she saw Byron enter. He was dressed in his steel-gray Burberry suit and looked very much like a Greek god that had decided to live amongst the mortals. Maribel kicked herself for still yearning for him, despite the situation. He looked around a bit, then pulled a small jarred candle from his jacket pocket and set it on the bedside table. After lighting the candle, he proceeded to use the restroom to piss and brush his teeth. When he was done, he came out, sat on the edge of the bed, and turned on the television.

Byron flipped through the channels for a bit, turned the volume to mute, then looked at his watch and yawned. Several minutes passed with him just sitting and rechecking his watch over and over. It became clear to Maribel that he was clearly waiting for someone. Suddenly, the door flung open to the motel room, then slammed shut. The candle's flame flickered wildly, and Maribel guessed that the room's door hadn't been shut properly and the wind took it. Shortly after, the lamp went out on the nightstand beside the bed, leaving only the light of the TV and candle. Maribel leaned in when Byron took off his jacket and slung it behind him. A wolfish smile lit up his face as he undid his tie and unbuttoned his dress shirt.

It was when he stood up, undid his belt buckle and slid his dress pants, along with his boxer briefs, completely off, that Maribel gasped. She could see that he had a budding erection. He stared down at it, smiling wider and laughing as it began to hit full mast. *From what?* she wondered. The weather channel wasn't exactly porn, and he wasn't even looking at his phone. She cringed when Byron sat back down on the bed and started to stroke his dick. Maribel mouthed, *What in the actual fuck are you doing, you lunatic?*

She continued to cringe as Byron pleasured himself, and at some point, she realized she'd chewed her bottom lip hard enough to draw blood. She paused the video, closed her eyes, and drained her glass. Her husband's frozen naked image—boner smacking in hand—on the edge of the ragged queen-sized bed made Maribel shiver. One thing was for certain: if she was going to get through the rest of the footage, she was going to need more scotch.

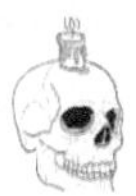

Maribel came back to the kitchen with the bottle of scotch and, this time, no diet cola. She sat down, tipped the bottle to her lips and drank, then poured some into her glass. The tip of her finger lingered on the play triangle for only a moment. Did Byron know what she'd done? Was this whole weird fucking show some kind of sick and twisted ploy to get back at her? Well, she had news for him. It wouldn't work. Maribel was afraid, but more than that, she was angry. She clicked play.

Byron continued to stroke himself, but as he did it, he began to talk. She couldn't hear much of what he was saying, as he had always been a low talker, but she froze when she heard him say, "Of course, you've always been more beautiful than her. She's nothing to me. She never was or will be anything to me." Then it looked as if he had been forced back onto the bed. He began to laugh, something he barely did around Maribel. Maribel vibrated with rage as Byron's tongue tasted the air like a serpent, flicking in and out in rhythmic motions. His hands were in midair, massaging and gripping an unseen thing.

Byron lowered his hands to the area above his crotch, where they rose up and down in slow motion, something Maribel was very familiar with. Next, he got on his knees on the mattress and began to pump away; at what Maribel wasn't sure, but he was definitely giving it to whatever it was. He slapped at what she supposed was an invisible ass and she could hear him moaning. That act went on for longer than she cared for, and tears began to flood her eyes. They slid down her cheeks, down her neck, and saturated the collar of her silk top.

Maribel watched in disgust and horror as Byron changed positions several times. Whatever imaginary person or thing he was fucking, he was giving it his all. He fucked it sideways, against the wall, missionary, and then doggie style again, until he cried out the same way he used to cry out with her. As he lay in the rumpled sheets panting and slick with sweat, he said something loud enough for her to make out and it made the marrow in Maribel's bones freeze. She backed the video up three times and yes, she'd heard him right the first time. He'd said it. Tender and intense, he'd said, "I love you, Angelica. Forever and always."

Maribel ground her teeth as she resumed the video. She stifled the scream that was on the precipice of escaping as Byron whispered sweet nothings to his imaginary lover. The minute he started licking what looked like the pillow, she vurped and again hit pause so she could get ahold of herself. Angelica was dead! Or at least, that was what Maribel had been told.

Had Byron gone crazy when he couldn't contact her? Had he snapped? Maribel knew that he'd been seeing Angelica at least a couple nights a week, beginning less than a year after they'd been married. She'd caught him in a lie, and he'd confessed, but then swore it was over for good. Maribel had forgiven him, but she didn't believe him.

Maribel walked in circles with the phone in her hand. She'd memorized the number by heart so she hadn't had to write it down. Her hand trembled as she dialed the number and held her phone to her ear. It rang three times and then a voice as hard as diamonds but without any of the sparkle answered.

"Yeah?"

"Uh, this is uh … Maribel Wickhamp. I-I'm calling about the pest control you administered—"

"Why're you fuckin' callin' me? I told you to never contact me again. I only do one and done jobs."

"I-I know, but … listen, where did you, um, get rid of the pest?"

"You already know the answer to that."

"No, what I mean is, where was it when you offed it?"

"What? Why? If there's heat, it's all on you, because you know what'll happen if you even fuckin' mention my name. I mean, if you so much as give a description of my fuckin' eyebrows, you, your family, your friends—"

"There's no heat! I paid you nearly everything I had and now I just need to know this! Please!" Maribel shouted into the phone, surprising herself.

It was silent at first but then the man said, "Look, I'm not gonna give you the exact name of the place, but I'd been followin' that roach for a few days, lookin' for the right moment, and this one night, that roach took a cab and was dropped off at some shitty motel. I figured it was as good a time as any, so when I was sure the roach was alone, I knocked on its room door, pushed my way in, and clobbered it over the head before it could even scream. Then I dragged the thing to my car. The rest is history. You need my bowel schedule for that day too? Look, I gotta go. Lose my number and remember what I told you will happen if you squeal." He hung up.

Maribel felt sick. She felt more than sick. Her stomach churned and churned until the contents made their way up her esophagus and crowded her mouth. She gave up trying to hold it in and spewed the vile chunky mixture all over the floor, where it splashed up and speckled the bottoms of her white pants. She sobbed in between upchucks, calling Byron a bastard and a piece of shit, then she composed herself enough to go back to the computer and continue the self-torture. She had to finish the video.

Back in front of the computer, Maribel washed her mouth out with more scotch. She gurgled with it then swallowed, letting the bite of the alcohol singe away the rankness of her barf. She felt like she was losing her damn marbles. It was becoming more and more likely that Byron knew about what she'd done, and he was getting her back for it. That had to be it. That was the only thing that made any logical sense. Byron never did play fair, and he could be wicked and cruel. He'd been with Angelica for five years—married for two of them— before Maribel had waited on him at a golf clubhouse. They'd had hot and wild sex behind the pro shop and then for almost three whole months before Angelica caught them together. Never in a million years did Maribel think it would end up where it had.

Maribel decided to plug the USB into the ninety-inch flat screen television in the living room. "The better to see you with," she growled. After turning on the TV and plugging in the drive, she grabbed the remote from the coffee table and recommenced the video. She watched as Byron whispered out loud. She turned on the surround sound and pumped the volume up to see if she could hear him better, but she still found it difficult to hear what he was saying. The whispering went on for a while until he got up from the bed and began tugging at his dick again. When he was fully erect, he began pumping away at the edge of the bed, hard and fast, causing the mattress to lift up off the frame. She wanted to look away from the giant screen but found she couldn't. The grunts he was making sent shockwaves throughout her body. And then she saw it. The glowing semi-transparent image of a curvy naked woman bent over the bed being pounded by her husband. The glowing woman's figure flickered in and out.

Maribel gaped at the woman's long, straight hair, but it didn't register at first. Then the flickering woman turned around to look at Byron as he held onto her hair like a rein and grunted animalistically behind her. There was no mistaking who the woman was. Angelica looked up toward the camera and smirked. Her face filled the screen and Maribel's heart stopped, fluttered, and then went into a full sprint. As her pulse throbbed in her ears, she thought she might faint. It was Angelica—with her almond eyes and full cupid's bow lips—and she knew she was being filmed. She'd been duped. By the hitman, by the private detective, by her husband, and worst of all, by Angelica. Maribel knew that it was only a matter of time before she was going to be arrested. Byron had wanted to teach her a lesson before they destroyed her life, and he had spared no details.

Angelica's beautiful form faded in and out, but Maribel had come to the conclusion that it was all an act. The only other possibility was implausible. Angelica wasn't a ghost. *Was she?* "There're no such things as fucking ghosts." Maribel chortled. "Well, this ghost fucks, apparently." With technology being what it was, they simply edited out Angelica where they had wanted to, and then made her look like a ghost. It was too much. They wanted to fuck with her. They wanted her to know they were getting back together and wanted to hurt her before they completely ruined her. Maribel started to laugh, quietly at first, then it turned into a full-bellied laugh that racked her entire body. She banged her hand against the wall and laughed until her sides hurt, until she coughed, gagged, and threw up again.

With the sounds of their pleasure booming around her, Maribel continued to laugh. She found it all so hilarious. The two of them putting on a sex show for her. It was so damn corny, the whole thing.

They had her going for a while, they really did. They'd almost sent her packing. But she'd show them. The video of Byron slapping the ass of Angelica's *ghost* as he screwed her continued to play as a snorting and cackling Maribel left the room. "You two are a riot," she roared.

She still had the bank card from their mutual account, and she had a couple of credit cards of Byron's that she knew had crazy high limits on them. She knew how to disappear. She'd done it before, like the time she'd worked that short stint as a Hooter's waitress and stolen all the horny old men's credit card numbers.

The only thing was, she didn't know how long it would be before whoever was coming for her would arrive. She also didn't know if the mutual account they'd shared had already been canceled along with the credit cards. She went back to the living room and tried to shut off the television, but no matter what she did, the video wouldn't stop playing. The volume grew louder and louder until it rattled the pictures and paintings on the wall. Maribel covered her ears, then shrieked and threw the remote at the TV, hard enough to crack the screen. Her phone. She would use her phone to check the account. She hoped it wasn't too late.

She thought she'd left her phone on the counter after she'd called that revolting hitman. But it wasn't there. It wasn't anywhere in the kitchen that she could tell. She could barely think with the racket of the two of them fucking echoing around her, each moan and bedspring squeak a knife to her heart. A snarl erupted from her throat as she continued to search. It couldn't be upstairs; she hadn't gone up there the entire time. She figured the current situation had scrambled her brain and that maybe she left it in the living room. In a rage, she knocked over a Tiffany lamp, flung the cashmere pillows from the couches, and looked underneath everything. It had to be in the kitchen. She pulled at her hair, strands of it coming loose between her fingers. "UGH! The two of them have driven me fucking insane!"

Back in the kitchen, Maribel rifled through the drawers and cabinets. She moved all the chairs away from the table and even looked in the oven and refrigerator. By the time she was done, she was breathing like an angry bull and her lips were curled over her teeth. She picked up the almost empty bottle of scotch and threw it at the wall, reveling in the sound of the shattering glass. That gave her an idea. She screeched as she ran back to Byron's stash and grabbed more of his precious liquid gold. Snot dripped from her nose and spittle flew from her mouth as she hurled more priceless bottles of scotch against the walls.

She flew to the living room, and every insult against Byron and Angelica imaginable was hurled along with the last two bottles at the TV's screen. It didn't matter that her throat was raw from screaming, or that her ears felt like they could begin to bleed at any moment from the cries of lust and bed squeaking that pervaded them, she kept screaming and finding things around the room to throw at the television. The screen was smashed to bits, but still the video played and the volume got even louder. She tried with all her might to pull the USB from the port, but it wouldn't budge. And just when she thought she might pass out from all the straining and panting, it stopped. Not the video itself, but the sounds of fucking. Now all she heard were the quiet murmurs of lovers who were resting side by side. It made her sick that she actually felt grateful to them that they'd finished.

As she was catching her breath, she heard her phone ringing. "Moonlight Sonata" by Beethoven. It was Byron.

Maribel was disoriented by her rage. She went to run and ended up slipping on the slip 'n slide made of glass shards and scotch. The palms of her hands and soles of her feet were riddled with glass, but she got up and power limped to the kitchen anyway, leaving trails of blood in her wake. Tendrils of her hair hung loose, so she smoothed them back with the blood from her hands.

She could still hear the phone, but she didn't see it. Somehow, the footage had rewound itself and was back on the two of them fucking. The sorrowful sound of Beethoven mingled with every moan, bed squeak, and grunt. Maribel decided to ignore them and search for her phone instead.

The phone stopped ringing in the midst of her looking for it and Maribel dragged her fingernails down her face and howled up at the ceiling, "Where the fuuuuck are yoooooou?"

The room grew frigid then, and the scent of jasmine, musk, and sweet rot permeated Maribel's nasal passages. She could see her breath rise in plumes around her as she choked on the cloying odor. She'd lost her mind, and she knew it. This was what they'd wanted, and it's what they got. Something akin to fingers made out of ice trailed the back of her neck and she whirled around. There it was. Her phone. It was suspended in midair and she could see that it was recording her.

Goose pimple upon goose pimple rose on every inch of Maribel's flesh and she swallowed the bile in her throat as she stared back at the wreckage of her own face on the phone's screen. Bloody scratches and mascara lined her face. Her hair was disheveled, strands of it ripped out in her fit of rage. She looked exactly how she felt. Insane. Then she felt the hand that belonged to the icy fingers grab her own and force her fingers to curl around the end of one of the broken bottles of scotch.

Maribel struggled, but she was no match for whatever had ahold of her. As the phone still recorded just inches above her face, Maribel's hand plunged the broken bottle deep into her own jugular. Blood sprayed and gushed from her wound, but she managed her last words before she slid to the floor. "F-fuck-you, Angelica, you filthy whore," she rasped, then she spat a bloody loogie at her invisible foe. When Maribel's eyes finally closed, the recording ceased and the grisly video of her death was sent to Byron with the message, *See you when you get home, love.* Then the phone dropped with a thud on Maribel's chest and the television in the living room exploded.

HEART-SHAPED BOX

I'm a piece of shit. But you would've done it, too, if you smelled your loved one rotting from the inside out. I didn't believe it was real at the time—I mean, with the lack of sleep and everything else—I just thought it was a hallucination or my overactive imagination. To give you an idea, when I was four, I freaked out because I thought I'd seen eyes staring at me from an old potato and this other time, I ran away screaming after I spotted a cabbage patch doll's head in a bundle of cabbages at the grocery store. See what I mean? Anyway, at first, the memory of *that night* clung to me like a ghost, haunting my every move, but as time went by, I began to believe it was never real. Turns out it was always real. So, now, I'm fucked, and, well, someone else I love is fucked too, and it's all my fault.

I sat by my father's bedside and plucked the strings of my Washburn. He turned his head toward me and tried to speak. I set the guitar down and grabbed his cold hand. His sunken eyes fluttered before they closed again. Cancer is a dirty whore, but unless you've seen firsthand what it can do, you don't truly *know*. A nurse and CNA came in and I stood up to give them some room. They smiled and nodded but said nothing. The nurse removed the dressings from my dad's neck, and I winced and tried not to gag but failed.

The area of blackened necrotic flesh reminded us that the cancer had progressed to the point of no return. Even though my mom had placed bags of charcoal under Dad's bed, it'd done nothing to mask the smell, and the room remained ripe with the pungent aroma of impending doom. I looked at my watch and wondered when my mom would be back. She'd said she'd gone home to shower, eat, and take a nap, but I knew she needed time to herself to come apart— something mothers don't like to do in front of anyone.

We were taking care of Dad at home with the help of a nurse, but when it got to be too much we decided to move him to a hospice. He was too weak to use his walker and despite the weight loss, his fragile body was still hard for us to carry back and forth to the bathroom. Of course, Dad also refused to wear diapers and kept trying to pull them off. I squeezed my eyes shut when the CNA pulled down the blankets from his emaciated body, then walked out of the room for fresh air. "Fuck God and fuck cancer," I'd whispered once I got outside. Then I added, "Fuck it all the way to Hell."

The sky started to turn a shade of sherbet. I looked up and spotted several buzzards in the trees. "God's sanitation workers," my mom always called them. *Jeesh, do they smell Dad too?* My cell buzzed in my pocket. *Mom.* I held the phone to my ear and waited.

"Talia? You there? I … I'm not coming back tonight." She choked up.

"What do you mean, you're not coming back? I need you here, Ma." I began walking in circles.

"I just can't … I'm so tired, honey. Look, I need to rest and it's not comfortable there and with your Aunt Jackie coming tomorrow, I need to get the house together. I'll be back in the morning and you can leave. Did you eat any dinner?"

"Dinner? No, I didn't, and I forgot about Aunt Jackie coming. I really wish you'd come back tonight, Ma."

"I know you do. Just be there with Dad and play him some cool tunes on that guitar of yours. He likes that. He always did … anyway, I love you both."

"Ma?"

"Yeah, honey?"

"Never mind. We love you too … and get some rest." I knew she needed it. We both did.

I wanted to ask Mom if she thought tonight would be the night. Every morning Dad managed to peel his eyes open was a miracle, though he'd wanted to believe he had a chance all along. He was stubborn and hadn't gone to the doctor until it was too late. We pestered him again and again when he complained of an earache, sore throat, and swollen lumps in his neck until he finally broke down and went. It took a few different doctors, but they all suspected the same thing: cancer. Head and neck cancer, to be exact.

The cancer then spread to the nearby lymph nodes, coiled around his carotid artery, and eventually forked its filthy fingers into his lungs. When he told my mom and I, my ears had started to ring. All I heard were hoarse snippets of what he'd said. "Squamous cell carcinoma. Shouldn't have smoked all those years. And I just got my own office closer to home. What on earth are we gonna do now?"

Dad promised to fight tooth and nail even though his chances were slim. There were surgeries, radiation, chemo, and even immunotherapy, but none of it did a damn thing. The whore kept spreading itself and reached out to different parts of his body. Dad lashed out and started to spend money on things he'd never get to enjoy. He got a new truck, fishing gear, and a top-of-the-line BBQ grill.

Mom tried to keep her mouth shut during this time, but when Dad said he was thinking about getting a boat, she went ballistic. She'd carried on and cried about the money and, finally, Dad had conceded. He had asked my opinion when I was changing his feeding tube and when I said that I agreed with Mom, the look in his eyes crushed my eggshell of a soul. It was like the last thread of hope he'd had, had been extracted and set on fire. From then on, his stare became the vacant look of never again. I wished in that moment that I'd had a sibling to share the burden with or a maybe just a friend to cry on.

As his cancer progressed, Mom resigned from her teaching job to help take care of him. Dad worked in insurance for years and his company had opened up an office nearby that he was supposed to manage, but as things stood, he'd never get the chance. During all of this, I was still trying to figure myself out. College wasn't for me and my parents never forced me to do anything, which sometimes I wish they had. Shit happens the way it does for a reason, though, right? At least I was free and able to help out.

Back inside, I paused outside my dad's room and applied another thick layer of peppermint lip balm. Guilt racked my body. I didn't want to go in there and had begun to wish he'd just pass already. *Why was he hanging on like this?* I wondered. Mom always said Dad was bad at goodbyes and she was right. I took a deep breath and went in.

My chair had been moved, and it annoyed me more than it should have, so I noisily dragged it back to the side of the bed. I picked up my guitar and played "Heart-Shaped Box" over and over until my fingers hurt. Dad stirred a few times, but his eyes didn't open. All he did was sleep. Not being conscious of the fact that you're on your way out is a sort of gift from whoever oversees that sort of thing, I guess. Someone opened the window earlier, and I was thankful for the breeze that swirled in and aerated the stench.

That night, as I was nodding off in the chair, I tried something. I tried the one thing I hadn't done since getting kicked out of Catholic school—I prayed. I prayed for Dad to either wake up or die, though I wasn't sure which one anymore.

"Fuck God and fuck cancer all the way to Hell, you say?"

My eyes shot open. *Dad?* But his eyes were still closed and his chest rose unevenly. Somehow, all the lights had been turned off, and the room felt like a meat locker. I peered around the blackness and whispered, "Who's there?"

"I am." The voice boomed around me.

When my eyes adjusted, I saw the outline of a looming shadow in the far corner of the room. It almost reached the ceiling. *Who the hell could be that tall?* Suddenly my blood was crushed ice and goose bumps rose over every inch of my flesh. Even though my teeth chattered and I was both scared shitless and scared enough to shit my pants, I'd managed to say, "You have two seconds before I scream like a banshee. You do realize this is a hospice house and that people are in and out of here all the time, right? Look, I don't know if you got lost looking for someone else or what the hell you're trying to pull, but—"

"I'm here for your father." The voice grated the marrow in my bones.

"You're deranged! I—" My hand involuntarily flew to my mouth and stuck there.

"Scream and I'll go away, which means you'll never get the chance to know whether or not I could have done something about the stinking carcass that is your father. I am going to let you remove your hand, so that maybe we can discuss my terms like civilized beings."

"I'm dreaming. Whatever you are ... you're not real. You're not—"

"Oh, but I am indeed, child."

"Well, who are you then? You can't be God? So, are you a demon or the actual Devil?" I paused, then murmured, "Are you ... Death?"

"I am one and the same. Stop resisting the shiver going up your spine, child, and pay attention."

"You're him—you're Death," I gasped.

"I can be many things, and I work in mysterious ways. Now, if you agree to what I ask, then your father will wake up tomorrow and his cancer will be fucked, just as you wished."

Still convinced I was asleep and that it was all a bizarre nightmare, I played along. "All right, what's it you ask then? I'm not sacrificing anyone, drinking any kind of blood, or having your ugly spawn, so ..."

"I do appreciate your sarcasm and choice in cinema, but nothing like that, no. You only have to agree to never fall in love. If you can consent to that, then we have a deal."

I snorted in spite of the situation. "What? Why?"

A sound similar to hundreds of cicadas filled the room and then it hissed, "Because it pleases me!"

When I found my voice, I asked, "And what happens if I do fall in love?" I was only nineteen years old and the prospect of never knowing true love frightened me, but then again, it wasn't like anyone was banging down the doors to be with me.

"Then you will have to watch them suffer until they shrivel up and die!" Its words were acid.

"That's so messed up." I swallowed the dry lump in my throat.

"But you would have your father back, and he is still relatively young. Think of your poor mother. Besides, you can still take your pleasure with whomever you wish. You cannot love them, but you may fornicate to your heart's desire. Plenty of you mortals do that already."

I didn't think I had ever fornicated before anyway, so what would I really be giving up? I loved my parents and would do anything to take away their suffering. Though they had never said it, I felt like I had failed them in so many ways. This could be the one thing I made right.

"Does fornicate mean to have sex? Or is that copulate?" I asked.

I heard a long sigh, like a door creaking, then it replied, "They are one and the same."

"You sure like that saying, don't you? Look, how do I know you're not messing with me? Like, this could be some devil in the detail mumbo jumbo and once I accept, you steal my soul and my dad still dies. Maybe you even go after my mom." I squinted to try and see it better, but still couldn't make out much in the dark.

I thought I heard a chuckle before it replied, "You have my word. Just say you accept and thy will be done."

"Fine … I'll do it. I accept. Fuck love all the way to Hell!"

"Indeed. Until next time."

The sun came through the window and baked my cheek and the annoying sound of chirping birds pecked my ears until I peeled open my eyes. *Ugh, morning.* I yawned and grimaced. My mouth tasted like I licked the inside of a turtle tank. The first thing I noticed was that my dad wasn't in his bed. *Dad?* I panicked and stood up. *Did he pass in the night? Why wouldn't they wake me?* "Dad? Daddy, where are you?" I cried.

The bathroom door opened, and I almost hit the floor. My dad stumbled out the door and had a lopsided grin on his face. Somehow, he had managed to get out of bed and take himself to the bathroom. He hadn't been able to do that for weeks. This was impossible. I ran over to him, grabbed his noodle of an arm, and led him back to the bed to sit down.

"Daddy? Is that really you?" I still had a hold of his arm.

"Far as I can tell, it's me. You look like you seen a ghost, you okay?"

"Am I okay? How in the … how did you … how did you get up out of bed, Daddy?"

"I don't know, I just got up. Woke up and had to pee. That damn Depends stuck to my ass when I tried to pull it off, hurt like a bastard!" He coughed when he laughed.

"Dad. I … I missed you so much," I sobbed.

"I missed you, too, Sugar Pop. I don't even remember how long I've been gone for. I know I was really sick and then all the sudden it was lights out … I had a dream, I think, but I don't recall what it was. Anyhow, I opened my eyes this morning, and I just felt … better. It's a damn miracle, Talia. You must've been praying real hard last night, Sugar Pop."

"I think I was …" I shook my head and tried to remember.

"It was you and your ma's love. Love, love, love. Love is all you need!"

Love? What was it about that word? Then I remembered something and my stomach turned, but it had to be a dream, right? "It was definitely love, Daddy." I squeezed his hand and let the tears fall.

"Where is your ma?"

"She was getting some rest and waiting for Aunt Jackie to come. I'll call and tell her you're awake. I can't believe it! Let me get you some water. Are you hungry? Wait, let me get someone—"

"Slow down, Sugar Pop. One thing at a time. How's my hair?" He patted the sparse patches that he had left on his head and my heart swelled with joy.

That day was a complete whirlwind of people, in and out. Lots of tears, smiles, laughter, and pure disbelief. No one understood how Dad suddenly started to recover. In the weeks to follow, his wound started to heal, but then his cancer started to disappear too. It was months later when he had a scan, and they found no evidence that it was ever there at all. He started to put weight on and even grow his hair back. Dad started to resemble himself again, and we did too.

Our lives went on as before, Mom went back to working as a teacher and Dad was eventually able to get his old job back. I'd begun working as a cashier at a drugstore and taking a few classes at the local college. After a couple of years crept by, I had started to forget my end of the deal. It had been a bad dream, I told myself … but then I saw her. She wore big gold hoop earrings, a purple sundress, and yellow Converse. Her earrings swayed with her hips when she walked. I hadn't been with anyone since *that* night, hadn't even thought about it, but then she walked in and it was like I'd stuck my fingers into an electrical socket.

The first thing I thought was, *but she's a girl?* I didn't know what or who I was attracted to, because I hadn't really explored it. I mean, in school, I had found people attractive, but never enough to feel the magnetic pull most teenagers have toward each other's loins. For the first time in my life, at twenty-one years old, I felt the pull, and it was strong! My eyes followed her around until she disappeared into one of the aisles, but I could still see her beautiful distorted image in the convex mirrors that were up around the store.

She was in the card aisle, then she went over to the nail polish, and finally to the lotions and bodywash. My mouth was full of cotton by the time she sauntered over to me and placed her basket of items down. I looked up at her perfect face and my lips parted, but no words came out. Laughter bubbled up from her throat and it startled me. Her mouth spread into a smile.

"You all right?" She raised her eyebrow.

"I … yeah, I uh … I thought you were someone else," I lied.

"Oh really? Who?" She pursed her full cupid's bow lips.

"Wh-what?" She caught me off guard.

"Who did you think I was?" She tilted her head full of honey-colored curls.

Shit. "Oh, just someone I used to know from school. Was this all you needed?" I avoided her stare and instead focused on ringing her up. I noticed the card was a *Thinking of You* card and felt a stab of disappointment.

"I think so. You don't talk much, do you?"

I shrugged and put her stuff into a bag, told her the total and she handed me a twenty. She took the bag from me, but then stopped, and her fingers rested on mine like hot coals. "You know, I'm kinda new here. You wanna get a cup of coffee or something sometime?"

I looked up at her. My heart stopped for a moment before it went into a full speed sprint. Her skin was the shade of buttery toffee, and her eyes were the color of golden maple syrup. She was a goddess, and I was totally and completely smitten. "Yes," I said.

"Cool, alright then. My name's Sunshine."

"I'm Talia," I said.

"Pretty name. I've always liked that name … Talia." The way she said my name made my scalp tingle.

"I get off at seven." I could feel my cheeks burning.

She looked surprised, but said, "Okay then, it's a date! Where should I meet you?"

"Um, there's a little coffee shop around the corner from here. The Nifty Bean. They have a good cup and I can be there by seven thirtyish?"

"Sounds perfect! See ya then." She waved, and when she flashed another smile, I knew why her parents named her Sunshine; it hurt to look at her. I'd been living in the dark up until that moment.

I bought a toothbrush as soon as I got off and brushed my teeth in the restroom, then applied some watermelon lip gloss. Even though I'd showered before work, I still sniffed my pits, which to my delight, still smelled rather pleasant. My hair was up, so I pulled it free and let it fall over my shoulders and wondered why I was going through so much trouble to meet a girl? But I knew why. My body was a dowsing rod, and it was pulling me toward her.

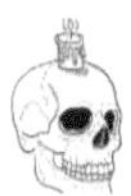

I walked in and saw Sunshine tucked into a corner on one of the plush couches. She sat with one leg underneath herself. A jean jacket covered her shoulders, but she still wore the purple dress. I felt creepy just staring at her, so I forced my feet to move. Her head shot up when I bumped a chair. Those amber eyes made my skin prickle, and I felt a longing I didn't know existed.

"Hi! I'm so happy you came." She stood up and hugged me like I was an old friend.

I awkwardly hugged her back, and she giggled. She smelled like vanilla and spice and everything nice. When she pulled free from our embrace, I caught myself from reeling backward. She smiled and said she was waiting for me before she ordered. We both got a lavender latte and orange scone. I followed her back to the couch, but when she patted the spot next to her, I froze.

"You gonna sit down?" She raised her eyebrow.

"Yeah, I just wanted to make sure there was room."

"I know I have a big butt, but it's not that big!" She laughed.

"Of course not! I was just …"

"I'm kidding, girl! Sit down." She patted the couch again.

I sat and Sunshine started telling me all about herself. She had a bad breakup and needed somewhere to go, so she moved here to live with her grandmother. Her parents had sold their house and bought a camper to travel in and although they offered for her to join them, she said she didn't want to live like a sardine in a tin can. She said she'd always liked small towns, and that's when she'd made up her mind. She was going to enroll at the college for nursing and was trying to find a job. She'd just turned twenty-two and her favorite movie was *Blue is the Warmest Color*.

"You ever see it?" she asked.

No. Never heard of it." I shrugged.

"Well, we should watch it sometime. You remind me of one of the characters, with that long brown hair of yours." She stared at my lips and my heart fluttered.

"Sure, I'd like that."

"So, tell me about you? I've been blathering on!"

"I like hearing about you. Plus, there's not much to me, really." There really wasn't.

"Of course there is. Just look at you … those pretty brown eyes tell a different story." Sunshine leaned closer to me and her warmth lit my insides on fire.

I bit my lip and looked away. "Um, well, I've lived here all my life. I go to school a couple days a week. I have no plan and no direction. You know where I work, which, by the way, they might need another cashier if you wanted to apply?" I looked up at her then. "I don't really have a favorite anything. Well, I like music. The Beatles, '90s rock, stuff like that. I play guitar and have an affinity for Doritos, the regular kind, none of those other weird flavors they keep coming up with. Just plain ol'—"

She did it before I knew what was coming. My whole face went numb, except my mouth. It was ablaze where she'd kissed me. I caught my breath and tried to say something, but before I could, she did it again until I joined in. I trailed her lips with my tongue and tasted the bit of orange icing left there by the scone. I found her tongue with mine, forgetting everything, and when we finally pulled apart, we sat and laughed until our stomachs hurt. And that is how I fell in love with Sunshine Johnson.

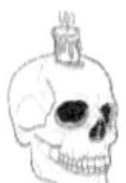

I hadn't thought about that night at the hospice house until after Sunshine and I first made love. We had just watched her favorite movie and then proceeded to do things I never thought I would do with anyone—let alone a female—and it was mind-blowing! Afterwards, we lay there covered in our own sweat, stroking one another's hair. I stayed silent for a long time. Sunshine asked me what was wrong, and I turned to her and told her I loved her and that I was scared. Tears streamed down my cheeks and she traced her fingers along my collarbone.

"Well, I love you, too, so don't cry, silly! Love is grand and some people don't ever get to experience it. Hey, why're you shivering like that?" Sunshine propped herself up on her elbow and rested her beautiful face in her hand. Her brows were knitted together, and she wiped my damp cheek tenderly. "Your face is paler than usual ... please don't tell me you're sorry we did this? Talia?"

"I am sorry, but not for the reasons you might think. I never thought I'd actually love anyone and now I do, and ... it's too late," I whispered.

"Talia, what the hell're you talking about? Too late?"

"It's so stupid. I never told you before because …" I couldn't finish. She knew that my dad was on his deathbed only a couple years ago, but that was all she knew.

"Goddamn it, Talia, just tell me!" Sunshine scooted away from me and crossed her arms over her breasts.

I sat up and recounted the entire story from that night. I told her every detail and winced when I was done, waiting for her response. Sunshine's mouth twisted and then she started to laugh. She fell back on my bed, slapped her hands on the mattress, and kicked her legs up and down. I was hurt that she found my story so funny, but also relieved she didn't go running for the door. I pulled on my shirt and told her to stop laughing.

Sunshine pulled me back down onto the bed and kissed me, then she said, "There's no such thing as the Grim Reaper or the Devil, Tal. What you all went through was a horrible, horrible ordeal, and your father was one of the lucky ones who somehow had a miracle, or whatever you want to call it. It happens sometimes. Haven't you ever watched those medical shows? Him getting better doesn't mean you struck a deal with some otherworldly creature! Look at me, I'm perfectly fine and lying in your Yellow Submarine bedsheets! Now, come here and kiss me again, Sugar Pop!" And then we were lost in each other's arms and I forgot about that night again for a while.

I had just come home from class and was about to take a shower when Sunshine called and told me she was coming over. When the doorbell rang, I jogged to open the door with a giant smile on my face, but that smile faded when I saw her.

Sunshine's eyes were red and puffy and she held a used tissue in her hand. I reached for her arm and her chin and lips started to tremble.

"What's wrong? What is it?" I asked. She let me pull her inside. I saw her glance around to see if anyone else was around, but my parents weren't home yet.

"Oh, Tal, I … I …" she sobbed.

I put both my hands on her shoulders and gently shook her. "What, Sun? Tell me!"

"I just found out. My parents are making their way here and I—I'm scared. I don't want to tell you. I'm afraid to." She looked down at the floor.

"Sun, tell me! If you don't spit it out, I'll scream at the top of my lungs until I combust!" I was serious. All I could think was, *she's breaking up with me and leaving, she's breaking up with me and leaving*. My body tensed up to prepare for the bomb that was about to be dropped on me.

She looked up at me and whispered, "I have cancer."

The words gored me in the guts. "What the fuck did you just say?" I looked at her and waited for her to continue.

"Metastatic breast cancer, it's spread to my bone, my arm bone to be more specific." Sunshine held up her left arm to show me, then looked at the floor again. "I need more scans and tests, but they think it might've also spread to other places. I'll find out more soon."

My entire body felt like it had been injected with colossal needles full of Novocain. "When? And how long have you known something was wrong?" The room had started to spin, and I leaned my hand against the wall in case I passed out.

"I didn't know, Tal. I started having bad pain in my arm a few weeks ago, thought it was from working out, but then it wouldn't stop hurting even when I rested and iced it. I went in and they did a scan and, well, now I know."

"You never told me your arm hurt?" I was beyond furious.

"I didn't think it was anything to worry about. Please, Tal … I need you." She reached for me and I backed away.

"I can't, Sun. I just can't," I said. "This's my fault—all of it! Don't you see?"

"Tal, don't be ridiculous. There's no such thing as that thing you described and even if there were, what would it matter now? We fell in love and there was no stopping that." She reached for me again, but I moved away from her as if her touch were full of venom.

"No stopping it? Are you serious? I could've stopped it! I should've never gone to that coffee shop and I should've never kissed you or fucked you or listened to you when you told me there was nothing to worry about!" I was yelling and crying all at once.

"How could you say that? Please, please stop shouting at me. I need you. I can't do this alone. I love you more than anything. I have to start treatment as soon as possible if I have a chance of beating this and I don't think I can muster up the strength without you by my side." Again, Sunshine reached for me, and again I pushed her away.

I laughed sardonically. "I have no right to be by your side. I did this to you! Me! That thing said to never fall in love. It said it! And I did, and now what? I'm supposed to fucking watch you suffer like my dad did? Just shrivel up and fucking die right in front of me? Is that what you want me to do?"

Sunshine's mouth hung open, then she hurled herself at me and slapped me across my face. "Stop it! Just stop being selfish! You're making this whole thing about you! This is hard for me, and I know you're hurting, but I really need someone right now and you're supposed to be there for me, damn you!"

She was right, of course, but I couldn't think straight. "I need some water," I croaked and left her standing there.

When I came back from the kitchen, she was gone. The front door was left open, and I ran outside in time to see her yellow Volkswagen Bug turn the corner.

I tried to call her, but she wouldn't answer. I saw her parent's camper and her Bug in the driveway when I went to her grandma's, but when her grandmother opened the door, she told me Sunshine wasn't home. I tried again and again for over a week, but I was told the same thing each time. This was all my fault. I needed to be with her. I wanted to be with her. To see it through to the bitter end.

After work, I went back to the house again and banged on the door until someone answered. A man opened the door and frowned at me. He was white, but he had the same golden maple eyes as Sunshine. The woman that came up behind him looked out at me with a furrowed brow. She was beautiful and tall, with familiar honeyed curls and toffee skin.

"I'm guessing you're Talia?" The woman took a breath in.

"Yes, ma'am," I said.

"I'm Sun's mom, Beatrice, and this's her father, Roland." She nudged the man's arm and he nodded at me.

"Nice to meet you both. Please … please, can I see Sunshine?" My eyes filled with tears before I could blink them away.

"That's not up to us, honey, that's up to her. You hurt her, you know. She loves you and what's she's going through, shouldn't nobody have to go through. She's just a baby. Our baby."

"I'm s-sorry." It was all I could muster.

"I'll go ask her if she's up to seeing you, but if she ain't, you need to just stop coming over here and calling. It's too much for her and Lord knows, she don't need more pain." Then Beatrice pointed her finger at me and said, "You get what I'm saying? No more coming over or calling if she don't want you to." I nodded and then she shut the door in my face.

I stood there for what seemed like years before the door opened again. It had only been a little over a week, but Sunshine already looked thinner and dark circles sat under her eyes. She stared at me, her angelic face drained of its usual color, and my soul teetered on the edge of a cliff, waiting to jump off and shatter into a million pieces.

"Sun, I … I really fucked up, and I was wrong. I want to be here for you, and I'm so, so, sorry. Forgive me, please."

'The thing is Tal, I don't know that I'll beat this. It's pretty bad. I'm not sure you can handle that, and that's fine. I get it."

"Sun, please—"

"No, you need to listen. I'm giving you what you wanted. I'm letting you go. I can handle you wanting to walk away because you're scared. But what I can't wrap my head around is the fact that you wished you never loved me … that's what hurts the most. You wished you never loved me, right? You wish we'd never met?" Sunshine searched my face and when I said nothing she shouted, "Answer me, damn you!"

"Yeah, but it's not like that, and you know why I—"

"Well, let me tell you something. You were the love of my life. I love you and I would've loved you no matter what, even if you'd told me that crazy-ass story on the first day we met. You think you're different when it comes to love? Nobody knows what the hell they're getting into when they fall, Talia! I'd never wish not to have fallen in love with you, because love, heartache, death, all of it … it's one and the same!"

"What did you just say?" I felt sick. *One and the same.* I'd heard those words before.

"I said it's one and the same. There'll always be a goodbye and you don't get to put your head in the sand when something bad happens without missing out on all the stuff in between. You're the one who broke my heart, you and you alone. I love you, always will, and always would have. Remember that."

I saw it then. The towering figure that materialized a few feet behind her. It had to bend to greet me and this time I saw it clear as day. It was skeletal, but there were bits of decomposed leathery flesh stretched across parts of its face and body. Dark fluid dripped from the corners of its gaping black hole of a grin and its shoulders shook with dry and dusty laughter, but no one seemed to see or hear it but me. When it placed its putrid hand on Sunshine's arm, I gulped and a hook pierced my soul and tried to pull it from my body. Sunshine started to close the door, but I put my hand in to stop her.

"No, wait! It doesn't matter anymore! I love you, Sun! And … I … I'll never love anyone else," I rasped.

"No, you won't. Goodbye, Talia," Sunshine said. Then she pushed my hand out of the way and shut the door, launching me back into the heart-shaped box of darkness she had pulled me out of.

SKIN TAGS

Originally published in *Midnight Beyond the Stars*
edited by Kenneth W. Cain

Lorna grumbled under her breath as she swept the various clumps of hair on the floor into the dustpan. She'd been doing hair for over thirty years and had yet to be given her first client since being hired over two weeks ago. It was true that she'd only worked at chain haircutteries over the years, but that didn't mean she wasn't capable of the same level of service as the other stylists at the highfalutin salon. She was starting to think they'd hired her to do their dirty work, and it wasn't sitting well with her one bit. The broom slipped from her hand when she looked up and saw a man sitting in her chair.

"Hello? May I help you?" Lorna gave the man her best smile.

"I was told you could give me a haircut," the man said. He didn't smile back.

"Oh, well, of course. Just give me a minute." Lorna picked up the broom. She was annoyed no one had alerted her that she had a client and pretended not to see the smirks on the faces of her coworkers in the mirrors as she went to wash her hands.

The man in her chair was fidgety, like he had a terrible itch he couldn't scratch. His clothes hung from his rail-thin frame and he was as pale as watered-down milk. A full salt-and-pepper beard covered most of his face and he had a head of thick white hair that looked like it hadn't been combed or cut in some time. Lorna introduced herself as she put a cape around him. He nodded, but didn't offer his name. He said he didn't want his hair washed, so she sprayed his bird's nest of a mane with water and tried not to meet his bloodshot eyes in the mirror.

"I got back not too long ago … I was on a mission," the man said.

Lorna stopped spraying. "Excuse me?"

"I was on a mission. That's why my hair hasn't been cut. I should've shaved, I know, but I actually grew to like the beard and I'm not too sure I want to see what's underneath."

"Well, the beard suits you. Do you mind if I ask what kind of mission you were on?" Lorna combed through the man's tangles and feigned interest.

"Space … I was in space."

"Did I hear you right? Did you just say you were in space?"

"Yes. Space." The man sighed a long-exaggerated sigh.

"Wow! Now, that's really something. What were you doing all the way up there?" Lorna had heard a lot in her years of cutting hair, but this was something completely new.

"I'm sure you may've heard or read recently about a few certain big shot entrepreneurs getting involved in the field of asteroid mining."

"I don't have cable right now, but I do remember seeing a news article or something on Facebook about platinum mining—"

"Platinum? Ha! Precious metals! They aren't the only things these people are interested in. Water … that's the real meal ticket."

"Water? Who would've thought? Well, a big kudos to you for being brave enough to go up there and help those who're doing God's work for the good of the country!" Lorna met his haunted gaze in the mirror and suddenly became uncomfortable.

"God's work …? For the good of the country?" The man scoffed.

Lorna frowned. "Did I say something wrong?"

"Those greedy narcissistic bottom-feeders didn't care about the good of the country, the world, or even the galaxy. They sure as hell didn't think about who or what else might've already been on those ugly rocks! All they wanted was to become trillionaires and the poor bastards they sent to do their dirty work had no idea what awaited—never mind. Anyway, I wasn't sent there to mine. Mistakes were made, and I was supposed to save them from themselves and it all went to hell in a handbasket."

"Jeesh, that sounds like an absolute pickle for sure." Lorna could tell the subject was upsetting the man, and even though she normally let her customers get things off their chest, she didn't think it was a good idea to continue the conversation. She was also starting to think he was a bit off his rocker and wondered if he'd ever really been to space at all. She parted his hair and asked, "Well, um, all right then. So, how would you like your hair cut?"

"My hair?" The man stared off into the distance for a few seconds then said, "Just get rid of it all."

"We can do that," Lorna chirped.

She began to focus only on his hair. First, she had to cut away the bulk, then she could use her clippers to do the rest. The man had closed his eyes and seemed to fall asleep, which wasn't unusual—clients did it all the time. She noticed as she was cutting away that he had several large skin tags clinging to his neck. Most were flesh-colored, but some were a rusty brown and reminded her of pieces of cooked ground beef. She looked up, and upon further inspection, she could see some of the flesh-colored stalks protruding from his eyelids as well.

A shudder rippled through her body.

The guard she chose for the clippers was a four, which would give him a short cut but leave enough so as not to expose his scalp too much. Lorna wondered how previous stylists got around all the skin tags at the base of his neck and wasn't sure how she was going to, but she would worry about one thing at a time. The buzz of the clippers didn't seem to stir the sleeping man, and she was glad for that. She ran them over his head once without incident, but then her clippers hit a snag and got stuck. When she tried to gently pull it free, blood spurted like a geyser into Lorna's eyes and rained down her face.

A piercing scream erupted from her throat, causing the man's eyes to pop open. He looked at Lorna's blood-splattered face and sprang from the chair.

Everyone in the salon was frozen in horror, including Lorna, who stood motionless except for her slick, trembling hands. The clippers hung from the wild-eyed man's head, still caught on whatever had snagged them. He looked around as if he was lost, then his breathing became labored and he bent forward with his hands on his knees until he could catch his breath again. Suddenly, he ripped his cape off, threw it to the floor, and shouted, "I shouldn't have come back … you're all doomed!" Then he fled from the salon, leaving a trail of his blood behind him.

At first, everyone was too stunned to breathe a word, afraid that if they did, the man would hear and run back in. Seconds felt like hours as they looked around at one another with their hands to their chests, then everyone began moving and speaking all at once. They checked on one another and made sure everyone was okay and then went to grab cleaning supplies to help clean up the mess the man left behind.

After washing up as best she could, Lorna tried to explain through frantic sobs what she thought must've happened. The manager wrote up an incident report, but didn't call the authorities because, she said, she wasn't sure an actual crime took place. Still in hysterics, Lorna replayed the incident over and over and tried to explain to her dismissive manager about the man's large skin tags. "They were all over his neck, but I didn't know they'd be on his scalp. I thought I was being so careful," she cried.

The manager looked at her coldly, then spat," Well, you should've been even more careful. I need you to go home until further notice. Let's just hope we don't end up with a lawsuit on our hands."

Lawsuit? *Been more careful,* she thought. *What about me? His blood went into my goddamn eyes! I could contract something … He didn't look well!*

Lorna shivered the whole way home. She had become a hairdresser when she was just twenty years old, and not once in her career had anything like that ever happened. Not to mention being reprimanded by a woman who was young enough to be her daughter was humiliating. She wondered if she should go to a doctor. What if some of his blood went into her mouth when she screamed? Why hadn't the manager instructed her to go to the doctor? She was forced to sign the incident report, so why shouldn't she go get checked out too?

First thing tomorrow, she would call the salon and tell them she wanted to go to the doctor and that they were going to pay for it. She might even call a lawyer. After all, she was genuinely traumatized by the incident and none of her coworkers seemed to give a rat's ass.

Once home, Lorna scrubbed herself pink in the shower, then stood under the hot water until it turned cold. Still wrapped in a towel, she downed four shots of Tito's, hoping the vodka would race through her veins and kill whatever cooties could've gotten into her. A couple more shots later, Lorna was feeling somewhat better, but she wished she had someone to talk to about what had happened. With no parents, kids, or siblings, she wondered who she could trust to listen to her worries. Most of her so-called friends were too busy with married life to ever give their full attention to their single burden of a girlfriend. There was her ex-husband, but he was an ex for a reason. Still, she wanted to call someone, anyone, but in the end, she chose to go to bed and deal with it in the morning.

Morning knocked on Lorna's brain like a sledgehammer. Not only did she have a pounding headache, but she couldn't turn her neck without wincing. It felt like her lymph nodes might be swollen. Her eyes felt like dried figs in their sockets, and she could barely peel them open against the laser beams of sunlight coming in through her blinds. There was a fleeting thought that she should stay snuggled up in her blanket and go back to sleep, but it evaporated when she remembered why she was still home in the first place.

She hung her feet over the bed, yawned, and consoled herself. *The man was an astronaut or something, right? How tainted could his blood actually be?*

Lorna looked in the bathroom mirror and cringed. Her normal rosy complexion was pallid, and her eyes were bloodshot.

Maybe I am sick?

All she wanted to do was go back to bed and forget about everything, but she needed to phone work and see what was going on. She couldn't afford to be without a job again, plus, she still wanted to go to the doctor.

The work phone was busy, so she dialed the doctor. They told her they couldn't get her in until the following Monday. She could go to the emergency room, but she wasn't sure if it was an actual emergency. She dialed work again and finally got through. It was her boss that answered.

"Yes," she snapped.

"I was just wondering when I could come back to work? Also, I'm not feeling so well, and thought I should go—"

"Take the rest of the week off, Lorna, and on Monday morning we'll have a meeting to see what we're going to do."

"But I ... okay, all right then. See you Monday morning." Defeated, Lorna ended the call. The salon was closed on Sundays, but that meant she'd be without tips for several days.

By Thursday morning, Lorna noticed a few skin tags on her wrists and along both sides of her neck. They sprouted from her skin like rows of corn. Fright tickled her innards like ice-cold fingers. She'd had a few small skin tags already, but these weren't ordinary skin tags. They were bigger, for one thing, and they looked similar to the ones that had been on the astronaut. She began to think maybe it was a virus of some sort and decided she might need to go the hospital after all. But without decent insurance and limited funds, she wasn't sure how she'd pay.

"Besides, skin tags aren't contagious," she told herself. "I probably had some of these all along and just now noticed because I'm paranoid. Better to wait until Monday, have that meeting, and then go to the doctor so they can pay for it."

Hot tea with honey and a healthy dose of the internet consoled her. She read that skin tags were harmless and found nothing about viruses that could cause them. She'd searched enough Google images to reassure herself that what she had, were, in fact, harmless skin tags. Though most of the articles said not to cut them off yourself, she'd cut a few off before with a pair of nail clippers, and other than a little blood, nothing bad had happened. Lorna decided she'd only clip the bigger ones. *Isn't that what the doctor would do, anyway?*

After a shower, Lorna glugged some vodka to prepare for her procedure. She laid a towel on the bathroom floor, then she sanitized her nail clippers and the areas she wanted to cut with rubbing alcohol. She needed to egg herself on so she wouldn't chicken out.

All I have to do is snip and they'll be gone. They don't grow back. Just do it!

She took a deep breath and squeezed the clippers. It really hurt, but she found that if she took a deep breath before each snip, it was manageable. One by one, they fell like heads from a guillotine onto the towel.

When she was finished, she examined the little blobs stuck to the towel, then shook them into the bathtub. Most ran down the drain when she sprayed them with the stream from her shower head, but a few of the larger ones stuck to the tub like glue. Lorna shrugged and decided she'd get rid of them later. Miraculously, many of the spots had stopped bleeding almost immediately after she'd clipped them.

She chuckled. *Who needs a doctor when you have the internet, a good pair of nail clippers, and a bottle of vodka?*

It was still dark when she sat up in her bed. Her tiny wounds throbbed and itched something fierce. Her throat was raw, like she'd been screaming in her sleep.

Probably shouldn't have had all that vodka before bed.

She groggily wandered to the bathroom to pee. When she turned on the hall light, she shrieked. More skin tags, bigger than the last, had cropped up on her wrists. Her hands flew to her neck and she could feel several of them roll under her fingers. She raced to the bathroom in a panic.

They were on her eyelids, under her armpits, and on the sides of her stomach. Some of the larger ones were engorged, like overfed ticks. She touched one, and it jiggled. Then she pinched it between her fingers, and it fell off onto the floor. Lorna's mind reeled with fear. She'd have to go to the hospital. There was no other choice.

Queasiness caused her to lift the lid on the toilet, where she hung her head and eventually threw up buckets of foul-smelling goo. Stars danced in front of her eyes and dizziness overwhelmed her. She caught her breath and leaned against the wall to keep herself from fainting.

"What's happening to me," she whispered.

A strange sound from the bathtub startled her. It sounded like the squelch of a wet mop. All she had to do was peel back the curtain and look in, but she was afraid to. More chunky acid rose in her throat as she moved her feet.

It's nothing, it's nothing at all. The squelching continued. *It's something, it's definitely something.*

Lorna closed her eyes and gripped the curtain. Slowly, she peeled it aside. She opened her eyes and gasped. What she saw moving around the tub made no sense.

"I'm asleep," she murmured. "This isn't real and I'm asleep."

Lorna pinched herself until tears sprung to her eyes. *I'm definitely not asleep.* The skin tags that hadn't gone down the tub drain had somehow merged and morphed into a large blob and it was rolling around in a frenzy.

"What the fuck is happening?"

Who should she call now? The police? The military? Maybe a fucking mental institution? It was the spaceman; he had something to do with this; she was sure of it. Lorna continued to watch in horror as the thing undulated around her tub. Like rising bread dough, the gelatinous mass seemed to be getting bigger by the second. When what looked like two small limbs poked out of it, the single thread of sanity she'd been holding onto snapped and she hit the floor.

She was cold and her eyelids were almost too heavy to lift. *Where am I?* Lorna remembered she was in her bathroom and had passed out on the tile. Then she recalled why she had passed out and shot up.

Her ears rang as she looked around. She didn't see anything. *The tub.* But there was nothing in there either. She started to giggle, and then it turned into a full belly laugh that echoed around her. *None of it was real! None of it!*

Except she still had the skin tags, and she still felt like hot death warmed over. Her legs were wobbly when she stood, and she felt weak. She couldn't remember when she ate last, and despite the alarming situation, she was ravenous. The reflection in the vanity made her recoil. It was her face, but it was gaunt and dark circles underlined her sunken eyes. Every single strand of hair on her head had turned white. Lorna's shoulders shook as she tried to cry, but no tears fell.

A sound like glass shattering came from inside the house and she stiffened.

Someone was in the house. Lorna was sure of it. They were walking around and knocking things over. She needed to get to her phone. It was charging in the kitchen on the counter where she left it. Why hadn't she ever gotten a gun or even a dog? She looked for something to defend herself with, found a pair of scissors in the bathroom, then tiptoed out.

Whatever Lorna was looking at, she wasn't sure if scissors would cut it. She didn't dare move a muscle or take a breath as she watched the grotesque human-like figure move around her kitchen. It was hairless with no discernible face, and its flesh reminded her of melting candle wax. The refrigerator doors were open, and the floor was littered with its contents. The thing's foot slipped in the slime of some broken eggs, but it caught itself from falling.

Lorna watched as it grabbed an entire bunch of bananas off the counter and pushed them into where a mouth would be. Then it ate a roll of paper towel and a bottle of dish soap. It seemed to pick items at random. Most of the stuff stayed in, but some of it came flying back out as if it found it unappealing. It pulled her phone from the wall and consumed it, cord and charger still attached. It must've liked it because the phone didn't reappear.

A million thoughts raced through Lorna's head. What the fuck was this thing? How could this be happening? Whatever it was, it wasn't human. It may've slightly resembled a human, but it wasn't one. With her phone gone, she had to get out and find help. At the time, renting a secluded bungalow on a dead-end road seemed perfect. Not so much anymore.

She tried to creep quietly backwards, but she tripped over her own feet and bumped the wall. The thing looked in her direction. Lorna wasn't sure if it could see her since there were no eyes on it anywhere that were detectable. It made an earsplitting noise like a squealing pig and, with surprising speed, it moved toward her as she raced to get away.

Lorna's legs buckled and she fell. She was too weak. The thing was on her in an instant. It held her down with its gummy hands. When Lorna cried out, it squealed in return. It seemed to be blindly studying her, moving its fingers over her skin, until it reached what it was looking for. A soft gurgle similar to a cat's purr came from it as it tenderly caressed and stroked each of her bloated skin growths. It lowered its featureless face only inches from her own, and a thick snot-like substance reeking of blood and rotten mushrooms dripped from it, saturating her.

Dry heaves racked Lorna's stomach, and she tried once again to fight, but her body just wouldn't put in the effort. The thing forced two of its slimy fingers into one of her eyes, and she screamed. As it rotated its fingers around like a drill, she shrieked over and over until it felt like her eardrums would bust with the effort. When it ripped her eye from its socket, Lorna alternated between bloodcurdling screams and choking on the acidic vomit that scorched her esophagus as she watched it—with her remaining eye—push her eyeball into its face. It looked down at her with one familiar blue iris and squealed with what sounded like delight. A moment later, it held up one of her bloated skin tags for her to see, then gently placed it down beside her.

Lorna's chin trembled as she turned her head and watched the ball of mutant flesh roll around and begin to morph. "Oh my God," she panted. Though she knew no God was coming to save her. As the thing squealed and began to dig out her other eye, she screamed and screamed until the blinding darkness consumed her for good.

CATCH AND RELEASE

Originally published in *The Jewish Book Of Horror*
edited by Josh Schlossberg

It was a cold evening for September, and the wind whipped off the water and bit into Raz's cheeks like tiny teeth made of ice. He'd been standing on the pier over the dark choppy waters of Lake Ezra for quite some time, looking down into its gloomy murkiness, trying to decide when to empty his pockets of the crumbled bits of bread he'd stuffed into them. His tears had long dried, but his shoulders still shook, both from the chill and with remorse.

He hadn't meant to hurt Beth, but she'd asked him to do the unthinkable; leave his dear Sera. Raz had enjoyed Beth's company, more than enjoyed really—he'd been fooling around with her for months, how could he not?—but she wasn't Sera and never would be. Then she said she was going to tell Sera everything, and he'd lost it. His hands acted of their own accord and wrapped themselves around Beth's swanlike neck.

It didn't take long for Beth to die. She didn't even struggle. The fact that Raz wanted her dead took the life out of her before his hands ever did. She'd loved Raz with her whole heart and didn't care to live without him, anyway. If Raz saw the yielding in Beth's eyes, he ignored it. His only motive had been to keep Sera ignorant of his unfaithfulness. Even when the blood vessels broke and peppered the whites of Beth's bulging eyes, he'd kept squeezing. Panic only set in when he'd stood over Beth's lifeless body and wondered what he was going to do to cover his tracks.

When his cell rang, he jumped in his skin and held it up with shaky hands. It was Sera. He answered, his voice strained. She asked him what was wrong, and he told her he was tired, that work had been extra stressful. There was a pause—of disbelief, maybe—but then Sera accepted his explanation and asked him when he'd be home. Raz told her he was leaving the office as soon as he finished up a few things and that he'd be home in about an hour or two.

Before he hung up, Sera murmured, "I love you so much, Raziel. You're a good husband. I just wanted you to know that."

And with that, all the guilt that had been chomping through his guts like a ravenous worm in an apple tunneled its way to his heart. *There's no turning back now*, he thought, and then scrambled to clean up his mess.

Beth's corpse was somewhere in the choppy water below. It had been a couple months, but Lake Ezra was vast and deep, and her body had probably drifted quite a ways by now. Raz shuddered. The fact that a woman who he'd cared about, fucked, and laughed with over bottles of wine was having her pale olive flesh plucked away from her bones by ravenous marine life was too much to think about. After he'd dumped her, he'd actually hoped her body would be found and that he'd be caught, but it never happened. She ended up just being another missing person.

Raz looked across the water and choked, "I'm so, so sorry, Beth. Forgive me, please …"

It wasn't too long after what happened that a troubled Raz went to his rabbi. While he didn't tell him what he'd done, he confided that it was something horrible, and that there might not be any amount of prayer that could save his soul. But Rabbi Robens insisted that he was wrong, that God heard all, and that no sin could overcome His forgiveness. He told Raz that if he felt true regret for whatever he'd done and never did it again, he could then begin the process of teshuvah by righting his wrongs and asking for forgiveness.

Raz asked what he was supposed to do if the person he'd wronged refused to hear his pleas for forgiveness, but he stopped short of telling him why.

Rabbi Robens reminded a distraught Raz of *Micah* 7:19, and spoke in a firm but gentle voice as he recited it, "He will take us back in love; He will cover up our iniquities. You will hurl all our sins into the depths of the sea."

Raz had come to Lake Ezra as a child with his parents and then as an adult during the Jewish New Year of Rosh Hashanah to perform the ceremony of Tashlich. Before the following week of Yom Kippur, he and others would recite biblical verses of repentance and forgiveness and cast their bread—which symbolized a person's sins—into the deep, murky water below.

Lake Ezra had always been the one place he could tell his secrets without any judgment, and this particular secret was the biggest he'd ever had to tell. But he was ready to rid himself of the bread in his pockets, which felt more like stones. Standing by the water, he did not feel the presence of God as he'd hoped; instead, the presence of something sinister.

He and Sera had already performed Tashlich earlier that afternoon. They'd met with other friends and shared a lunch of Sera's fresh-baked raisin challah and apples dipped in honey before they began the ceremony. After their prayers, they threw leftover bits of challah to the fish below in hopes of starting anew.

But Raz hadn't actually thrown any of his bread; he knew he needed to be alone to truly complete his. So later that evening, he told Sera he was going to the office to sketch out ideas for an ad campaign he was working on. When he returned to the lake, he stared at the rippling reflection of the moon on the water and found he was struggling to begin. Each time he went to open his mouth to speak, something seemed to reach up into his throat and cut off his voice.

Since Beth, Raz hadn't been sleeping well, and he lashed out over any little thing. Then he began to refuse all of Sera's sexual advances, blaming it on everything from work to her most recent push for a baby. But really, it was because each time he lay atop his wife, he saw Beth's face. Though she had to have been wounded by his lack of interest, Sera still ran her hands through his thick, dark hair each night and whispered that she wanted to try for a baby before it was too late.

"You're only thirty-two," Raz replied. "We still have some time."

But Sera insisted she was ready and that they now had the money for the fertility doctor they'd been saving for. Raz finally gave in and agreed they'd start in October, which meant he was more eager than ever to cleanse himself of the evil fungus that was continuing to spread.

Raz tried to ignore the moaning of the cold wind and focused on the water instead. He cleared his throat again and again and attempted to speak. Eventually, he was able to produce a whisper, which would have to be good enough. He pulled the bread from his pockets and made fists over the water, then closed his eyes and concentrated.

First, he saw Beth. She was still in the purple dress she'd worn the night he'd taken her life. Her long, blonde hair bobbed in the water, and she beckoned for him to jump in and join her. A milky film had settled over her honeyed eyes, and her full lips were cracked and set in a grim smirk.

Raz cried out and almost took a step forward, but he shook his head clear and pictured Sera. Sweet Sera, with her bright green eyes and the waves in her soft brown hair. She was what mattered now. Only her and the baby they'd make together. Not himself and not Beth. The smoke of his breath was like living tendrils as he recited *Micah* 7:19. Then he whispered, "L'shana tovah," as he unfurled his fists and let the bread tumble into the water below.

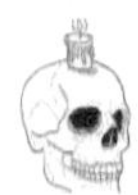

It was a walleye that ate it. It gobbled up every crumb of Raz's horrific sins, then swam away. Over a span of weeks, the three-pound fish grew larger, and its belly swelled—so much so that it begun to have trouble swimming. It was sluggish and lethargic, and its keen vision was off, which is probably why it went for the wriggling crankbait.

The day was crisp but humid and overcast, and the lake's surface had the right amount of ripple that was perfect for fishing, in Asher's opinion. He'd set out on his own for an afternoon to himself. He preferred to fish alone—fewer distractions and more chances for a catch.

His boat had been drifting on Lake Ezra for a while without any luck, and he began to wonder if he should've brought along some nightcrawlers instead of the crankbait his wife, Naomi, had bought him for his birthday. He'd have felt guilty, though, if he didn't use them at least once. Plus, he knew she'd ask him, and he didn't feel like lying to her—he'd done enough of that in the past. He took a sip of the lemonade iced tea she'd filled his thermos with and sighed. Life was pretty damn good.

Asher had been daydreaming when he felt a tug on his line. He fumbled only for a second, then stood up and began to reel in his prize. Whatever it was, it had to be pretty big because its weight was bending the rod to the point of snapping, and it was a sturdy pole. Luckily, he had a good leader on.

Beads of sweat formed on Asher's forehead, and his hands became slick too. But he steadied his legs and kept reeling as the thing used the water's current and its own strength to try to win its freedom. The boat was being towed towards the center of the lake, and Asher wasn't sure how much longer he could keep his grip on the reel. He was afraid the line would snap if the battle continued much longer.

Just as Asher was about to cut the line, the violent tugging came to a halt, and he was finally able to reel in his catch. Asher whistled when he caught sight of the walleye. It was enormous! The biggest he'd ever seen. It had to be over thirty pounds or more, and it was easily over three and a half feet long!

Asher had to use both hands to pull the mammoth into the boat. He cut the line, and left the bait hooked into its mouth, which hung open, revealing rows of its pointy canine-like teeth. It gasped for air every few seconds, then flapped its fins and tail half-heartedly, almost like it knew it had been defeated.

Asher couldn't be sure, but he thought maybe he'd done the thing a service by catching it. Maybe it wanted to be put out of its misery. It had to be ancient in walleye years, as huge as it was. The cooler he brought was not going to contain the behemoth, so he used it as a sort of table, hauling the fish across it, and letting it hang over the edges. He could've cut it to fit, but he didn't want to mutilate it since he wasn't sure of his plans for it.

Asher felt a little bad about keeping the fish. He imagined it must've had one hell of a life. *It sure ate like a king,* he thought. Still, releasing it wasn't an option. The fish was just too awesome to let go. He thought about who he was going to get ahold of to have the thing looked at. He was positive it'd be a record breaker. Having his picture and name in the paper would be sweet. Then he'd have it stuffed and mounted on the wall in his office so he could gaze at it whenever he pleased.

But then Asher's stomach growled loud enough to nearly rock his boat, and another thought came to mind. He knew smaller walleye was best for eating, but his mouth watered at the thought of a thick fillet of the big fish, pan fried and swimming in lemon. The thought of consuming its delicate white flesh overtook him, and he decided right then and there that the fish would be dinner.

Asher made his way back to land and was glad he'd forgotten his cell phone, which was probably still plugged in next to his computer. The urge to call someone would've been too great, and he wanted to wait. He lifted the cooler with both hands—fish still slung over it— and hauled it to the bed of his pickup. He bubbled with excitement. He'd have to snap some photos before he cleaned and filleted it so that he could share them on social media. Otherwise, no one would believe him. With the cooler and fish loaded into the back of the truck, he hitched his boat back up and set off for home. He couldn't wait to show Naomi!

"What the hell is that thing, Ash?! It's freaking huge!" Naomi stood at the top of the steps that led to their front door and stared at the monster her husband was holding. It sort of looked like a walleye, but the biggest she'd ever seen. She brushed her unruly red hair away from her light blue eyes and padded down the steps to get a better look.

"It's supper, baby! And I caught him using the bait you bought me! It's a walleye, biggest I've ever seen, maybe the biggest caught in Lake Ezra. Hell, maybe the biggest caught, ever! I fought him hard and eventually he just gave up. "Whaddya think?"

"I … I don't know what I think. What do you plan on doing with that thing?" As Naomi walked toward her husband and the fish, a series of tingles traveled up her back and rested on her scalp. She'd seen plenty of walleyes before—her father used to catch them all the time—but none were as big as the one Asher was holding. As petite as she was, she was sure she never would've been able to reel that mutant in. The thing's color was weird too. Instead of the usual mix of gold and olive, this one's coloring was more like that of a rotting banana. And its large glassy eyes were completely black, not the opaque and cloudy color she remembered. No walleye she'd ever seen had black eyes like that. She winced, then gagged when she caught a whiff of it, vile and putrid, like rotten eggs times ten. "Ugh! Ash, it freaking reeks! I think it might be bad or something."

"What? It's not spoiled, it hasn't even been dead that long. Smells like lake water and fish. I don't think any fish smells pleasant, honey."

It was then Naomi looked into the fish's ink-black eyes again. She suddenly felt overwhelmed with deep despair and didn't know why. "No, but they don't smell like that thing does. I'm not eating it. No way!"

Asher frowned. "That's all you got to say? I was all excited to bring this home and you can't even pretend to be happy about it?"

"I'm sorry, Ash, you're right. It really is an awesome catch. I'm proud of you. Only a true fisherman could've bagged that sucker." She knew blowing smoke up his ass was the only way to keep things from getting too heated.

"So, if I clean and fillet it, you'll maybe cook it for us, then? I'd try to, but you know I can't even make shit on toast."

"I don't know, Ash. It doesn't look right. I mean, look at its eyes! Maybe you should have it stuffed instead. Show it off, ya know? Who knows what kinda pollution is in that lake nowadays?"

Asher sighed and spat a loogie in the grass, then he tutted and said, "I can't think of a single body of water on Earth right now that isn't polluted in some way, and we still eat all the shit that comes from most of them. Look, the thing's probably old. Humans look like shit, too, when they live past their shelf life. Age spots, bald spots—you name it, we've got it. Hell, we even smell kinda funky when we get old. I thought you'd be thrilled, I really did. Guess that's what I get for thinking, huh?"

She knew by the rise of color in his cheeks that things were headed back south. "Alright, Ash. Alright, then. I am happy that you're happy. Go on and clean it up, and bring me some of the fillets when you're done."

Naomi and Asher had been having problems, and she didn't want to disappoint him. Twenty years of marriage was too much to throw away. If cooking her high school sweetheart some fish would make him happy, then it would make her happy too. She shivered and hugged herself when a gust of chilly wind blew across the lawn and passed over her as she turned to go inside.

The fillets looked disgusting, and the smell of them was worse. It permeated the air in the small bright kitchen like a sulphury smog, and she was sure the odor would stick around long after it was cooked. The gifted *I JUST BAKED YOU SOME SHUT THE FUCUPCAKES* sign on the wall that normally made her chuckle suddenly wasn't funny. Naomi couldn't believe Ash still wanted to eat the fish. She pointed at the dark blemishes and spots weaved throughout its white flesh and pressed her finger into one of them, causing a black slime to ooze out.

Even that didn't deter Asher. He set a sweating bottle of beer atop their new, speckled granite counter, took a closer look, then shrugged. "It's probably just from what it's eaten. Or they might be varicose veins. Nothing to worry about."

But Naomi wasn't so sure. She was afraid roundworms had burrowed into the meat. "Ash, are you really sure you wanna eat this? I have a bad feeling about it. I could heat up some leftovers …"

He put his hands on his hips. "Just go on and make it. If I take a bite and it tastes funny, I'll throw it and all the fillets in the garbage."

Naomi was still trying to shake off the gut deep despair she felt as she set the table. She placed a platter of golden fried fish down, then surrounded it with wedges of lemon. She poured herself a third glass of wine and sat down in front of her dish of leftover lasagna.

Asher had gotten out of the shower and hollered from the bedroom that he'd be out as soon as he put some clothes on. She had to admit the fish didn't smell that bad now that it had been seasoned and fried. Still, she wasn't going to eat one bite of it. Not for all the fucking tea in China.

Asher beamed as he sat down at the table. "It looks delicious," he said, loading his plate with a few fillets. After squeezing lemon over them, he shoveled a forkful into his mouth and made annoying sounds of satisfaction.

Naomi glared at him but said nothing. She couldn't tell if he was being dramatic or really enjoying his meal that much. Neither one spoke a single word as they ate. The only sounds were Asher's intermittent moans and Naomi's fork grazing her dish.

Two pieces of fish remained, but Asher couldn't eat them. He started to feel queasy. Why had he felt compelled to gorge himself? After the first bite, the insatiable urge to eat as much as he could had overwhelmed him. What had he been trying to prove? As bubbles of indigestion loomed, he looked over at Naomi. She stared back at him; her mouth slightly twisted in confusion. He stared so long and hard, his eyes glazed over and his mind went blank.

Asher squeezed his eyes shut and then shook his head clear. He looked back over at Naomi. She looked completely different. Her hair was smooth and blonde, instead of curly and red. He squeezed his eyes shut and shook his head feverishly. He looked at her again and panic set in. Her blue jean eyes were now the color of golden honey and her thin lips were full and pouty. She was speaking to him, but he couldn't hear a word she was saying. His hands balled into fists and he pounded the table hard enough to cause everything on it to jump.

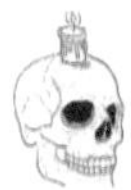

Naomi yelped when Asher banged the table, and when she saw his eyes, she became frightened. They were huge and black and he stared at her in a way that made her heart freeze and her bowels ache. When she could swallow the lump in her throat, she managed to ask, "What is it, Ash? What's wrong? Are you alright?"

Asher continued to stare at her. Then he began to breathe fast and hard through his nose and mouth. "Bettth," he snarled.

"Asher, you're really scaring me," Naomi whined. "Please tell me what's wrong?"

Asher stood and threw his chair across the room. "Beth," he growled, "I thought you were dead and rotting at the bottom of the lake. The flesh on your carcass picked apart! I thought I was done with you!"

Naomi ignored the frantic beating of her heart and forced herself to get up from the table. She backed into the living room to get her phone.

Asher grinned the grin of a madman and trudged after her. He threw his head back and laughed a terrible laugh that made Naomi's blood run cold.

His lips curled back from his teeth, and he shouted, "Where're you going, Beth? You gonna call Sera? Tell her all about us? I don't think so!"

He ran full speed toward a panicked Naomi, who raced to get away, but it was no use—the former college running back was too quick and too strong.

Naomi looked up into her husband's eyes, which were now completely black. Thin black veins ran along his temples, across his face, and down his neck. His sweat and breath stank of rotten eggs.

She wiggled in his grip. "Please, Ash, let me go and let me get you some help! Please … you're hurting me!" He laughed maniacally and placed his hands around her throat.

Asher spat a gob of blackened goo to the floor, then sprayed Naomi's face with foul spittle as he screamed, "I couldn't ask you for forgiveness, could I? Because you were dead! But here you are, right where I want you. Do you forgive me, Beth? Huh? Tell me you fucking forgive me!"

Naomi had no idea what was happening. She choked back cries as Asher's hands tightened around her neck. With her air running out, she rasped, "I love you."

Asher's grip loosened, and he fell backwards. He looked at his hands, then back at Naomi, shaking and sobbing on the floor. His chin trembled. He didn't understand what was going on. What had he just been doing to his wife? Asher whimpered out loud, "Naomi?"

But as soon as she looked up, a force, powerful and dark, began to consume him again.

Asher shrieked as his joints popped and his nerves twitched. As his body contorted, he pulled at the hair on his head to try and get whatever it was inside of him to stop. But it fought harder, reaching through his tissue, muscle, and bone until it found its way to what felt like the depths of his soul.

When Asher realized he was losing the fight, he leapt from the floor and fled from the house. Naomi had run after him, but didn't follow him to his truck. She stood just outside of the front door with the phone to her ear and shouted to him over and over, but her words sounded distorted and distant to his ears.

Cramps flayed Asher's insides, and his head throbbed. Hot coals rode up behind his sternum, then climbed his esophagus until an eruption of what felt like hot lava crowded his mouth. He had to keep spitting gobs of thick mud-colored rank stuff out in order to breathe, but it kept coming up. Asher let out a cry that was guttural and inhuman, and it pierced the night as he got into his truck. Naomi had finally run down the steps and was still shouting at him. He looked at her and ground his teeth, then put his foot to the gas and peeled out of the driveway.

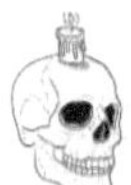

Asher parked his truck in an area of overgrown grass hidden from the road. There was a warped and rotting wooden picnic table surrounded by a smattering of Jack pines. He swung open his door and tried to make it to the table, but fell to the ground. He curled into in a fetal position, then writhed in agony as the darkness swirled around in his mind like a hurricane. It was feeding on his warmest memories, using them to try to gain strength and take control. When the dizziness subsided, and he could muster the strength, he got up and began to run.

He stopped only when he hit the water. A thick, eerie fog surrounded Lake Ezra. Asher's blood hummed in his ears. Every bit of his flesh felt like it was burning, and all he wanted was to put out the fire. The water was cold, and it lapped at his feet, summoning him to come in.

He was in up to his chin, and his teeth chattered as he treaded the freezing water. His legs hurt, and he was getting tired. But he still felt the urge to continue, so he kicked away and struggled to stay afloat.

A woman's voice, soft and gurgly, filled Asher's ears, startling him to full attention. "These sins aren't yours," she said. "They belong to Raziel. And only him. He's the one who put me here."

Before he could process the woman's words, he felt hands like bony weeds wrap tightly around his ankles and pull him down. He kicked out and cried out for Naomi and for his mother. But it was too late, and the lake swallowed him whole.

Asher couldn't see much of anything under the water, but bony fingers pried open his mouth as wide as they could. He tried to clamp down but couldn't. A few of the fingers jammed into his mouth, then tunneled past his uvula, causing him to violently gag until he threw up the entire contents of his fish supper. He wanted to breathe in, but knew he couldn't.

Just when he thought he was going to die, something propelled him to the surface. He wasn't far from land, and with the little strength he had left, paddled back to it.

Back on dry land, Asher fell to his knees and began coughing up a lung. Once he could breathe without hacking, he stood up and looked back out at the lake. A woman—her badly decomposed face and skeletal shoulders somewhat visible in the moonlight—stared back at him. She waded closer until he could see the purple garment that clung to her bones. He didn't need to see any more of her, it was obvious that she was not among the living.

Asher began to shiver uncontrollably, then turned away and refused to turn back around. He stumbled back to his truck and leaned against it. Tears streamed down his face. Who was that woman in the water and what had happened to her? And who the fuck was Raziel? Just the thought of the name gave him awful indigestion.

He didn't understand any of it, but as soon as he got back to his wife and called the police, he sure as hell was going to find out.

MATERNAL DRIVE

Gayle knew something was wrong when Jeremy didn't come back in time for dinner. He went for a run around the same time every afternoon, and he was always back in time to shower before she set the table. Bill arrived home from work around 6:00 p.m., as he always did. He set his briefcase down, took off his oxfords, and whistled a happy tune as he sniffed the roast-chicken-scented air. He was still smiling and whistling as he walked into the kitchen, but then he frowned when he saw his wife's face.

"What's wrong?" he asked.

"Jeremy … he hasn't come back from his run."

"Oh. Well, he's sixteen, Gayle, not six. I'm sure he ran into one of his friends or something. You know how he is. Mr. Popular!"

"He always comes back in time for dinner. He wouldn't just go somewhere and not tell me."

"Well, did he take his phone? Call him."

"I tried. His phone's on his dresser. He did wear his watch, though, but he isn't answering my texts. I just know something's wrong … I feel it in the pit of my stomach. I kept telling him not to take those winding back roads. People fly down them like they're in a race car!"

"Calm down, hun. Like I said, I'm sure he's—"

When the doorbell rang, Gayle almost fell to her knees. She knew. Like a bullet to the heart, it hit her. She knew something had happened to Jeremy. Bill touched his wife's shoulder, then went to answer the door. It was their neighbor, Murphy, and he was in uniform. He looked down at his feet as Gayle looked over Bill's shoulder.

"Murphy? What is it? Is everything okay?"

"I'm so sorry, Gayle ..."

"Sorry for what?"

"Jeremy, he ..." Murphy's chin trembled. "He was ..."

"He what? Tell me, damn it!" Gayle moved in front of her husband and looked up into Murphy's face.

"Gayle, calm down, honey. Let Officer Murphy gather his thoughts and speak."

"I will not calm down! It's my son he's talking about!"

"We ... someone found Jeremy on the road. We believe it was a hit-and-run. He's being transported to the hospital right now. If you'd like me to take you—"

"He what? He's been ..." Gayle heard Officer Murphy, but as soon as he said Jeremy was hit by a car, her ears put up a sound barrier. Everything anyone was saying sounded far away. She shoved Bill back when he tried to comfort her. Her blood rushed and her vision blurred. Her baby boy had been left to die in the road! Someone had hit him and then left him there like roadkill. The being she'd carried in her womb, who still called her mommy when he was upset, was left for dead.

"Gayle? Listen, we need to get to the hospital ..." Murphy had stepped inside when Gayle shoved Bill.

"Gayle and I will take the Jeep and follow behind you, Murphy. If that's okay?"

"Absolutely. Gayle I ... I'm sorry."

Gayle didn't realize she was moving backward, away from Murphy and Bill, away from the words they kept speaking. She hit the floor before anyone could catch her.

The hospital smelled as sterile and cold as it felt. It'd been five days since Gayle sat down in the ICU in the uncomfortable chair as close as she possibly could next to Jeremy's bed. His body reminded her of a machine, with all the tubes and wires coming out of it. She held his limp hand in her own, trying to rub warmth back into it. Friends had come and gone, most of them unable to handle seeing Jeremy the way he was, and Gayle's own best friend, Lillian hadn't picked up her phone in days, which was unusual, but she didn't have room to worry with that. Bill left to go get coffee, and she was grateful for his departure. She knew he was trying to be helpful, but he didn't understand. Jeremy was *her* son. Not his.

When they married five years ago, Bill had never tried to act like Jeremy's father, and Jeremy had refused to call him by any name other than Mr. Hendry. They got along well enough, but Jeremy never warmed to him the way she'd hoped. Gayle knew she probably wasn't being fair to Bill. She was sure he had to be upset, too, but this was her pain to feel, not his, and she wanted to feel every bit of it. If she thought it'd work, she'd slice into her own flesh, dig through her bones, and rip forth her soul so that she could give it to him. There was nothing more painful than seeing your child this way. Nothing. Her beautiful boy, swollen, bruised, and broken beyond repair. Even if he woke, they said he'd probably never walk again.

Officer Murphy, as well as other investigators, came to talk with her and Bill. They asked questions about his normal running routes and times, and she and Bill answered as best they could. They assured her they were doing everything they could to find who'd hit her son. Bill thought it wasn't a good idea to listen to the details of what they believed happened, but Gayle insisted. She needed to hear it.

She felt the bile rise in her throat as they discussed something they called throw distance, which is the initial point of when the car might've hit him to the resting place of his body. They said even though there were no witnesses yet, they believed whoever hit him was going extremely fast, as it appeared his body was thrown quite a distance. Then they went on to discuss how there wasn't much evidence to go on yet, but they were working on it. She listened with numb eardrums and swollen eyes. If Gayle was breathing, she didn't notice. Her wounded heart thudded in her hollow chest from the gallons of caffeine and lack of sleep.

When everyone left the room, she put her son's hand to her lips and whispered. "Please wake up. I love you so much. If I ever find out who did this to you, I will kill them …"

Bill brought her a change of clothes and barely kissed her goodbye before he left. He'd tried to get her to come home with him, but she'd refused.

"At least wash your hair, Gayle. It looks like someone rubbed cooking oil in it," he said.

"I don't give a rat's ass what my hair looks like, Bill. Just go home and worry about yourself. In fact, since it's such a hassle, don't come back anymore if you don't want to," she spat. She knew it sounded harsh, but she meant it to.

He pursed his lips but said nothing, then he turned and left the room without another word.

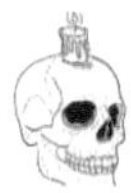

She fell asleep watching Jeremy's chest rise and fall like swells in an ocean, up then down, up then down. The purr of the ventilator was almost calming. She began to dream the same dream she'd been having since being at the hospital. It was her finding out who hurt Jeremy and obliterating them. She never saw the person's face. It was always a shadow, but she burned that shadow to the ground every time she closed her eyes. Gayle stirred when she heard his voice, soft, then loud and warbly, like he was speaking to her underwater. "Mom? Mommy! It was Bill! He did this! It was Bill! You're next! MOM!"

Gayle's head snapped up from its slumped over position. She winced at the ache in her neck and shoulder that she knew was a part of her now. She looked at Jeremy. His eyes were closed, but she could see that they were moving rapidly behind the thin veils of his eyelids. Her heart was in her ears, and her breaths became stunted by the rush of anxiety she felt. She'd heard him. That's what woke her up. She'd heard his voice.

"Jeremy?" she croaked, then she took his hand. "Baby, are you there?"

Bill hadn't come back since she told him to leave, and she was glad, because she didn't like talking to Jeremy when he was in the room. She gently stroked the part of her son's head they'd shaved before they carved into it to relieve the pressure on his brain. As she stroked the dark fuzz that was already growing back, the room began to grow colder. Goose pimples rose on her arms and legs as she watched Jeremy's eyes move faster and faster, like he was watching a movie that only he could see. She took his hand, and though it was brief, so brief it could've been imagined, she felt him squeeze her fingers. Adrenaline flooded Gayle's body, and she shot up from her chair, his hand still in hers. "Jeremy? Jeremy! It's me! It's Mommy! Are you coming back to me? Open your eyes! Come back to me, come back!"

Her cries alerted staff, who entered the room to see what was going on. Gayle ignored their pleas for her to step away and calm down. It was a whirlwind of doctors and nurses as she tried to keep hold of her son's hand. Someone had eventually moved her away from the bedside, and they were gently but firmly holding her in place. Her eyes felt like marbles in her head, seeing but unseeing. There was a cacophony of sounds—shouts, beeps, shoes squeaking, more shouts and beeps, and then there was nothing. And when the doctor looked at her watch, Gayle saw her. It was like her eyes zeroed in on that exact moment. He was gone, her baby was gone.

She'd laid her head atop her son's still body as long as they'd let her. Everything that happened after was a daze. All of her actions, everything she said or did, felt unreal. Someone contacted Bill, and he arrived after they wheeled Jeremy from the room. His presence made her angry, and she looked at him with disgust. She wished she could recall what Jeremy had said to her while she slept. She knew he'd spoken. Her head was too fuzzy. Maybe if she got some rest, she'd remember.

Bill had taken her Jeep again instead of his BMW. She hated when he drove her car, because each time he'd drive it until there was hardly any gas left and then he'd forget to fill it back up. When he opened her car door for her, she glared at him, then yanked it shut. Anger consumed her. It leaked from her pores like hot lava. As Bill got behind the wheel and turned the key in the ignition, she bared her teeth, ready to attack.

"Listen, I know you're upset, but—"

"Upset? Upset?!" Gayle laughed, then screamed at the top of her lungs, causing Bill to shut the car off.

"Jesus H. Christ, Gayle! I'm trying to be here for you, I am, but you have to let me. You're acting like a lunatic!"

"Screw. You."

"Right. Okay. I'm going to take us home, and once we're there, you can scream all you want, but please, let me get us home safely. We don't need any more accidents."

"You bastard. I fucking hate you," Gayle whispered, her eyes brimming with tears.

Gayle seethed as she watched the trees whiz by through the window. Her parents were due back from their Rhine River cruise soon. They were still ignorant of their only grandson's death. She wondered if it was selfish to not want to have to tell them. Couldn't he be alive in their minds for a while longer? Jeremy's birth father, Ricky, died from an overdose on pain pills when Jeremy was only two, and Ricky's parents and siblings never wanted to be part of Jeremy's life, so she didn't see a need to inform them. If they didn't have any part of his living life, she certainly didn't think they needed to know of his passing.

So now what? All she had was Bill. She was supposed to love Bill. Why was she feeling so much disdain toward him? Was she projecting all of her grief onto him? That had to be it. Though she was still furious, she decided to get some rest and see if she could get to a place where she could speak to Bill without wanting to rip his heart from his chest and take a bite out of it.

Once they pulled into the garage, her body went rigid. If she got out of the car and went inside the house, it was real. Jeremy wouldn't be inside. His room would still smell of him, only it'd be empty. His clothes would still be in the hamper. His backpack, his running shoes, his saxophone, his video games, his phone with filled voicemail messages wishing him well and hoping for his return. The house was filled with beacons of his existence, but he didn't exist in this world anymore. Going in there would be like sticking a salt-covered dagger into her fresh wounds, then stirring it around until the pain made her collapse. How could she go inside that house?

"Are you going to stay in here or get out of the car?" Bill got out and stared at her with a look of impatience.

"I will … just not yet. I need a minute. Just go inside and leave me alone."

"Fine."

Bill slammed the car door and Gayle wished right then that she could slam his head in the same door hard enough to decapitate him. She'd never had such violent thoughts in her life. After Bill disappeared inside, she let herself cry again. Fat tears stung the raw skin around her eyes. When the snot dripped from her nose onto her chin and joined the tears that rolled down her neck, she opened the car door and got out. And when she got out, she noticed Bill's car was not there.

Gayle stormed into the house, her fury guiding her like strings on a puppet.

Bill was in the kitchen eating what looked like a bologna sandwich. When he saw her flared nostrils and red face, he rolled his eyes and said, "What now?"

Gayle struck like a cobra and knocked the sandwich from his hand with enough force to send it sailing across the room. Then she slapped him hard across the face. Bill grabbed both her wrists and shouted for her to stop, but Gayle kept shouting about his missing car.

"Listen, I know you're upset. I am too. But you have to stop this! You can't go around hitting people and throwing tantrums. It solves nothing!"

"Answer me, Bill! Where is your goddamn car?"

"This is ridiculous, Gayle. You know where it is."

"No, I don't, because while you were here eating bolognafuckingsandwiches and doing whatever the hell else, I was beside my son's hospital bed, praying and begging for his return. So, again, where the fuck is your car?"

"If you recall, I hit a doe a couple days before Jeremy was … listen, Gayle, my car's in the shop. I took it to the shop while you were at the hospital. I didn't want to bother you with that, but I had to take it. Fuck. I feel like I'm being accused of something here, and I don't like it."

Gayle trembled, both with defeat and despair. He was right, he had hit a deer. She remembered him showing her the damage to the front of his BMW. There'd been bits of hair and gore caked onto the grill and hood and some stuck to the broken headlight. She remembered Jeremy coming into the garage to look at it, telling Bill how lucky he was that the deer didn't go through the windshield.

"I'm … s-sorry, Bill," Gayle said, then she turned and walked away, toward their bedroom. She refused to look in the direction of Jeremy's room. With his door closed, she could pretend he was in there, playing his game, or listening to music. Maybe he was in there right now, his dark curly hair plastered to his head from a run, his blue eyes—the spitting image of her own—intent on his computer screen. If she opened the door, he'd look back at her the way he always did when she opened without knocking, then she'd say sorry and make a funny face and he'd laugh and forgive her. But she wouldn't open the door. Not now. Not yet.

The walk down the hall felt like an eternity. She lumbered into her bedroom and realized she really did need a shower. She could smell herself. But how could she worry about her own hygiene when her son was inside a freezer waiting to be drained and prepared for burial? Pain climbed her arm and radiated across her chest. *Good*, she thought. She hoped she was having a heart attack.

Gayle peeled her clothes from her body, then brought them over to the hamper. Before she dropped them in, she noticed one of Bill's expensive shirts at the bottom, tangled up with a pair of his good jeans and boxer briefs. *Why would he be wearing that?* She knew her husband liked to look dapper whenever he could, but he didn't wear his good clothes just anywhere, especially not at a time like this. Her stomach cramped as she retrieved the shirt and jeans. The perfumy odor that wafted from the clothes struck her like a brick to the teeth. She froze. Only one person she knew wore Lily of the Valley. *Lillian.* She hadn't been answering her phone, and now she knew why. And just like that, Jeremy's voice was deafening. *"Mom! It was Bill! He did this! You're next!"*

"The hell I am," Gayle said.

She wasn't crazy about guns, but after Jeremy was born, she'd gotten her CCW and got one. Being a mother, especially a single one, leads you to do things you wouldn't normally do. Bill didn't even know about the gun, because she'd forgotten all about it, until now. Gayle could hear the television from the living room. She put some fresh clothes on, went into the closet, and found the small gun where she'd left it—in an old purse. She put the gun in the waistband of her pants and left the bedroom.

Bill had made himself another sandwich and was eating it in front of the television. When he saw Gayle staring at him, he stopped chewing.

"What the hell're you doing? Gayle?"

"I'd like to go get ice cream. Can you take me?"

"I'm not—ice cream? We have some in the fridge."

"I don't want that kind."

Bill dropped his sandwich, then stood up. He put his hands on his hips and sucked his teeth. "Fine. Let's go."

She waited until they were on an isolated road to pull the gun. Bill swerved and almost lost control of the vehicle.

"Are you outta your goddamn mind?! Where'd you get that thing?"

"Pull the Jeep over, Bill." Gayle cocked the hammer back. "Now."

Bill pulled over.

"I know what you did."

"I wish I knew what the fuck you were talking about. Our son just died, and you need help. Let me help you—"

"Our son? That's really cute. If you say one more word about *my* son, I'll blow your fucking head off. You don't get to speak his name. You're a murderer and a coward! If you deny it, I'll shoot you in the dick."

Bill looked down at his lap and ground his teeth as Gayle spoke.

"You killed Jeremy. Maybe you didn't plan on doing it the way you did, but when you hit that deer, you were inspired. You and Lillian. Was it her idea?"

"I have no idea—"

"Deny it one more time and like I promised, that dick of yours, the one you've been giving to my best friend, is toast. So, I ask you again, was it her idea?"

"No," Bill rasped.

"But she knew?"

"Yes."

"You got insurance policies on us, didn't you?"

Bill closed his eyes and nodded.

"So, what? You thought you'd kill my son, then me, and what, you get to live happily ever after with Lillian in a house with a picket fence?"

Bill shrugged. "I don't know, Gayle. I wasn't going to do it, but then I saw him running and I just, I did it and … I'm sorry."

"You're sorry? Sorry!"

"Yeah, I am, believe or not."

"Get out of the car."

"Gayle. C'mon—"

"Get. Out. Of. The. Fucking. Car."

"I'm not getting out—"

Gayle fired the gun at his crotch and Bill howled in pain before swinging open his door and falling out of it, hitting the ground like a sack of potatoes. When he stopped rolling about and crying in pain, he got up and limped away from the Jeep, looking back every so often to assure his safety. Gayle drove ahead slowly, as if she were finally leaving, then she put the Jeep in reverse, hit the gas, and backed into him. As soon as he hit the ground, she ran over him several more times, enjoying the feel of his treacherous body under her tires. She smiled a real smile and left him lying on the road, hoping something might come along and pick his bones a little before his pathetic body was found. At that, her stomach growled, so she decided to get her ice cream after all, before heading over to pay Lillian a little visit.

RAGGAMUFFIN

Lori felt at peace as she finished working in her backyard. She'd just finished planting various veggies and herbs in the planter boxes she had constructed. The act of sifting the moist soil between her fingers was more gratifying and relaxing than she'd thought it'd be, and she needed that. After going inside to wash up and grab a snack, she noticed several birds and squirrels loitering by the tender plants. She slid open the sliding glass doors, walked out onto the back porch, and glared at the critters. Something would have to be done or else her plants would never stand a chance.

On the porch, she tapped the glass on the windows, but the critters didn't care and continued hopping through the plants. She didn't want them destroying all her hard work. It was times like this she wished Tim was still around. As much as he was an asshole, he'd been handy. She'd mustered up the courage to kick him out after years of torment. He'd asked her to marry him too many times to count, and she was glad she'd never said yes, or else getting rid of him would've been even harder.

It was only a few months after their split that Tim went and got himself killed. He had crashed his motorcycle on Halloween night, and typical Tim wasn't wearing a helmet. His head had been smashed open like a jack-o'-lantern, and bits of his brain had decorated the asphalt. His family hated Lori and blamed her for his death. They said he wouldn't have been drinking and being reckless if she hadn't broken his heart. Lori expressed how sorry she was for their loss and left the funeral without saying goodbye. She'd felt terrible about what happened, but she was furious too. Tim had always been reckless, and his death could've happened at any time. To blame her was ridiculous.

She still had some of his personal things and was going to give them to his family, but after their interaction at the funeral, she just couldn't bring herself to call them. And now, almost a year later, on the anniversary of his death, the box of his stuff still sat in the guestroom. It was filled with Tim's flannels, a few pairs of pants, his Yankees hat, and a pair of Harley-Davidson leather boots. He'd also left tons of work tools in the shed. Lori'd called him several times to collect all of it, but he said he wouldn't, not unless she took him back. When she'd refused, he had screamed into the phone that she was a fucking cunt and hung up.

Anger consumed Lori as she stared out into the backyard. It wasn't her fault Tim had been who he was. Fuck him, and fuck his dysfunctional family. She was alone now and didn't need any man to help around the house. She could do it herself. It was Halloween weekend, and other than handing out candy, she didn't have plans of any kind. As she crunched the ice in her drink violently between her teeth, an idea formed.

What if I make a scarecrow? Wouldn't that be fun and keep the birds and critters away? She didn't really have friends to speak of. Tim hadn't liked any of them and after years of neglect and keeping her distance, they'd parted ways. She'd tried to restore her relationships once he was gone, but most weren't interested.

She went to the guestroom to pull down the box of Tim's stuff. As she opened the closet door, something leapt at her and she screamed as it ran between her legs. Her heart slowed, and she chuckled when she realized it was only Petrie, her cat. He looked back at her with wide yellow eyes, flattened ears, and his hair on end.

"Petrie, you nut! Mommy almost had a heart attack! I didn't know you were in there. Too bad you couldn't go outside and keep all those naughty birds and squirrels away. But it's not safe for you out there."

Petrie had been a rescue cat she'd brought home from the local shelter. He had long orange-and-white fur and was a ball of nervous energy. He never liked Tim, but that's because he knew Tim didn't like him either. The first night he was home, Petrie had curled up on top of Lori in bed. Annoyed, Tim knocked him from the bed with such force that Petrie cried out when he hit the floor. That night was one of the many rabbit-hole arguments between them.

Petrie meowed and skittered away as she brought the box down and sat on the carpet. She pulled out a red-and-blue flannel, khaki pants, his hat, and the leather boots. She was pretty sure she had the stuff in the shed to build a cross frame. Excitement bubbled around in her chest. *There're old garden gloves in the shed, too, and I could use a pillowcase for the head!* All she needed was some string and straw. *Well, I know what I'm doing tomorrow.* Lori grinned, then shouted, "Happy Halloween to me!"

Sleep came easier than it had in weeks, and she woke early the next morning. She was excited to get to the craft store. Luckily, they had all the items she needed, and she rushed home to start her project. The cross frame was easier to make than she thought. When she was finished with it, she grabbed the mallet and knocked it into the ground near the planter box. Satisfied with where it was, she went inside and fetched the rest of the materials.

She started by feeding a horizontal piece of wood through the shirt arms and securing it, then she took a length of string and tied it tightly around the bottom of the shirt to create a waist. She did the same to the sleeves and made hands out of the gloves. After stuffing the shirt with straw, she pulled bits of loose so it would poke out of the buttons and arms. She stuffed the pants, then attached them to the body. It was coming along nicely.

Lori hesitated as she held the boots. She had to put holes into the back of them. She whispered, "Tim loved these boots." *Well, Tim's dead,* a voice shouted inside her head. A smile plastered her face. "That's right, he is." She made the holes, then tied the boots to the base of the pants. She stood back and admired her handiwork. *Now, for the head.* An old pillowcase dangled from her hand. She stuffed it with straw, then pulled it down over the top of the frame. Once it was molded the way she wanted, she secured the hat using a needle and thread and used the rest of the straw for hair.

Lori thought the scarecrow needed a name. She looked at it with her hands on her hips and wiped the sweat from her brow. The old flannel, wrinkled pants, and dirty garden gloves made it look like a ragamuffin. *Raggamuffin, that's a good name!* Its blank stare was eerie, so she grabbed a few felt pieces to create a face. She chose the pieces carefully, even giving it eyebrows. It wasn't until later she noticed who the face reminded her of.

After a hot shower, she grabbed a book, a glass of wine, and went to read on the back porch. It was raining and Petrie purred in her lap. She'd fallen asleep and woke to the sound of Petrie growling and hissing. "What're you growling at?" Then she saw it. The book fell from her lap as she sprang from the chair. A soaking wet Tim stared at her through the window. Her heart thrashed in her chest. Petrie hissed one final time before he ran to hide.

She stumbled, rubbed her eyes, and then looked again. Her breathing calmed, her heart slowed, and then she laughed. *It's only Raggamuffin! But why's he facing the windows? I faced him away from the windows … didn't I? Must've been the wind.* She walked closer to the window and stared back at the face. It did sorta look like Tim. The dark eyes and menacing smile spooked her. She shook her head and scolded herself. "Lori, you're a big dork! It's only a scarecrow, remember?"

She slipped on her shoes, went outside, and turned Raggamuffin away from the windows. The sky was growing dark again and rain began to pelt her head. She wondered if she'd get any trick 'r treaters in this weather. After one last look at the scarecrow's eyes, she turned away, shivering. Tomorrow, she'd change its face. Back inside, she poured another glass of wine, sat down on the couch, and turned on the television to watch whatever spooky movies were on.

Even with the rain, there were knocks and doorbell rings. The bowl of candy was thinning before 7:30 p.m. The final knock came from a group of teens dressed as the living dead. They stood at the front door, patiently awaiting their sweet spoils. Lori raised her eyebrow, but said nothing as she handed them the last of the candy. Goose bumps rose on every inch of her body when one of the teens said, "Whoever that dude is outside of your house in the scarecrow costume looks sick as hell. Straight fire! We almost shit our pants! Is that your husband?"

"W-what?" Lori swallowed hard, but the lump that formed in her throat wouldn't budge.

"The dude in the scarecrow costume stumbling around outside of your house, he's just standing there all SUS and creepy AF! He got us, that's for sure. We all jumped when he groaned. He, like, for real, scared us!" The teens all laughed and nodded their heads.

"I-I-um, I don't know what … never mind. Be safe out there, and … Happy Halloween, guys." Lori shut the door with a trembling hand and tried not to faint as she leaned against the wall. Her heart was going so fast she was sure it'd explode. Could they've possibly gone around to the back of her house and seen Raggamuffin? She wasn't sure how else they'd have known about him unless they had. Why would they do that, though? She convinced herself that the teens had gone around back, seen her scarecrow, and decided to try to scare her. That had to be it. She refused to let a bunch of teenagers get to her. It was Halloween, and she should've known better than to let them scare her so bad. But still, fear flooded her senses. It stole her appetite and caused her insides to ache with an artic chill she couldn't warm.

For dinner, Lori made herself a tuna salad sandwich but couldn't eat it. She put food out for Petrie, too, but he hadn't come out from hiding, not even when she opened her can of tuna. Since she couldn't eat, she showered and got into an oversized shirt and sweatpants. Tim hated when Lori wore those types of clothes. He said she looked like a fat hobo. She combed her hair, took her contacts out, and put on her glasses.

Petrie still hadn't touched his food, so she called to him. "Petrie! Mommy's little Fur Man Choo! Where are you?"

He still didn't come running, which worried her. She searched for him and finally found him under the guestroom bed. He growled as she peered at him. His eyes were huge, and he hissed when she reached for him. "Hey! What's gotten into you? It's Mommy. C'mon, Fur Man Choo, come out." Lori reached further under the bed and he swatted her hard enough to let her know he meant business. She pulled back, hurt and concerned. "Petrie, Mommy's not gonna hurt you. You okay, buddy?" Petrie growled until she put the bed skirt back down. *Maybe all the knocks, doorbell rings, and candy beggars had scared him,* she thought. That had to be it.

After cleaning the scratches on her hand, Lori decided to call it a night. She got into bed feeling lonely and depressed as she thought about everything she had and didn't have, weighing it all out, torturing herself with all of her shortcomings, 'if onlys,' and 'what ifs.'

She wanted to call her mother or sister, but it was late and then they'd be worried. She tossed and turned, thinking about what the teenagers had said. It replayed in her mind like a movie, over and over. *"The dude in the scarecrow costume stumbling around outside of your house, he's just standing there all SUS and creepy AF! He got us, that's for sure. We all jumped when he groaned. He, like, for real, scared us!"*

She hadn't gone to check on the scarecrow after that happened, she refused to. She knew there was no way what they said was true, and she didn't want to scare herself any further before bed. She pushed the event to the back of her mind and thought about Tim. Despite everything he was, she had loved him. She didn't miss his unpredictable anger and destructive behavior, or his breath reeking of whiskey and beer, but she missed his calloused hands running down her body, his lips grazing her neck … oh, how she missed that.

His family put their nose where it didn't belong in their relationship. He'd wanted to get married and have kids, but Lori held back. She told him he had to change, to seek help for his anger and drinking, but he wouldn't. Tim had been a product of his environment. His father was an abusive alcoholic and his mother was an enabler. Though his parents had a volatile relationship themselves, they'd turn against anyone who tried to step in. The rest of his family, siblings and all, were angry at the world and everything in it.

Lori thought she could help Tim and, in his brief moments of tenderness, she would falsely believe that he could change. He just needed her to show him how, but as soon as he'd let her in, he would shut her out again. It was an endless cycle of emotions that she decided she couldn't deal with anymore. He was too damaged.

When she told him she wanted him to leave, he'd gotten in her face, so close that his dark eyes burned through hers like hot coals. He'd smelled of sweat and beer as he cupped her face hard with his hand and breathed through flaring nostrils. His eyes glistened and his face was almost purple. "You'll pay for this, Lori. You'll see it was a big mistake. I loved you. I loved you with all my soul. No one will ever want you the way I did—ever."

For a moment she thought about taking it all back, but then he'd shoved her into the wall and she threatened to call the police. He put most of his clothes into some garbage bags and left. He called several times, sometimes cussing her out, sometimes just breathing, and then she would hang up and cry for what they'd never have.

A few weeks after the breakup, she had started to get used to Tim being gone. And then she got the call. It was his friend, Kyle, from work. He wanted to check in and see how she was doing and asked if she needed any help with anything. She said she was fine and asked why she'd need his help. Kyle was quiet for a few moments, but then went on to tell her that Tim and him were out the night before and that Tim got into a fight with some guy at a bar. They both got kicked out, and then Tim sped off on his bike and wrecked it a few miles down the road. Lori said she hadn't heard about that, and asked if Tim was alright. Kyle had choked up. "No, he's not alright. He's … Tim's fucking dead, man. I thought you knew. I'm so sorry," he whispered and then hung up.

Lori cried into her pillow at that memory. She missed Tim's strong arms around her and his unshaved face brushing up against hers as they kissed. The sex had been fantastic. She had stayed so long, put up with so much, ashamed to admit for the sex. She felt a familiar longing and slid her hand down into her pants. In the middle of enjoying a little tryst, she heard a noise. A soft scraping noise. Frustrated, she got out of bed and went into the living room. She turned on the light but didn't see anything.

The noise came again, making her jump and turn towards the kitchen. Lori squinted at her reflection in the sliding glass doors. Her unkempt hair stuck up in all directions, and her sweatpants hung off her hips. She hadn't been eating right, and it was beginning to show. She was pulled from her self-hating thoughts by another noise. Walking closer to the doors, her breath fogged the glass. She didn't want to open it, but was unable to see anything, so she slid the door slowly open and stepped halfway out into the indoor porch. Lightning flashed and Lori screamed. Her heart spun out of control when she saw his face pressed against the window. Dark eyes pierced the glass and his mouth was twisted into a horrible grin.

Outside, the wind whistled and blew, and Lori watched Raggamuffin batter the window with his face and gloved hands, recreating the horrible sound. Her breath slowed, and she got a grip. *How did he get all the way over here? I put him in the ground pretty good when I moved him back earlier.* There was no way she was going to go out and move him again. *And why not? It's a scarecrow, not a monster.* "Because," she murmured out loud in the darkness.

She turned and walked briskly back into her bedroom and locked the door. *Why am I letting a damn scarecrow scare me so bad?* But she knew why, deep inside, she knew. She pulled her weighted blanket over her face despite it being too warm. She felt pathetic as she began to pour sweat, but she refused to remove her blanket shield.

A pounding headache roused her from her fevered slumber. She smoothed sweat-damp hair from her face and looked up at the ceiling, or where the ceiling would be if it wasn't so pitch black. She looked at the clock; it was 3:00 a.m. exactly. Fingers of fear climbed her neck and settled atop her scalp, prickling it like tiny needles. *It's the witching hour.* Her grandmother used to talk of it all the time when she was little. "It's the time of night when the veil between life and death is thinnest, allowing spirits and ghosts to travel between two worlds," she'd say. "Jesus was crucified at 3 p.m. as you know from the bible, and the inverse of that would be 3 a.m., and so that's why it's an hour of ghosts and demonic activity. Even more so during Halloween!"

Lori knew what her grandma said was horse pucky, but she couldn't ignore the feeling in the pit of her stomach. Her mouth was dry, and she was in desperate need of a drink, so she dragged herself out of bed. Groggy and half asleep, she padded down the hall, careful to keep her eyes straight ahead. She froze when she heard a sound. It was coming from inside the house. Her breath caught and her eyes popped fully open. It sounded like someone was softly knocking on a door with mittens.

Lori's hand shook as she turned the hall light on. She gasped and jumped out of her skin when she saw paws coming from under the guestroom door. Petrie! Relief overtook her as she opened the door and Petrie darted out like a rocket. She didn't remember shutting him in there, but she decided she must've.

She made her way to the kitchen, refusing to glance in the direction of the glass doors as she got some water. As the water filled her glass, her grandma's voice blared in her head. *The witching hour, the witching hour, the witching hour.* "Ugh! Shut up, Grandma," she said.

Something on the kitchen tile felt strange and wet under her feet, but she chose to ignore it and chugged her water instead. On her way back to bed, she felt more strange wet stuff poking into the bottom of her feet. *Don't look, don't look, don't look.* She looked. Bits of wet straw littered the floor and there were boot prints that led into her bedroom.

Lori shook her head. Her stomach cramped. She covered her mouth with her hand to stifle any sound and moved backwards. She felt like she was going to be sick. *Should I call the police? Call the police for what? My scarecrow?* Then her grandma's voice, *The witching hour, the witching hour, the witching hour. Even worse, during Halloween!* She tiptoed to the kitchen and grabbed her phone. She had to check, she had to. She had to know. She grabbed the biggest knife from the knife block and opened the sliding glass door quietly, and walked toward the windows. The moon shone into the yard, but she saw nothing. He wasn't there. Raggamuffin was gone.

I'm either crazy or this is real. What other explanation is there? Could someone be trying to scare me? Who? Those kids? Then how did they get into my house and get straw all over, Lori? The witching hour, the witching hour, the witching hour! Petrified, Lori gripped the knife and stood in the kitchen for what seemed like an eternity. When she finally moved, she went as quietly as one could, then waited in the living room. She didn't want to confront whatever it was in the dark, but she didn't want to turn on a light to let it know she knew it was there. She crouched down beside the couch and waited.

She was nodding off when she heard it. The sound of wet boots and stiff straw. The crunch and squeal of wet boots was coming down the hallway. The knife handle was slick with sweat in her hand. She dried it off and got ready. As it got closer, she saw its shadow on the floor. *Crunch, squeak, crunch, squeak.* She didn't dare breathe. The shadow stopped.

Lori became furious. *Fuck this!* She stood up and crept closer to the hall. The shadow didn't move. She could smell it, the wet straw. She raised her arm, closed her eyes, and shrieked as she turned the corner. But there was nothing there. *Yup, I'm crazy!* She was crying and laughing at the same time as she slid down the wall and dropped the knife. She looked around, but didn't see any boot prints or straw.

Her mother had told her that she should see a grief counselor after Tim's death, but she had waved it off and said she was fine.

Maybe not. She got up and forced herself to look. Raggamuffin was right where she left him—pressed up against the porch window. She let herself laugh again, then she put the knife back in the block and went back to bed.

Lori woke to a strong odor in the bedroom. It permeated her nostrils and stole her breath. The banket atop her was soaked. *Gasoline.* She shot up in bed, tried to reach for her glasses, but knocked them to the floor. She slid in the liquid on the floor and felt her glasses snap underneath her weight. *NO!* Her pulse quickened as she squinted around the room on all fours. She strained her eyes, frantically searching the dark. She heard a noise like a dry chuckle. It was Tim. She knew it. She sputtered and coughed, trying to scream through the caustic fumes.

Lori heard the strike of the match and that's when she saw him, his twisted grin and black eyes. She cried out and tried to jump back on the bed as a lake of fire spread across the floor. The flames chased her, licking at her heels, and finally climbing her sweatpants. She was engulfed in seconds. The pain as her flesh was cooked on her body was too intense, and she collapsed to the floor. The fire smothered the bedroom and surrounded Lori's burning body on all sides. Somehow, as her eyes broiled in her sockets, she caught a glimpse of scarecrow Tim standing over her, and before she succumbed to death's embrace, she heard his voice, dry and hoarse, but crystal clear. "Remember that I said I loved you. And I loved you with all my soul. No one will ever want you the way I did—ever."

The house was partially burned to the ground before the fire was put out. Inside, firefighters and police found what was left of the horribly charred body of Lori Milfred, and beside her, a pair of Harley-Davidson leather boots.

ROLY-POLY

Originally published by Blood Bound Books in the anthology
Chew On This! edited by Robert Essig

The day was hot, and sweat gathered in all her fleshy crevices. Margot trudged into a coffee shop and bought herself two cherry cheese Danishes. A table with three chairs was free, so she sat down and ignored the people who stared at her. She could feel their judgment, *the fat girl who eats two Danishes, and then she needs a table all to herself to do it. The nerve!* She could see the round peaks of her cheeks with each calorie-loaded bite. A tiny burp escaped when she licked her fingers free of icing, relishing the last of her sweet treats.

When she stood up, she could feel her dress stuck in her butt crack, so she pulled it free. She turned around when she heard murmurs and glared at the two college-aged girls gaping at her with smirks on their perfect skinny faces. "Is there a problem?" Margot asked, but the girls just shook their heads. She could hear their bubbling laughter as she threw her trash away. *Fuck 'em.*

Margot wished she had opted to Uber, but the last time she did, the driver kept looking at her thighs in the rearview mirror like they were juicy sugar-cured hams. Her tacky feet slid about her flip-flops and sounded like a fart when she walked. *God, I hope no one hears that! Should have worn sneakers, Margot! Only a couple more blocks, you got this!*

The building was an old brownstone, but it looked well kept. She had never been to her friend's new apartment. They hadn't even seen each other in a few years. Even though they lived in the same city, their conflicting schedules never seemed to match up. When Pammy called Margot out of the blue, they talked for over an hour, and by the end of their conversation, Pammy offered to give her something that she said would change her life. When Margot politely declined, Pammy begged her to come see for herself, because seeing is believing. Though she was skeptical, Margot decided to take her up on the offer.

She climbed the steps and pushed a button. "Margot?" Pammy's voice rang out. "Is that you?"

"It is I, the one and only, Roly!" Margot sang out. She wondered why Pammy called her Margot instead of Roly.

Margot's shoulders slumped when she spotted the stairs. Pammy was on the third floor and there was no elevator. *How do they even get fucking furniture up there? I'd probably be a damn bikini model if I lived here for a year!* She sighed, then slowly began to climb them. Her thighs burned, and she had to keep wiping away her sunscreen-tinged sweat before it dripped into her eyes. When she finally reached the third floor, she was breathing like an angry bull. She gripped the top of the railing and fist pumped in silent victory. It smelled funny on the third floor, like boiling root vegetables, garlic, and spoiled bologna. *Ugh, gross,* she thought as she made her way down the hall.

The door opened before Margot even knocked.

"Margot! I heard you coming! My smiley friend, how are you?" Pammy beamed. "Come in, come in!"

Margot gasped when she saw her. It didn't even look like her. "Pammy Cakes? You look … phenomenal!" Margot wrapped her arms around her friend.

"I know, right? I feel so good too. I'm a completely new person! Come, sit down, have some herbal tea, and I'll tell you all about my magic pill!"

Margot shook her head and wondered how Pammy did it. She must have lost over a hundred pounds or more. She was acting so weird, though, overly happy. *That's not like her. She's usually pessimistic and sarcastic. Well, if the key to being optimistic is being beautiful, I'm screwed.*

Also, when did she start drinking herbal tea? We always drank fizzy Italian sodas or iced coffees; she hated herbal tea. Margot sat down and felt a pang of jealousy as she watched her formally obese friend pour hot water into two mugs.

"So tell me, Pammy Cakes, will this magical pill do the same for me? And how much is the damn thing?" Margot snorted.

"What's a Pammy Cake?" Pam tilted her head.

"Seriously? Did the weight loss melt your brain?! You were Pammy Cakes, and I was Roly-Poly since elementary school! How could you forget that?"

"Oh—yeah, yeah, I recall. Well, I guess I chose to forget that. Shed those painful memories along with my weight, ya know?" She looked at Margot in a way that made her feel uncomfortable.

Margot squirmed in her chair. "Sure, I guess. I get it. So, this pill, is it expensive? I don't have a lot, but I do have some money saved …"

"I won't hear of it! I have an extra one, just for you! No charge. I want you to have it." She smiled so wide Margot thought she could see her epiglottis.

"Why?" Margot asked.

"Why?"

"Yeah, why? I mean, I haven't seen you in ages and now you call me outta the blue and offer me this … this weird weight loss pill. Why?" Margot searched her friend's gorgeous face.

"Well, you're given two pills in case the first one doesn't take. Obviously, it took for me and I have the extra, so I thought of you because you're my friend." Pammy shrugged. "What're friends for?"

"You mean I'm your only *fat* friend."

"Well, yeah, but you won't be for long!" She grinned.

"Alright, Pammy—sorry, Pam, I'll bite. What is it and what does it do? Where'd you even find out about it?"

Pam brought the steaming mugs to the table and sat opposite from Margot. She slid a bottle of honey across and then exhaled before she spoke. "Well, I was tired of being fat. I tried it all. Exercise, diet programs, shakes, pills, and you know the whole rigmarole. My insurance wouldn't cover a lap-band surgery, so I felt out of options. I was making my way through a bag of cheddar and sour cream Ruffles when my phone buzzed. You remember Lita?"

Margot nodded. "How could I forget her? She was the other fat girl in school, except she was well-liked due to her very popular and attractive older brother."

"Well, anyway, she called me and we chatted about the old days and all that. Then she told me she lost a bunch of weight. I, of course, asked how, and she told me that while on vacation in South America with her friends, she came across a man who was selling these miracle diet pills out of this little bodega. She said there was a long line of people waiting, so she asked them what they were waiting for, and they told her."

"So, you went to South America?" Margot probed.

"No, silly! Let me finish. So, anyhow, I did some extensive research and got my own online. Cost me a thousand bucks! And now, here I am, paying it forward."

"It feels wrong, though, like, not legit. Is this one of those freaky pyramid scheme things? I mean, is it even FDA approved? Did you get it from the Dark Web? This shit could hurt people, Pammy!"

"Dark Web—ha! It doesn't hurt people; it makes people better. Do I look hurt?" Pam stood up, twirled, and ran her hands down her perfect body.

Margot shook her head, "No, but ..."

"Look, you don't have to take it. I just thought I'd offer it to you before anyone else. I have friends at work who could lose a few—"

"No! No, I want it. I just want to know if there're side effects or warnings? Do you know what's in it?"

"There are some side effects, as with anything. Cramping, loose stool, maybe some gas, but nothing too major. No worse than those pills we took in high school that were practically legal speed." She sat down and covered Margot's hand with her own. "As far as what's in it, don't freak out, alright? It's a ... it's like a ... tapeworm."

Margot pulled her hand away. "A tapeworm! Are you nuts? Have you lost your damn marbles? You swallowed a tapeworm pill? Those are so bad for you and banned here for a reason! This's fucking crazy, Pam! A worm? A fucking worm? I'm out. No thanks!"

"Calm down! It's like a tapeworm, only it's not. It's a safer alternative. It doesn't hurt you. You lose the weight as it absorbs some of what you eat and when you have reached your goal, all you need to do is eat a bunch of garlic and drink tons of water to flush out your system and voila, it's gone and you're a new person! No pill from the doctor, no anything."

"How do you know that, huh? Lita told you this? For all you know, it's a money-making scheme, and she roped you in and now you wanna rope me in! How do you know you don't have a giant googly-eyed worm inside of you right now? Have you checked the toilet after you take a dump, see if there's any wiggly worm segments doing water ballet? How about your butt? Does it itch? Do you drag your ass across the floor?" Margot stood up from the table and crossed her arms. "I'm out. No thanks."

"You're being dramatic!" Pam's face was beet red.

"You just offered me, your friend, a pill with the potential to fill me with fucking worms, Pam!"

"Yes, but they're not bad. Look at me, Margot." Pam stood up. "Just look at me!"

Margot had to admit that her friend looked incredible. It wasn't just that she lost so much weight, either. There was no skin baggage, no stretch marks, and she practically glowed. Margot wished to look like that her whole life, to not be the fat girl. She bit her bottom lip and then sat back down. "How do you know this pill will work for me? If it's so damn effective, why aren't more people using them?"

"Well, you know how our government is. They don't want people better. They like people fat and sick. It provides doctors and big pharma with more money and decreases the population. Look, this pill will change the future. I think it'll even be on the market in parts of Europe very soon. And you know how these things go. Once it's approved over there, we'll get on board too. Monkey see, monkey do. We'll just charge an arm and a leg for it and then make people jump through giant hoops to get their hands on it. Capitalism, it could use a lap-band, right?" Pam sat back down and sipped her tea, her perfectly French manicured pinky pointed outward.

"Fine, I guess I'll try it."

"Good choice! Because to try and get your hands on it once it does become a thing will be a lot harder, if not impossible. You're going to be so happy you did this." Pam reached over and covered her hand again.

"I guess so. It's just that, well, maybe it won't work for me like it did for you?"

"It will. One pill worked for Lita and I both. She gave the extra to her mother, I believe. Her mother was a real plumper, remember?" Pam chuckled.

"Yeah, I guess. Well, alright. So, can I just swallow it now or should I do anything special before? Like eat a bag of potting soil or something?"

"Very funny! You can take it now if you want. There's no special before stuff or anything. I have it in here." Pam got up and put her mug in the sink, and grabbed a small container from the kitchen cabinet. She brought it back to the table and rattled it around. "This's about to change your life, girlfriend. It takes some time, but it will work miracles!" She opened the lid and took out a small cream-colored pill. "Here it is. Your future."

"It looks like a Tic Tac. Well, bottoms up!" Margot swallowed it, then clawed at her throat as she coughed and gagged.

"Margot? Are you okay?" Pam came around the table.

"I'm fine, you ninny! I was joking!" Margot snorted.

"Oh, you scared me!"

"So, about how long do you think it will be before I look as fabulous as you?"

"I don't know," Pam said. "I assume everyone is different. For me, it took several months, but you should start to notice a change within a few weeks. Try to eat well and stay away from alcohol. You can call me anytime and we can talk about anything that's going on."

"Well, it's too late now. I took it."

"Yup, you did. It's gonna be great, you'll see!"

Margot wasn't totally sure it would be great, but at this point, what did she have to lose other than half of herself? They talked more about possible side effects and what foods to eat to help ease them. They walked around her new apartment and Pam showed her all her new clothes. By the time Pam hugged her goodbye, she was feeling giddy and optimistic.

Walking down the stairs was easier, but it was still muggy in the building. Margot almost slipped out of her sweaty flip-flops and tumbled down the steps but caught herself. *Pam seems healthy and looks so fantastic. I feel completely fine right now. Maybe this will work, maybe I will be a new me months from now too. I can't even imagine being that thin. No more Roly-Poly.*

She picked up some fruits and veggies at the farmers' market, including multiple bulbs of garlic, just in case. Overhead clouds took some of the afternoon heat away and the walk home felt delightful. Her thighs still burned from her trek up the stairs, but she ignored it. Once home, she made herself a big green salad and chopped up some strawberries for dessert. *A new me, I can already feel it.* Then she let out a gargantuan fart and belch. "Oh, my lawd! Jeesh, excuse me! Must be the worm!" She cackled, then flopped down on the couch with her salad and turned on the tube.

Weeks passed and though she'd lost a few pounds, it wasn't anything as dramatic as she was expecting. She was constantly tired, bloated, and ravenously hungry. She was mildly disappointed when she didn't notice any wiggling worms in her stool. The frequent gas was embarrassing. At work she blamed it on her squeaky chair or rushed to the restroom before letting it all out. She was grateful for the lack of smell. She called Pammy and told her all about the symptoms, but Pam told her it was all normal and to be patient. *Easy for her to say, Miss Flawless.*

A few more weeks went by and Margot was irritated. She did everything she was supposed to. She ate fairly healthy; she drank loads of water, and stayed away from alcohol. She had lost fifteen pounds, but that was only a dent. When the weekend rolled around, she decided to say fuck it and order a pizza and drink a six-pack of beer. *I'm eating for two, aren't I?* She even asked for extra cheese and garlic knots.

Five slices in and three beers later, she sat back on the couch watching a documentary about Inuit people in Alaska. They were eating something they called Muktuk, which was whale blubber and skin. Children giggled with blubber glistening on their faces, eating the stuff like an ice cream cone. Margot's stomach churned. Her hand strayed under her loose shirt and she grabbed a handful of fat. *My Muktuk. I wonder if you could eat human blubber?* She gagged, then farted. *Of course.*

She'd fallen asleep on the couch and woke up to stomach cramps. She wobbled to the bathroom and sat on the toilet. The cramps were ruthless. It felt like she was trying to shit a stalactite. She leaned forward and moaned. Tears sprang to her tightly shut eyes. "Maybe I shouldn't have eaten all that pizza." She grunted. "Or those garlic knots. Ugh." A colossal fart echoed off the bathroom walls and then she was finally able to go.

She couldn't remember a time where taking a shit had caused her to sweat. It worried her. She wiped and gasped when she saw drops of dark blood on the paper. She stood up and examined the toilet, other than the most monstrous turd she ever made, nothing out of the ordinary. *Maybe I should just go to the doctor and tell them what I took?* Exhausted from the strained bowel movement, she decided to call it a night and decide what to do later.

When she woke the next morning, she felt lighter, and when she ran her hands down her belly, it felt flatter. She burped, then rolled on her side and let out a few farts that ruffled the sheets. The smell was foul, like rotting meat, and she gagged. A piercing cramp stabbed her abdomen and caused her to jump up and flee to the bathroom, but by the time she got there, it ceased. She looked in the mirror and gasped. Her face was thinner, her hair shinier, and her skin glowed, just like Pammy's. *Maybe I'll give it more time.* She was beyond pleased with the progress, even though she knew in the back of her mind it made little sense. The rest of her weekend was a shit fest, but in the best possible way.

By the time Monday rolled around, the transformation was phenomenal. She knew the amount of weight she lost over one weekend was insane, but the pill must finally be working. She strutted into work wearing heels and a red dress she hadn't worn in ages. It was even a little loose. She beamed as all the compliments rolled in. *So, this's what it's like?*

Guys in the building who never looked her way, smiled at her, and female coworkers gathered round like clucking, pecking hens and asked her how she did it. She told them she'd been dieting and working out. They eyed her suspiciously, but she insisted that was all she did. They told her to keep up the good work and give them tips some time over cosmos. Margot basked in the attention. She'd been a ghost at work only last week. Now she was front and center by the end of the day, popular even.

She must've lost over fifty pounds in one weekend. And with the previous fifteen or twenty she'd already lost, that was almost eighty pounds total. She still had quite a bit to go, but she felt incredible. It's remarkable how much your face changes when you begin to lose weight. She had cheekbones, *actual cheek bones!* She'd always wanted them. Her double chin was barely there.

At home, she gave herself a facial. She plucked her eyebrows for the first time in years and swooned at her own reflection. *Pam was right. This is a miracle, too good to be true!* Something moved inside her eye and made her jump. "What the fuck was that?" She leaned back in. "What the …?"

Margot held her eye open and watched a thin black tendril creep along. There was a slight pressure, and it tickled her cornea as it stretched out in several different directions, like a tiny dead tree. *This can't be good. Whelp, it was fun while it lasted; I guess.* The other eye did the same. Tiny black lines crowded the entire whites of her eyes. A cramp shot up from her lower abdomen and raced up into her chest. She clutched her side.

In the kitchen, she held her phone with a shaking hand as she found Pammy Cakes in the contact list. She wanted to punch the screen. It rang twice before she heard her friend's chirpy voice.

"Hello? Is this Margot? Are you there?" Pam asked.

"I'm … here. My eyes—they're fucked up! My vision is blurred and the cramps are intensifying. I think I need a doctor!" Margot sobbed into the phone. "Pammy, I … is this normal? Please tell me, this's normal?"

"Calm down, it's normal. It all happened to me before the big change. Have you recently lost a lot of weight in a short span of time?"

"Yeah, but—"

"Listen, it'll all be fine soon. Trust me. The new you, it's right around the corner. How exciting! Hooray, you!"

Margot couldn't believe what she was hearing. She gritted her teeth. "Pammy, my eyes look like something out of a fucking horror movie! My cramps are next level, and I'm pretty sure I might be dying! How could you be so happy for me at a time like this?"

"But you're not dying, you're just changing! It'll be over soon enough!"

"You're sure? Like, really sure?" Margot choked.

"Yup, surer than a heart attack!" Pam chuckled.

"Not funny, Pammy. Listen, this's is a lot harder than I—"

"Take it easy, Margot. You'll be fine. Let it take its course. You've come too far." Then she abruptly hung up.

The phone call did nothing to quell her fears, but she was too invested to up and go to the doctor only to be flushed out before she reached her goal. Also, she could only imagine how they would look at her when she told them what she did. She chugged a beer and lay on the couch. "Fucking worm!" she wailed. "You're a damn terror!

She called into work the next day, unable to hardly move from her bed. Her body felt like it was being tattooed by a thousand needles from the inside out. On the plus side, she felt weightless, having relieved herself of yet another ginormous bowel movement after another night of painful stomach spasms and obnoxious farts. She'd crawled to the kitchen and grabbed a bottle of vodka. It would've been great at a time like this, but every time she took a glug, something seemed to lurch into her throat and gag her until she spit it back out. She put the bottle back under the cabinet.

"I can't wait anymore! I'll do the rest on my own!" She grabbed the garlic and began to peel clove after clove. The garlic went down easy. She popped several more cloves and downed a couple bottles of water. The burps were putrid, but she continued until she'd eaten almost a whole bulb. There was one tiny clove left. She chewed it and savored the pungent taste. "*Hasta la vista*, bitch!" She drank a third bottle of water.

An extremely sharp pang punched her gut, and she hit the floor. Breathing hurt. The worm was clearly displeased with her dining choice. It writhed around maniacally inside of her and she thrashed around the kitchen floor. She pulled down the dish towel, balled it up, and bit down on it to assuage her agony. She kicked her legs in a cycle motion, trying anything to alleviate the severe discomfort. It indignantly rebelled the more she fought. Her skin was cold and clammy as she lay flat on her back.

"Get the fuck outta me, you bastard!"

A brutal itching sensation covered her body. Her skin was being stretched taut in different directions. Her joints crackled and popped. Convulsions racked her body. She vibrated across the floor and tried to call for help, but she could only gurgle. Her tongue felt like a pork rind. It was as if all the moisture in her body had been sucked away. The great waves of pain were relentless. It was too much for her to even try anymore. Her limbs were rigid, like rigor mortis set in.

The body of Margot looked like a mummy that had been unwrapped. It began to separate, slowly at first, like a difficult pistachio nut, but then it swiftly popped open. The shell of Margot lay in thin crisp sheets. As the new Margot emerged, the sheets disintegrated like ash that had been blown by a gust of wind. She stood tall and tilted her head one way, then the other. She pointed her feet like a ballerina, then spun around, kicking the old Margot into to dust.

When she stopped spinning, she coughed several times. She felt something lodged in the back of her throat. It was forced out with several more urgent coughs. She burned with pride as she examined the sticky little cream-colored egg in her hand. It was exquisite. She carefully put it inside of a small container with a lid to harden, then twirled to the bedroom and admired her lithe body in a full-length mirror.

"I'm completely gorgeous!" She smiled. "How splendid!"

Back in the kitchen, she swept up the floor, grabbed the phone, and scrolled until she found a name that looked pleasant. She'd seen how it was done. Her finger lingered over the name, then she touched it, and put the phone to her ear.

"Hello?"

"Hi, Kiyah?"

"Roly? Is that you, girl?"

"It's Margot. Listen, I have something that'll change your life!"

ROOM FOR CHANGE

Donovan hated working on Saturday nights. He could be at home playing video games, or updating his Tinder profile. Who was he kidding? He still had his senior photo as his profile pic, and that was from six years ago, when he looked like a poor man's Adam Sandler. He sat back against the pleather office chair and began to swivel around. He'd only been working at the Slash Pine Inn for a few months, but Johann—his chode of a boss—was always leaving him in charge. Being in charge was something he wasn't good at.

The worst part was, if any issues arose, he had to call Johann's cell. It'd ring a gazillion times before Johann picked up, and the conversation always went the same. "There's an issue and you need to come up here, man. I'm not the boss," Donovan would complain.

Then Johann would snap, "And with that goddamn attitude, you never will be. Shit happens—deal with it!"

With the exception of some distant thunder, the night had been quiet, at least. With Thanksgiving over, everyone had gone home to a better place. North Florida wasn't Donovan's cup of tea and he imagined it wasn't anyone else's either. He stopped spinning and checked his phone. *Nothing interesting.* He began to spin again when the bell above the office door ting-a-linged. *Freaking people, always ruining my fun.* He turned and gulped.

"Can I h-help you?" Donovan stammered. The most stunning woman he'd ever seen glared back at him like he was a human turd. Her hair was like dark golden honey and it poured down her shoulders. It took all he had not to ogle the nipples on the teacup breasts that were cutting through her thin sweater. He barely noticed the tall, gangly guy beside her.

"We need a room, please." She nudged her companion, causing him to jump, then he handed her some money. She held out a crisp one-hundred-dollar bill.

"Uh … yeah, sure. I just need some info and I'll get you hooked up."

"Can't I just pay you and get a key to a room? This isn't The Ritz, it's a rest stop motel." She snickered.

"I need the basic info in case—well, in case anything." He really didn't need much if they were paying in cash.

"Fine, I'm April and this's Sebastian. We need one room with one bed. And you can keep the change. Satisfied?" She raised her eyebrow and waved the money.

Extra money in my pocket? Hells yeah! Donovan took a second glance at the Muppet-looking dweeb she was with and noticed the sweat that peppered his forehead and ran down his temples. The guy wiped it away with his catcher's mitt of a hand. *What a goober! No way is this smoking hot chick his girlfriend. She must be a hooker or something … that or he probably has a bunch of money.* Donovan looked at the guy's watch and confirmed his suspicion. *A Rolex? Fucking A! He could've at least sprung for a fancier place!*

"Alright, *April*, room 112. It's pretty clean in there. One large king bed too." Donovan wiggled his eyebrows.

April sighed and rolled her cognac-colored eyes. "Whatever. Can we get the key now, please?"

Donovan turned in his chair and pretended to look for it, but he knew exactly where room 112's key was. "Ah, here it is! Check out is by ten in the morning. There aren't any restaurants that're willing to bring food this far out, but there're vending machines if you need anything and—"

"We'll be fine. Thanks." April yanked the key from Donovan's hand, grabbed the dweeb's arm, and pulled him out of the office.

Donovan let a smile creep across his face as he watched them go. He drank in April's long tan legs and apple of an ass. A low whistle escaped his lips as he cracked open a diet soda and picked up his phone. Spying on people wasn't right, and he knew that, but he was lonely and bored as hell. If he couldn't live a fulfilling life of his own, he'd have to live vicariously through others.

Mostly, people were predictable and he wouldn't watch for too long, but sometimes something interesting transpired that would intrigue him. He hoped tonight would be one of those nights. He tapped the phone's screen until room 112 came into view, then settled into his chair.

April opened the door to their room and immediately sneezed. It smelled like mildewed carpet and stale cigarette smoke. She pulled Sebastian in behind her and told him to lock the door. When he turned around, she was pulling her top off. She flung it to the floor and told him to get undressed. When he didn't move, she sauntered over and ripped open his flannel. He finished peeling it off himself, then pulled his undershirt up over his head. She kissed his hairless, concave chest, then walked over to the humming heater to turn it off.

"We won't be needing this old thing later, believe me. It'll get plenty hot," she purred.

"Is it ... gonna hurt?" Sebastian winced.

"I don't think so. I mean, my first time hurt a little, but we're all different. You won't remember all that much anyhow. It's always a blur." April unbuckled his belt and pulled his khakis down. She stared at his budding erection and moaned as she traced her long, pointy black nails over it. "I see you're rising to the occasion."

"Kinda hard not to."

"Ugh, clothes are too confining!" April unhooked her bra, then shimmied out of her pants. She wore no underwear, and Sebastian reddened when she caught him looking.

"You like what you see? Most men do, but you're not most men, are you?" April licked her full lips.

"I suppose not, no. Can I ask, how'd you know?"

"I got a nose for these things, honey. I knew it the moment I laid eyes on you. Oh, and take your watch off. Not a good idea to have that thing on."

"Dang, I didn't even think about that. So, how long do you think it'll last?" Sebastian set his watch on the nightstand.

"Depends. With it being your first time, it's hard to say, but I'll be with you every step of the way."

"What if someone hears it … happening?"

"You won't even care at that point. It'll be fine. I promise," April chirped.

"If I'm being honest, I'm not just nervous, I'm scared."

"Don't be. Look, it's only ten thirty, and we got time to kill, so why don't we relax a little? Let me calm your nerves. It's what I'm here for." April took Sebastian's hand, then tugged him down onto the threadbare comforter.

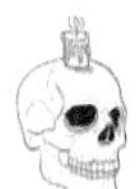

Donovan almost choked on his soda when she took her clothes off. *Holy shit, she didn't waste any time! And, daaaamn, that dweeb is sportin' a Swiss Colony Beef log. Good for him!* He was proud of himself for installing the cameras. There was one in the smoke detector, one in the alarm clock, and even one in the heater. He didn't put any cameras in the bathroom, though, because he had some scruples. As he watched the beautiful woman lie beside the gangly dweeb and begin to run her fingers tenderly through his mop of hair, his sense of pride in his handy work vanished.

All he felt now was a sense of shame. Here he was, spying on two people about to get it on, and they had no clue. He could turn it off right now, and watch YouTube or play solitaire, but he didn't, instead he ripped open a candy bar with his teeth and continued to watch the couple in wide-eyed wonderment.

April gently moved Sebastian's hand from her breast. "Not yet, honey. We gotta wait. You want it to be good, don't you?"

"I'm sorry, of course, yeah, it's just … you're so gorgeous."

"Oh, you're just saying that! Just wait, you won't say that when things get hot and heavy—I can make some pretty ugly faces!" April crossed her eyes and stuck out her tongue.

"I'm certain my face won't be flattering either. But nothing could ever change how beautiful you are."

"Well, you sir, are the absolute sweetest." April leaned over and kissed Sebastian.

At first, Sebastian froze, but then he began to kiss her back as she pulled his lower lip down with her teeth and emitted a low growl. April climbed on top of him and raked her nails down his bare chest, drawing beads of blood all the way to his belly button. When she brought her fingers to her mouth and licked them clean, Sebastian moaned. Then he reached for April and rolled her onto her back. He held her wrists and kissed her hard on the mouth, biting her lip the way she'd bitten his. April pulled away for some air, then grinned as she wrapped her long legs around him.

"That's what I'm talking about! Let's get this party fucking started!" April bucked underneath his grip. "Why, you might just be a natural, cowboy. Yee-Haw!"

Donovan licked the chocolate from his fingers and gasped. He was pretty sure he'd just seen the chick scratch the shit out of the dude's chest then taste his blood. It was weird, but also, he found it kinda hot. He reached into the desk drawer and fumbled around for another candy bar, but came up empty. With nothing to distract him, he eyed the bottle of lotion on the desk. "For my eczema," he'd told Johann.

He knew what he was about to do made him the lowest common denominator of a human, but it was all he had. He got up, locked the office door, and pulled the blinds shut. *If anyone needs a room, I'm on break.* The zipper on his jeans was stuck, and he cussed out loud as he tried to pry it free. "Seriously? Now, really? Ugh, you rusty ass bastard!" When he got it down, he breathed a sigh of relief.

Donovan pumped the bottle of lotion. It squelched, but nothing came out. He tried a few more times. Squelch. Again, nothing. *Are you fucking kidding me?* He looked back down at his phone. The chick's long legs were wrapped around the dweeb, and she was bucking like a bronco. Donovan snapped his fingers. *The console! There's more lotion in there! You're a genius, Don! Always prepared.* He pulled his pants up, but didn't bother zipping them as he hurried out to his car.

"I feel so itchy. My skin … it's on fire! I think … I think it's—it's happening!" Sebastian rolled off April and arched his back. His skin started to stretch and peel away in bloody sheets, revealing the slick red sinewy tissue and muscle underneath. He clenched his jaw as all his bones and joints began to crack, pop, and snap.

"Yeah, let it happen, baby! Oh, yeah, you're so sexy right now," April said, then she sprang up on all fours and got face to face with Sebastian. She bared her teeth as her back arched, then she began to writhe and undulate, her skin shedding around her. Their shoulders, necks, and backs contorted and bulged, the sound a jarring harmonious symphony.

Lightning struck and a loud crack of thunder vibrated the walls of the room as Sebastian's eyes yellowed. Thick, dark hair sprouted from every follicle on his body as he gripped the mattress with both hands. April threw her head back, gnashed her teeth, and howled at the ceiling, causing Sebastian to snap his head back and do the same. More thunder rattled the walls as both faced each other in full form. They were panting, and long strings of saliva dripped from their eager, hungry mouths. He sniffed her, and she sniffed him and they made yipping and whining noises back and forth. When she made a move to get on top of him, he swiftly and savagely turned her around. What was Sebastian looked up toward the ceiling and bayed as he seized what was April from behind.

Donovan shivered against the rain that had begun to fall outside. It pricked his bare skin like cold needles. When lightning flashed, he ducked, then clumsily jogged over to his car. He noted that his car was the only one in the parking lot. *What, they walked here? Prolly they Ubered.* He shrugged, then looked up at the night sky and shook his head when he noticed the enormous golden moon peeking through the storm clouds. *Oh, great. A full moon. That always brings out the crazies.*

His car door was open, and the lotion was right where he knew it would be. "My precious," he rasped. He was walking back when he heard it. The lotion slipped from his grasp and slapped the pavement. Every hair on his body stood on end, and his heart began to thud. "What the fuck was that? Was that … howling?"

Donovan was bending to pick up his bottle when the sound came again. It pierced his eardrums and guts like an ice pick. Howling. And it was coming from the direction of none other than room 112. *Oh shit, what am I missing?* He held his falling pants up as he trotted back to the office, locked the door, and waddled back to his chair. Feelings of desire possessed him as he pumped the new lotion into his hand. Then he looked down at his phone. *Wait—what the fuck?*

Two massive hairy animals were going at it on the bed. One was considerably larger than the other. He couldn't tell if they were mutant dogs or something else. *But what else could they be?* The larger one was pumping away at the other one from behind with violent thrusts. Several thoughts swam through his head. *What in the world's this shit? I need to call Johann. No pets allowed! They must've snuck 'em in! Are those even dogs? What kinda shit are these two into? Are they dressed in gorilla costumes? They don't look like costumes. Is it bears? Jesus Christ, I hate bears!*

Donovan wiped the lotion in his hand onto his shirt and pulled at his hair with trembling hands. He needed to call his boss. He wasn't dealing with this. Not a chance. No fucking way! He picked up the office phone and dialed. It rang several times before he hung up. *Fucking asshole.* He tried again. No luck. He glanced back at his phone and yelped. The things were off the bed now and standing on their hind legs. "Holy Shit," Donavan breathed. His teeth chattered in his head and when the office phone rang, he almost shit his pants. The caller ID read Johann.

"Oh, thank fuck! Listen, Johann, man, you need to get over here right now! There's an issue—a big one! There's some whack jobs that brought their giant crazy dogs with them and the dogs are going at it—"

"You let them bring in animals? Are you an idiot?"

"What? No! They must've brought 'em after I checked them in!"

"Go to the room and tell them they need to leave."

"You don't understand—"

"What's to understand? You told me what the issue was, and I told you what to do, so handle it. I'm not coming all the way out there to do what I pay you to do. If they don't leave, then call me back."

"But ..." Donovan slammed the phone back in its cradle when he realized Johann hung up. What was he supposed to do? He wasn't going to that room, that was for sure. *I could leave, just get outta here and never look back.* He patted down his pockets. *Fuck, where're my car keys? I must've dropped them jogging back in here!* He checked the office door again and made sure it was locked. He turned all the lights out and turned on the No Vacancy sign. Then he grabbed a chair and wedged it under the doorknob. "Better yet still ..." he strained as he pushed the heavy desk towards the door. White light slipped through the blinds and thunder cracked like a whip, sending Donovan's heart into double time. When rain began to spray the windows and roof like bullets, he grabbed his phone and locked himself in the office restroom.

The pungent odor of piss stung his nose, and he kicked himself for not cleaning the toilet as often as he was supposed to. He really was a lazy sack of crap. What if he called their room? What would they do? Then they'd know he knew. If he called the cops, they might find out he put cameras in there. It was already climbing up to midnight, so he decided to try and ride it out. *Maybe I should keep a gun in the car and not lotion and useless bags of candy!*

He forced himself to look down at his phone. The things were getting busy again, this time up against the wall. He set the phone on the floor in front of his feet. "Are they—could they be werewolves? Do those even exist?" *No. Of course they don't! You are an idiot!* Just like Johann, his father had always called him an idiot. Said since he was dumb, he'd better be tough. Except Donovan wasn't tough, not at all. He could hear himself whimpering as he watched the phone's screen. If there was ever a time he needed to step up to the plate, it was now.

Donovan had somehow nodded off, but thunder jarred him awake. When he looked down at the phone, the screen was dark. He unlocked it, saw the things weren't there, and panicked. *Where'd they go?* Then he saw the door to their room was open and his bowels knotted together pretzel style. Tears sprang to his eyes. Every crack of thunder was followed by howls so loud, he was sure he felt it echo off of his bones. He knew they had to be right outside of the office.

"Fuck whether or not they find my cameras, I'm calling the cops!" Donovan picked up his phone to dial, and it went dead. "Holy fucking shit on a stick! Are you serious?"

He didn't have his charger. He'd have to exit the restroom and get to the office phone. Even if he could manage that, what was he going to say? "Hello, 911, there're two hellhounds on the run outside of the Slash Pine Inn. No, it's not a prank, yes, I did say hellhounds. Could you kindly send some reinforcements? Maybe send the coastguard and make sure they come with cannons that blast out silver cannonballs!" Just then, the office phone began to ring.

Donovan army-crawled out of the bathroom over to the desk. The phone's cord was a tripwire, stretched across the room, and he had to be careful to slide under it. He stood up like his body was an overfilled gravy boat, picked up the phone, and whispered, "H-hello?"

"Donovan? Why're you whispering? What the hell's wrong with you? Did you get those people to leave?"

"Johann, you gotta listen to me! It's not dogs! They're some kinda monsters or werewolves or I don't even fucking know! I closed down for the night and I'm about to call the cops. I'm locked in the office and—"

"You what? You closed for the … are you outta your mind? Are you smoking something? I'm on my way, and you better hope you're not high. You're such an idiot. And no police! You hear me? I'm going to get dressed, leave my hot wife in bed, and come all the way out there to take care of this myself, and do you know why? Because I'm a motherfuckin' boss!"

For the second time, Johann hung up before he could reply. Donovan knew that his boss was coming from town, which was about twenty minutes away. He wished he never applied for this job. He should've stayed in classes at the college and finished up his computer science degree instead of slacking off. If he made it out of this, that's exactly what he was going to do. Even if he had to move back in with his mother and asshole father, it was better than working at this dump. And he'd never spy on people again. He wrung his hands, stared up at the ceiling, and squeezed his eyes shut. "Never again. I swear, God, please, let me live. I'll never do it again."

Donovan decided against calling the cops and waited for Johann to arrive instead. The cell phone charger was on top of the desk, so he grabbed it and plugged his phone in before he slid back down to the floor. Peeking to see if those things were out there was out of the question. Even though he hadn't heard any howls for a while, he'd seen and heard enough. He hoped Johann heeded his warning and came armed. After a few minutes, he was able to turn his phone on and see room 112 again. The door was still open, and the room was still empty. *Maybe they aren't coming back? But won't they need their clothes?*

Donovan knew the woods across the street were dense with slash pines and sharp palmettos. He also knew a ton of wild animals lived in those woods, as their dumpster was constantly being mauled by them. *Maybe those things'll kill some deer or raccoons and leave me alone?* How could such a beautiful woman turn into that hideous, hairy beast? He was confident that those monsters were the two from earlier. It had to be them. There's no way they brought those things with them. He didn't understand it, but some things were just not to be understood. His heart stopped when he heard a loud pounding.

Something's weight was being thrown against the office door. When the desk began to rattle and skid, Donovan fled and locked himself back in the bathroom. *This is the end, Don. It's prolly the end. You should've called the cops.*

"Donovan? It's raining cats and dogs out here. Open the damn door! You hear me? What do you have blocking it? Any damage is coming out of your check! Let me in, you idiot!"

At the sound of Johann's voice, Donovan's heart swelled and his breath caught in his throat. He never thought he'd be happy to hear his boss. He flew out of the bathroom and began to slide the desk back. As he went to remove the chair from under the doorknob, he heard it. Howling. Then, his boss began to scream and throw himself against the door again.

"Donovan! Let me in! There's some sort of animals along the edge of the woods—hurry up, damn it, they're coming! What're those fucking things? What the hell are they? If I have to break the glass, you're paying for it in more ways than one! Open the damn door you id—oh my god, they're running! Let me in! Heeeelp," Johann screeched.

Donovan shoved the desk back. He didn't dare breathe or move a muscle. The howling was right outside the office door. Johann's urgent screams turned to wails and then to gurgles, and Donovan was sure he heard the things tear his boss's flesh and chomp down on his bones like a Nestle Crunch bar. *Crunch, crunch.* As the things ate, they were yipping and snarling and Donovan had to shove his knuckles into his mouth to keep himself from vomiting. His knees grew weak, and he started to sway. He clung to the last bit of sanity he had and dragged himself back into the bathroom. Somehow, he pulled the door shut.

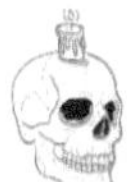

When Donovan woke, his cheek lay in a puddle of cold drool. His whole body hurt. He stumbled when he stood up and had to steady himself on the sink before he turned on the light. He was afraid to open the door, but the faint yellow light coming in from underneath gave him some reassurance. *Holy fuck! Was it all a dream? Please, please let it have been a dream.* When he opened the bathroom door and saw the state of the office, he freaked out all over again. It wasn't a dream. *Johann!*

The wall clock read 7:30 a.m. Donovan picked up his phone and brought up room 112. The bedsheets and mattress cover were missing, but other than that, almost everything else had been straightened out. There was no sign of the beasts. He shuffled to the window and peered through the blinds. Nothing but a gang of buzzards. It took all his might to drag the desk back. Then he opened the door.

The morning sun was brighter than it needed to be, and he had to shield his eyes from its assault. He shooed the giant ugly birds away, but they didn't go far. Most of them loitered atop Johann's car and the rest sat on the inn's roof, waiting to resume their breakfast. Before he even looked down, he smelled it. It was the reeking stench of blood, guts, and baking death. Donovan squeezed his eyes shut for a few moments, then forced himself to look.

Right away, Donovan recognized his boss's shredded clothes among the carnage. Flies and other hungry insects buzzed about the gnawed-on bones and crawled over the meaty clumps and entrails stuck to the ground in congealed globs. In a puddle of bloody rain water, he spotted something. He kneeled down and watched for a minute, mesmerized by the thing as it bobbed in the sickening mixture. At some point, Johann's blue-green iris stared back into his own and Donovan's hand flew to his mouth. He tried not to puke, but it shot through his fingers like water through a dam.

He needed to get a hold of himself, so he took several deep breaths. *It served him right*, Donovan decided. He tried to warn Johann. He'd tried to tell him. "You never listened to me," he said as he pointed down at his boss's eyeball. "Now, who's the idiot? Remember what you always told me? Hey, shit happens, man—deal with it! Now who's the motherfucking boss, huh? Me, that's who!"

Donovan stepped around the gory sludge and, with a swagger in his step that he'd never had before, he headed toward room 112 to get rid of the cameras before he called the cops. He didn't know yet what he was going to say happened, but he'd survived the night and that was all that mattered.

SQUID'S INK

Amelia adjusted her hair and her blue blazer, then she sighed a sigh of defeat and shrugged at herself in the mirror. When she majored in journalism, she thought she'd be a serious journalist who'd cover serious topics, but instead, she'd settled for a small-town newspaper where she was interviewing local business owners or writing the occasional piece about wackadoodles who saw Jesus in their pastry. She hoped today would be interesting, at least. She was meeting a tattoo artist who was creating a lot of buzz with his bodies of work. She'd heard he could see into his client's souls and put what he saw on their skin. As she applied a second layer of lip gloss, she felt a cold shiver travel up her spine. *I certainly hope he can't see into my soul,* she thought, then blotted her lips on some toilet paper.

In the car, Amelia practiced the questions she wanted to ask and reminded herself not to mention her own tattoo. She'd gotten it in her junior year of high school. It was spring break and her parents took a few of her friends and her to Panama City Beach, Florida. After begging her parents, they caved, and she became the proud owner of a butterfly tramp stamp. She hated the phrase tramp stamp and found it unfair, but she still used it to describe her own tattoo.

She pulled up to the shop front and studied it. It didn't look like anything spectacular. In fact, it appeared to be the type of place that someone wanting a tattoo might avoid. There was an oversized brown tabby cat curled up in a folding chair by the door and a blue neon sign in the window that spelled out: SQUID'S INK. She knew that was the artist's name, and she rolled her eyes. *Oh, how I'm gonna love calling him that! Hello, Mr. Squid, is it?* "I hate my life," she whispered, then got out of the car.

The image of a ginormous burly bearded man who probably wore a bandana and sweat-stained tank top popped into her head as she made her way to the shop front. She hoped he was more the Jason Momoa type. A smile crept onto her face. *Or maybe he looks like Harry Styles, but he's wearing no shirt and he's covered in tattoos? I could get down with that.* Then she remembered she hadn't gotten down with anyone since *that night* and her smiled faded. The night where her whole life had been flipped upside down. The night that had turned her into a shell of her former self. The night that made her feel ashamed to be alive at all. She froze on the sidewalk and closed her eyes, hoping to will the memory away.

Amelia's hand paused on the rusty door handle and she took a deep breath before she pulled it open. A bell dinged as she walked in. No one was in sight, but she heard someone moving around in the back. It smelled good, an aroma of burning sage and other herbs. Two worn brown leather couches sat opposite each other and there was a coffee table in between them stacked with binders and magazines. She studied the pictures of customer's tattoos that were tacked to the wall. There were mythical beasts, magical creatures, and nameless faces, but some of the colorful designs were harder to figure out.

The skin of entire backs, arms, legs, and torsos reminded Amelia of the scenes on some of the tapestries she'd seen in art museums. She couldn't take her eyes off them and had to admit, the detail in every tattoo was astounding. A waterlogged voice startled her, and she almost tripped over her own feet as she turned to greet it.

It was a small old man with one cloudy eye and a mouth like someone who had just sucked a lemon. He had deep lines in his dark olive skin and sparse salt-and-pepper curls clung to his head. He limped toward her and held out his hand; she shook it but looked over his shoulder to see if someone else was coming. Amelia wondered where the famous Squid was.

"Hello, I'm Amelia Turner, from the newspaper? I'm here to interview a ... Mr. Squid?" She felt her cheeks burning. "Is he available?"

The man smiled and nodded. "I am Squid."

Amelia's mouth dropped. *How in the world could this little gimp-eyed old man possibly create those tattoos?* she wondered. "You're Squid?"

"You are wondering how an old man like me does tattoos, right? I still have one good eye!" He pointed to his unclouded eye, which was the color of a stormy sea, then threw his head back and laughed. She counted all three of his remaining teeth.

"No, I wasn't wondering that—well, yes, I was, but ..." She felt like an idiot.

"It's understandable. I have a mirror or two." He smiled warmly, and Amelia relaxed.

"You look ... fine, it's just ... I was expecting someone a bit more, I don't know, different. You don't have any tattoos, do you, Mr. Squid?"

"It's just Squid, please, and no, I have none. I never needed one. Come." He motioned for her to follow him.

Amelia wondered where he was from. He had an accent she couldn't quite place. She thought maybe it was Greek or Italian, but she wasn't sure. He brought her to a dimly lit room with a large desk and she took note of the various pencils, colored pens, and sketch pads that littered it. He pointed to one of two worn leather armchairs and told her it was the more comfortable one. Then he asked if she wanted a water or a soda, but Amelia declined and pulled a notebook from her bag. She was slightly annoyed when he sat down in front of her and began drawing in one of his sketchbooks.

How could he even see in this light—and with that eye? "Are you ready to begin?" Amelia tried to sound chipper.

"Yes." He didn't look up.

"First, I have to know, how did you come about the name, Squid?" Amelia asked.

"I have always been known as Squid, for as long as I can remember."

"Your parents named you that? Or was it a nickname given to you by someone?"

"It has always been my name." He shrugged.

Why is he evading my question? Maybe he doesn't like taking about his family? "Kind of like you were always meant to do this tattooing thing, huh?"

"How do you mean?" he asked.

"Squids? They make ink, right? And now you make ink!" Amelia chuckled.

"I see how that could be seen that way, yes." He stopped drawing and nodded.

Amelia realized the name thing was a dead end, so she switched gears. "Do you work alone here?"

"Yes. I work by appointment only, so I do not need many other people around to help."

"I see … so, is this where the magic happens? You come in here and sketch out your ideas before you do your tattoos?"

"I do not *do* tattoos; I tell stories. This is the place where I have a conversation with a client and I ask them questions. Sometimes I will sketch it out as they're talking. Some pieces can be done in a day's time, but others might take a lot longer to finish and they have to come back many times because their story is still unfolding."

"That's … interesting. Do you base their piece on what they specifically ask for or something else?" She fought the urge to shout at him for not looking at her when she talked to him and began tapping her pen against her pad.

"I draw what they show me." He smiled secretly to himself.

"Right, but exactly how do they show you?"

"Everyone has a story they want to tell and sometimes a tattoo is the only way they feel comfortable telling it. I put a piece of their story onto them for the world to see—or not see. Many people do not truly listen to what others have to say, but how many times has someone seen a tattoo and asked that person what it means? Then the individual can decide whether to tell their story. Some stories are tragic, some are adventurous, and some? Some are terrifying. The magic is knowing how to see which it is." Squid looked up at Amelia in a way that made her feel naked and vulnerable.

Amelia looked away from his gaze and tried to breathe normally. "And you know which it is, I suppose, right?"

"Usually, yes." He started to sketch again and this time Amelia was grateful for it.

"Can I ask you where you're from, Squid? I forgot to ask that earlier. I'm sorry."

"I am from a little place known as Malta. You know it?"

"I've heard of it, yes. I don't know much about it, though. Is it a province of Italy or Greece?"

"We are Sicilian Arabs I like to say, but we have had many different cultures on our island, Greek being one of them, but Malta is uniquely Malta. It's in the middle of the Mediterranean. Sicily is about fifty miles to the north and then a couple hundred miles to the west is the country of Tunisia—that's North Africa. It is very beautiful on my tiny island and if you ever get a chance to go, you should. You know there are temples there that are even older than the pyramids of Egypt? Stonehenge too."

"Wow, no, I didn't know that. Have you ever been inside one of these temples?"

"Once upon a time, yes, I was."

Amelia waited for him to continue, but he didn't.

"What was it like in there, the temple, I mean?"

"It was … a long time ago and I don't really recall."

Amelia wanted to know how old he was, but she didn't dare ask. Instead, she asked when he began doing tattoos, then corrected herself. *He doesn't do tattoos, he tells stories.* She wanted to roll her eyes, but refrained.

"It was only three years ago when I began." Squid shifted in his chair.

She didn't hide her surprise. "Excuse me, but did you say three years ago? I'm genuinely shocked! What did you do before that?"

"I have been many things."

Amelia pushed. "Can you tell me one of those things?"

"I was an oracle," he said.

"You mean … like a fortune teller?"

"A fortune teller is for movies. I *was* an oracle."

"I'm sorry, but I don't see the difference." Amelia finally rolled her eyes and snorted.

"The difference is that I actually see things for what they are, what they might be, and what they are not."

"That must come in handy when you first meet people, huh?"

"Yes …"

"Do you use that skill—or would you say method—when you work with a potential client?"

"Sometimes, yes."

"Do you think you would be as successful as you are without this ability?"

"I know how to draw, so maybe I would be alright, but successful? I don't think so."

"How about me? What's my story, Squid?" Amelia was beginning to think he was no different than the wackadoodle pastry prophets.

Squid stopped drawing and looked up at her, then he leaned forward and whispered, "When I shook your hand, I saw you. I saw *everything*."

"What did you say?" Amelia felt his words sink in, deep into her tissue and muscle, and then finally they crept into her bones. She began to tremble uncontrollably.

"You have been hiding for so long, no? That has to be exhausting. By the way, your butterfly is slightly off. I could see how at the time that you got it, it suited you, but now, something else lurks just beneath your skin." Squid smiled as he went back to his drawing. "Almost finished," he muttered.

Amelia's mouth filled with saliva, and she thought she might be sick. She tried to remember if she'd told him about her tattoo or if maybe she'd bent down to tie her shoe and her blouse had lifted. But she was wearing boots and a blazer and she knew she hadn't mentioned it. Maybe someone else told him? She racked her brain for answers. *That makes no sense, Amelia! He's probably seen me out before. That's got to be it. He's trying to scare me … he doesn't know a damn thing! Does he?* She told herself not to grab his pencil and snap it in half. It wasn't hot in the room, but sweat pooled under her arms.

It wasn't like she'd meant to hurt anyone. She was just having a good time. Drinking, and partying; stuff most twenty-one-year-old women did. The guy Amelia had swiped right on her phone said his name was Tucker. She'd Ubered to the bar they'd agreed to meet at and he'd bought her vodka soda after vodka soda. She should've gotten the hint when he sneered at her and said he liked her tramp stamp, but it had been a while and he was smoking hot and the place between her legs thumped. By the time she'd heard the bartender shout that it was last call, she could barely stand. Her date had grabbed her hand and dragged her out the door.

He'd stuffed her into his Jeep like a rag doll and peeled out of the parking lot. Though she was disoriented and wasted, Amelia tried several times to ask Tucker where they were going, but he wouldn't answer. When she tried to ask again, he'd shouted and slammed her head against the dash. She'd managed to fish her phone out of her purse, but he ripped it away and threw it out the window. His high-pitched maniacal laugh filled the car when she tried to grab his phone from in between his legs. He'd backhanded her and told her he was taking her to a place where he'd be able to punish her the way she deserved.

It was a blur after that. Amelia screamed at him to stop the car, but he continued to laugh and upped the speed. She begged and pleaded with him, but he wouldn't stop. That was when she'd decided to try to grab the steering wheel. He punched at her head several times, but she kept struggling with him. Then they hit something and went off the road into a ditch. Somehow, she was able to fling herself from the car, where she threw up in the grass. When she stopped puking and was able to get up, she saw a man lying in the road.

Amelia stumbled to the motionless man and saw that part of his face and head were smashed in. Blood splattered the electric yellow windbreaker he wore and there was a long rope that trailed from underneath of him. When she'd spotted the dead dog a few feet away, she fought to keep herself from fainting. She kicked pieces of a flashlight as she attempted to get closer. Tucker was still in his Jeep, revving the engine and yelling the word fuck over and over.

Amelia bent down next to the man and choked on her sobs. Blood seemed to leak everywhere from him and even though she knew he was dead, she checked for a pulse. She stood back up and ran over to the Jeep and screamed for Tucker to call 911, but he ignored her and kept revving and revving. His wheels squealed and kicked up the rank thick muck from the ditch, but the Jeep wouldn't budge.

"You can't do this! We can't leave them here like this!" she'd cried.

"We? Are you serious? You did this—if you hadn't grabbed my steering wheel, this wouldn't have happened! Now, get the fuck off and get away from my car or I'll run over you too!"

"Why're you doing this?" Amelia asked through choking wails.

"Because I can." He smirked at her, then revved his engine again.

Amelia went back to the dead man and fished out his wallet. There was a picture of a woman and three kids holding the same shaggy dog that lay lifeless just feet away. A whine escaped her lips and her hands shook so bad she couldn't pull out his license. She dropped the wallet and checked for a phone, but couldn't find one. Then she felt something. It was a holster, and it was attached to his hip. A fleeting moment of joy warmed her when she realized a gun was inside of it. She retrieved it, stood up, and marched back to Tucker's Jeep. The safety was off, and the gun was cocked and ready. Amelia aimed the gun and shouted for Tucker to turn his car off, but he acted as if he didn't hear her.

Tucker turned and laughed the same maniacal laugh from earlier. "Oh, you're gonna shoot me now? You've probably never even shot a gun in your entire miserable fucking life you stupid who—" the bullet ripped through his cheek. Somehow, he was still able to scream, and a geyser of blood spurted from the giant hole in his face. Amelia fired again until there was nothing but the click, click, clicking of an empty gun. Tucker's lifeless body slumped forward and his head hit the horn. Amelia ran to the Jeep, grabbed her purse, and took off into the thick woods that lined the sides of the road.

She grappled with herself to go back and use his phone to call the police. *They'd understand that I had no choice,* she told herself. *But you did have a choice. You didn't have to kill him! Two men are dead because of you! But what were his plans before the Jeep hit that poor man and his dog?* Amelia fell to her knees on a bunch of pine needles and cried out in the dark. She knew she had to make a choice: go back or keep running. *A car will come along soon and see the mess you left behind. You're fucked! Run, girl, run—and get rid of that gun!*

Fat drops of rain had started to fall through the trees. By the time she'd made up her mind to flee, the rain was falling in sheets. As Amelia made her way through the woods, she silently thanked the full golden moon for giving her light in the darkness. When she came out on the other side to a road, she almost collapsed with relief. She was soaking wet and cold, but she willed herself to get a grip enough to make her way ahead.

A few miles later, she hit a dingy gas station. She threw the gun in their dumpster and then lumbered inside. The clerk raised his eyebrows in shock when he saw Amelia's disheveled state, but he didn't ask questions when she asked to use his cell phone. An Uber arrived in less than fifteen minutes and when she slid inside the car, she crumpled into a trembling heap in the warm and dry backseat. The driver seemed displeased by her wet and dirty appearance, but like the clerk, they didn't want to get involved.

She had slept like the dead that night. It was only when she had woken up that she'd panicked. She'd kicked herself for not listening to her mom about having a landline. She had turned on the television and it wasn't long before she found a channel with the local news running the story about the man and his dog found dead in the road not far from another man found shot to death in his Jeep. Authorities weren't sure what happened, but they vowed to get to the bottom of it and offered a reward to anyone with any information. Amelia was sure it was only a matter of time before she'd be toast. She waited for the other shoe to drop, but when a few weeks went by and no one came knocking on her door, she had let herself breathe a little.

The guilt wormed through Amelia's insides, turning her guts to Swiss cheese. How they never figured out her involvement, she wasn't sure. Every day was a walk on a tightrope. She thought about coming clean—especially when her parents grilled her about being distant—but then the memory of that sicko's laughter pierced her brain and she refused to cave. She felt sorry every day for the family man and his dog, but that fucker Tucker, well, he could rot in hell!

It had been her last year of college, and Amelia buried herself in her studies. After a couple years without incident, she'd allowed herself to step off the tightrope. Then she got a job at the town newspaper and even if she did dislike being a small fish in an ocean of opportunity, she was still proud of herself. The fact that she'd dipped her feet in had been enough for her.

Now a strange tattoo artist knocked her for a loop and Amelia felt the familiar ravenous worm start to weave its way through her insides again as she stared into the old man's swirling cloudy eye.

"I d-don't know what you're talking about, p-please …" Amelia murmured. She wanted to curl into a ball on the floor and cry for an eternity.

Squid said nothing. He stopped drawing and turned his sketch pad around for her to see. On it was a woman. She looked fierce and beautiful. Her long wavy hair was tied back with the top braided and she wielded a bow, ready to shoot at an unseen enemy. Her armor was both feminine and masculine. The face looked almost like her own. Amelia's eyes filled with tears and when she blinked, they spilled down her face.

"This is just a start. I have more to add, but with or without color, this could be quite beautiful! Do you like it?" Squid asked.

"Who … who is that?" Amelia whispered.

"It is the likeness of Cynane, but also, it is you. You would've gotten along well with her, I think. She was an independent and very powerful woman, although most Illyrian women were. She was a warrior and a princess. As the daughter of Audata and King Philip II of Macedon, she was the half-sister of Alexander the Great and was famous for her outstanding courage and brilliance in battle. She was a survivor. And you, you are a survivor. So, I ask again, do you like it?"

"Y-yes," Amelia said and nodded. "I like it very much."

"Good. This is only part of your story. If you would like, I could make you an appointment and we can continue your story." Squid said, offering a mostly toothless grin.

"I think I'd like that."

"For now, I will keep your story some place safe until you are ready for it. Any more questions?"

Amelia shook her head and wiped her tear brined face with her hands. "No, no, I think I got what I needed. Thank you, Squid. For everything." She held her trembling hand out and Squid held it for a moment, then she smiled at him and realized as she turned to leave, that she felt more her true self than she had in her entire life.

133

DON'T GIVE IT AWAY

I stopped takin' my antidepressants a while back due to all the side effects, but honestly, being born has more side effects than any of those fuckin' pills ever did. Think about it, you ain't got no choice on whether you're born or not and then you have to wade through the thick muck of shit called life without a pair of damn rubber boots. When I was just eight years old, my ma told me I was nuttier than a squirrel's turd. I didn't know what that meant then, but, well, I do now. Another thing I know is, sometimes, we figure shit out when it's too late.

All last week my ma had been all over my ass about everythin'. She kept hollerin' in that screechin' voice of hers from upstairs.

"Levi, make sure you only use my checkbook to pay the bills I asked. I don't need you buying booze or anything else," or "Levi, I don't want you leaving this house and staying out all hours of the night and bringing back some filthy whore!"

If it wasn't one thing, it was another. Ever since she had the stroke, I had to help wash her, cook her meals, and even put lotion on her reptilian feet. I had to quit my menial job, move out of my efficiency, and come back home to live with the most hateful woman I'd ever known.

Ma couldn't use one side of her body as good as she used to, but she could still speak just fine, which was unfortunate. Do you know what it's like to rub lotion on your mother's feet and listen to her make all kinds of noises while you do it? How about having to lift your naked ma into a shower chair, dry under her saggy tits, and then havin' her tell you not to forget her ass crack? It's pure hell.

Don't get me wrong, I loved my ma—for the most part—but everyone has a breakin' point. Mine came early last week. I'd been out late the night before and she was mad as a hornet. I was asleep on the couch and woke up to her starin' at me. I swear I could feel the hatred comin' off her like heat from a stove. Her mouth was twisted up in an evil, lopsided grin. Then she made a sound like a hog before she spat a loogie right in my face.

I supposed she figured out that I'd been disablin' her stair lift. She must've called someone over to look at it. Could've been the home health lady that comes a few times a week, but I bet it was that damn nosy old coot from down the street, Miriam. She was one of my ma's bingo partners from before the stroke and was always droppin' by unexpectedly to check on Ma, but I suspect it's about more than that now. I guess I might as well admit I banged her a few months back after I had too many bourbons. She ain't that bad lookin' for an old broad, but I do got some scruples, so I never done it again.

So anyway, Ma was mad. She started hootin' and hollerin' about how I wasn't a real man, that I was no good and never would be. What really got me was when she said I was just like my daddy and then cackled in that horrible way she always did. She liked to say that a lot when I was growin' up and knew it stung me good, on account of my daddy being what you might call a murderin' psychopath. He strangled a few hookers and carved them up like Thanksgivin' turkeys back in the day.

My last memory of my daddy is when they arrested him in the kitchen while Ma was makin' his breakfast. I 'member 'cause I'd just poured cereal and was diggin' for the prize in the box when the sound of knuckles began poundin' our front door. Ma'd pushed me back down in my chair before I could go and see who it was. I looked at my daddy then, and asked him who it might be. He didn't look at me at first, but instead took a sip of his coffee and a long drag off his Camel cigarette.

When Daddy finally lifted his head, he rubbed his bloodshot eyes and looked at me. He told me to be a good boy and that he was sorry for all he'd done. Two policemen came into the kitchen, nodded at me, then grabbed Daddy from his chair and led him away in handcuffs. I scrambled from my own chair and hid under the table. My hands were over my ears as the law men swarmed our house like termites. Eventually, Ma pulled me out from under the table and told me to go up to my room.

I wasn't told exactly what he'd done until years later. Ma said he was no good and would rot in prison where he belonged. We never went and saw him, even though I asked to a few times. He died in his cell only a year later, but I don't know how and Ma never did say.

I was lucky enough after what happened to be spared from bullyin' by my peers, but I wasn't spared at home. Ma took out what she couldn't on my daddy, on me. I think I resented him more for that, than what he actually done. I grew up as if I was his second skin and Ma never let me forget it. I always wondered if I would've amounted to more if none of it ever happened.

I wiped her rank sputum off my face and told her I was nothin' like Daddy, but she kept on in that shrill voice of hers, cackling like a goddamn hyena. I told her I only came back to her house of horrors to help and could leave anytime if that's what she wanted. She grunted, then began to ram her chair into my legs over and over. When I tried to move, she flung herself forward and hit the floor. I couldn't help myself and started to laugh so hard it hurt my sides. She was sprawled out like a starfish and she was cursin' me something awful while tryin' to flip herself over.

When I went to help her up, I felt white-hot pain ride up my arm. Her teeth had sunk into the meat of my forearm, and she locked on with the grip of a bulldog. It hurt so bad and I yelled for her to let go, but she wouldn't, so I kicked her. I didn't mean it, but the pain was too much, so I just kicked and kicked until it didn't hurt no more. Well, she let go alright, 'cause I killed her.

Her head and face were covered in blood. I got down on my knees and felt for a pulse. There wasn't one, so I started doin' chest compressions until I felt several of her ribs begin to snap, crackle, and pop. My own heart began to sputter out of control and there were wasps in my brain. My breaths became hard to catch, and next thing I know I woke up on top of Ma, starin' right into her mangled face.

I screamed and tried to get a hold of myself. It was almost the afternoon, and I knew that the home health lady would be comin' soon unless I called and canceled. I dialed her up and told her we would no longer be needin' her services. She didn't question me, which put me at some ease. I looked down at the bite wound on my forearm, then at the blood caked under my fingernails and felt woozy all over again. What to do about Ma? I didn't know what to do. Then I 'membered the chest freezer in the basement. It felt so cliché—kill someone and store them in the freezer until you come up with a better plan—but it was all I had.

Ma's body wasn't hard to move. Even with rigor mortis startin' to set in, I was able to easily fold her up like a pretzel and stuff her in next to the pork chops and Omaha steaks. Ma always liked those steaks. I took a couple out to cook up for supper later, then let the lid go. A loud thud echoed through the basement as the lid dropped and I felt a weight lift off me. I know I should've felt terrible about what I'd done, but I couldn't help but feel happy that she was gone and I started laughin' as hard as I did when Ma fell out of her chair.

We were never rich by any means, but Ma managed to save where she could and her bank account had about eighty-five-thousand dollars in it. She also had some decent jewelry I could pawn and other family heirlooms that might bring in some extra needed cash. If I could get enough together, I'd hightail it out of the country and start over. By the time they figured it all out, I'd be long gone, livin' like a king somewhere in Mexico.

I didn't want to pawn everything; I thought that might look suspicious, so I decided to have a yard sale. I'd tell anyone who came by that I needed the money to help take care of my ailin' ma, and that we were thinking of getting her into an assisted livin' facility. Not all together a lie, since I'd actually been thinkin' about it recently and had the brochures all over the backseat of my car. I'd gather enough items to sell by the weekend, have the sale Saturday morning, and have my flight already booked.

By Friday afternoon, I'd closed out my mother's account and pawned some jewelry. My flight was booked for Sunday afternoon and I was pretty much packed. I had priced, separated, and placed everythin' I wanted to get rid of on small folding tables ready to go outside in the morning. Everythin' had been going so smoothly that I hadn't even really thought about Ma all week, but seein' some of her stuff layin' out on the tables made me feel sharp pangs of guilt. I decided I should go down and look in on her, maybe say goodbye or somethin'. I owed her that.

I was about to head down when the doorbell rang. *Fuck*. I peeled back the blinds on one of the windows and peered out at none other than that old coot. She was all dressed up and holding a tray of cookies. I wanted to strangle her. *Goddamn, Miriam! Nosy, no good horn dog … I wish I never put my dick in you!* I opened the door and smiled at her.

"Levi! How good to see you? Sorry I didn't call first, but, well, I wanted to surprise you. I made fresh cookies this morning and thought I'd drop by and share with you and Janet. How is your mother? I talked to her on the phone last week and she seemed in good spirits. What, with a big strong boy to help her, I'd be in good spirits too." She winked and looked down at my crotch.

"Miriam, now's really not a good time …" I felt myself wanting to drag her inside and stuff her in next to Ma. *Maybe I am like my daddy after all.*

"Oh? Why's that? Is Janet alright? Can I help in any way?" She feigned concern.

"No! I mean, no, thanks. I have it all under control. Ma's just restin' and I don't wanna disturb her. She has a bad cold. Maybe you could come back next week?"

"Well, I could just come in and share these with you if you'd like?" She tried to poke her head in, but I stepped in her way.

"Not today, Miriam. I am so grateful for you, but really, today's not good. I need to take care of Ma. Another time, though. You know how much I enjoy your cookies." I wanted to barf.

"Oh, certainly, I *know.*" Her smile reminded me of the moment the Grinch got his big idea. She looked at the bandage on my forearm. "What happened to your arm?"

"Oh, I grazed it on somethin' sharp in the basement." *Only half a lie.*

"Well, you be careful. We need you to stick around. Take these cookies anyways, won't you? I can't eat all of them. Gotta keep my girlish figure!" She shoved the tray of cookies into my hands.

"Uh, sure, thanks. Have a good day, Miriam," I said.

"Well, alright then. Next week. And you better not push me away again, Mr.!" She batted her eyelashes, grazed my forearm with her talons, and I told her I wouldn't.

I didn't think she suspected anythin' at all and that was a relief. My thoughts traveled back to Ma. The sound of my footfalls on the old basement steps seemed to creak more dramatically than usual, but maybe it was all in my head. The freezer looked like it always did, though I don't know what I thought it'd look like. I crept over to it, placed my hand on the lid for a spell, then opened it.

I gasped when I saw her. Ice crystals had formed over the gore and encased most of her head and face in a hard red snow. She was no longer Ma, but another piece of dead meat. One of her eyes was visible, and it reminded me of a spoiled fish, so I covered it with a package of lamb chops before I spoke.

"Ma, I'm sorry this happened, but you drove me to it. You made me the man I am today—I was scared my whole damn life 'cause of you! I never had any confidence or belief in myself. And now I'm a murderer! Look what you made me! I hope you're proud. Now you're as cold as you were in life!" I slammed the lid and slid to the floor as I cried. I swear I heard her cacklin'.

After makin' a few more signs for the yard sale, I drove around and stuck them in the surrounding area. I ate my steak in silence and pondered what my new life would be like. Would I end up with a cinnamon sweet lady or would I become a tequila-logged beach bum and sell shells to tourists by the sea? It didn't matter, both seemed just fine by me.

Her cacklin' woke me and I jumped up in bed drenched in sweat. I knew I must've been dreamin', but the sound of it still rang in my ears. It was only six, so I had two hours to set up. Ma's stair lift sat unmovin' at the top of the stairs. *Wasn't it at the bottom?* Chills played my spine like a xylophone. *Maybe it came up on its own.* Damn *thing had been actin' up*, I thought, and decided not to worry about it.

Since I did most of the work already, it didn't take me long to get everythin' where it needed to be. I put my chair out and held a thermos of coffee. There weren't many nearby neighbors, and it was quiet on our street, especially in the morning. Other than the birds chirping in the trees, you could sit in peace and not be disturbed. The sale was set to start at eight, and at seven fifty-nine a car rolled up and parked. Two old women got out and hobbled up the driveway.

"Hello and good mornin'," I called.

"Oh, yes, poor boy. You dear, dear, thing," they said. Both women made a fuss over everythin' they touched.

"Uh, well, everythin' should be labeled. I'll go down where I can, but some things are already marked way lower than they should be. My Ma, she had a stroke and now—" I choked up.

"We understand. No problem, no problem at all. We'll pay full price for whatever we decide to buy."

I nodded and said thank you. I scolded myself for chokin' up. I needed to keep my composure or this would all be for nothin'. I thought maybe they knew Ma from somewhere, but I wasn't going to bring her up again, so I kept my mouth shut. One of the women grabbed an antique silver mirror. I had it marked at fifty dollars. She came over and told me it was well worth it and handed me a crisp bill.

"You're sure you're okay with the price?" I was in shock.

"Of course, I'm sure. Take it, take it. Poor dear." She patted my hand and shook her head full of white curls.

I put the money in my metal box and watched them descend the driveway and get back into their car. They waved at me as they left. *What was that about?* I wondered. More cars started to park along the road. Strangers shook my hand, patted my back, and told me everythin' would get better and that time heals all. I was a little confused, but also grateful that they seemed to want to pay full price for everythin' on the tables without hesitation. They couldn't know about Ma, could they? *Of course not, Levi. How could they know?*

I'd already made over five hundred dollars and it was only nine thirty! There was still quite a bit of stuff left too. I was startin' to feel giddy. And then I heard her cackle, mean as ever. I turned and look toward the house, but no one was there. *Get it together, Levi. You can't snap now. She's dead, dead, deadski. But I heard her? No, no, you didn't.* But I did.

I shook my head to clear my thoughts, and a van pulled up. A man got out with a woman and they smiled at me as they walked up. I waved, but said nothin'. The woman picked up a frame. It was Ma's, made of crystal, but it hadn't had anythin' in it for ages. She used to keep her and Daddy's wedding photo in it, but it'd long since been ripped up. I priced it at twenty-five bucks, which I thought was a good deal considerin' its actual value. The woman fumbled around her fanny pack and brought out some cash.

"Hello …" She paused. "I would just like to say I'm so sorry for your loss." The woman cradled Ma's frame.

"My what?" I asked.

"Your loss. I'm so sorry. It's always so hard to have to get rid of our loved one's stuff. It must be hard. So many beautiful things too, so many memories."

"I'm not sure what you mean. My ma had a stroke, but she's still—" I jumped when the man started shoutin'.

"Honey, look here, there's a brand-new comforter and sheet set— never opened! Five hundred thread count and just thirty bucks for both!" The man held up the brand-new bedding Ma had me order, but I never got around to putting on her bed.

The woman turned. "That's fantastic! We'll definitely want those!"

"Excuse me, miss, but as I was about to say, I'm just gettin' rid of stuff 'cause—" The woman put her hand up and stopped me.

"It's alright. You don't have to explain a thing to me, sweetie. We all grieve in our own way. Sometimes their belongings are too painful to keep looking at. I get it. Just make sure you keep the most precious of items to yourself … well, anyway, we're gonna take this lovely frame and the stuff my husband has. Such lovely things, honestly."

"Sure, yeah." My stomach started to cramp and my head hurt. I wondered, *what is this woman talkin' 'bout? Why're people actin' so darn funny? Am I projectin' grief?* Several more cars parked along the street. I needed to get ahold of myself, so I forced a smiled and greeted people as they looked around.

An hour till noon, and things were still goin' well. When I saw Miriam's car pull up, I cursed under my breath. She was out of the car in a flash and was in tears as she trudged up the driveway. She was makin' a fuss and everyone started to look.

"How could you not tell me, Levi? Why did you not call? I'm just so sick about it! You said she had a bad cold, but I never thought …" She let out a wail and began trembling. "You turned me away the other day … I might've been able to help! She's dead—my best friend is dead!" she cried.

"Calm down! What're you goin' on about?" I grabbed both her frail shoulders.

"Don't tell me to calm down! Just days ago, she was fine and now … now you're selling all her stuff! What did you do, Levi? What happened to her? You did something! What are you not telling me?" She backed away from my grip with surprisin' strength and pointed her arthritic finger at me. Some people started leavin', but others stayed, rooted to the ground like trees.

"Damn it, Miriam! Stop it," I shouted.

"Don't you tell me to stop! When's her service? How could you not have a service? Don't tell me you're getting rid of her stuff and not even having a funeral … my God … you are! She always said you were a no-good monster! I wanted to believe otherwise, but now I see exactly what she was talking about!"

"Listen to me, I just need to gather up enough money to help put Ma—" She slapped my face.

"Liar! You took advantage of me, so of course I should've known you would do the same to your own mother! Worthless, lying scoundrel! You killed her, didn't you? You had enough of taking care of her, and you killed her! You told me how hard it was on you and how you hated having to take care of her! You're a murderer!"

I saw nothin' but stars, and then the wasps invaded my brain again. Rage guided my body like strings on a puppet. I shoved Miriam and her head bounced off the concrete. I heard distant gasps and screams as I ran toward the house. I locked myself in and tried to figure out what I was gonna to do. How'd this all happen? I needed to run. Just get out, take what I had, and run.

I froze when I heard it. Her cacklin'. It bubbled up the basement stairs and shook the walls of the house. It filled my ears, rattled my bones, and coiled round my innards. It turned my blood to ice. I fell to the floor, curled up in a ball, and pulled at my hair. "Shut up, Ma! Shut the hell up! Why're you always fuckin' laughin' at me! Stop laughin'!"

The cacklin' died and sirens whined in its place. Lots of 'em. Then I heard bangin' on the front door. I managed to crawl to the kitchen and position myself under the table. I sat there until the door was kicked in and I saw several pairs of feet come into view. I heard my name bein' called, but I couldn't speak nor move. Several police officers lifted the tablecloth and kneeled down to look at me. I was shiverin' like a wet dog, and though I heard them speakin', I didn't understand a word they said. They pulled me out and put me in handcuffs. It all felt like a nightmare that I couldn't wake up from.

The back of the police car smelled like stale piss and body odor, but I leaned my head against the seat anyhow and tried to drown out Ma's cacklin' that'd started up again. Numerous vehicles were parked at the house now. They kept tryin' to question me, but their words were gibberish through the sound of Ma, so I remained silent. I closed my eyes and didn't open them again until the car started movin'. When we turned the corner and I could no longer see the house, the cacklin' subsided. My head felt like it had a bowlin' ball on top of it, but at least I couldn't hear her anymore.

We were at a stop sign when I spotted it. One of my signs for the yard sale stickin' out of the ground. I slid over in the seat and put my face against the glass. I couldn't believe what it said on it. I'd spelled mornin' wrong! The sign read, "Mourning Yard Sale." I'd made a stupid mistake and now here I was, going to jail for the rest of my miserable life 'cause of it! *Mourning Sale … you goddamn idiot, you told on yourself!* Cacklin' pervaded my ears again, but this time, I wasn't sure if it was Ma's or my own.

PORCH PIRATE

Though it was midday, the sky was gray with rain. The holiday season was in full swing and packages that were too big for the mailbox littered doorsteps and front porches. Buzzards shadowed the mist, watching and waiting for the easy pickings. A car pulled up to the last house on a dead-end road and stopped. The car door swung open and a teenager with a ponytail stuffed through a hat got out and looked around with his hands on his hips. An unkempt lawn surrounded the house and several soggy newspapers littered its walkway. Satisfied no one was home, the young man walked up to the front door and picked up the red box that sat on top of a weathered welcome mat. He whistled a festive tune as he walked back to his car, then added the box to the pile he'd already collected that morning and drove off.

Bruce's back windshield was starting to become partially obstructed by all the boxes, and with his trunk and front seat already occupied, he decided to call it a day. It had been as easy as it always was: walk, never run, smile if someone sees you, and always pretend you're looking for your lost pet if approached. He hadn't run into anyone all day thanks to the chilly needle-like rain and all he had to do now, was go home and unload all his ill-gotten booty.

He hoped it was better than last week's stuff, consisting mainly of a lot of Instant Pots, Keto cookbooks, and *Star Wars* toys. There had been one exception though—a jumbo-sized hot pink double-headed dildo—and he was seriously considering repackaging that beauty back up and putting it under the tree addressed to his mom from his pop. He chuckled to himself as he imagined how that would play out. They'd get home and his mother would see the single gift sitting there and when she saw the tag, she would say something like, "Oh, Herb, when did you put this here? You sneak! You shouldn't have!" Then his pop would simply say, "I didn't, Silvia." Naturally, his mother wouldn't believe him and would raise her painted eyebrow and rip that sucker open and ta-da!

Bruce's parents were in Europe until the new year, so he had the whole house to himself. When he was done unloading everything into the living room, he appraised his haul. The red box stood out and he couldn't wait to see what was in it. He checked for a label when he carried it in, but there wasn't one. In fact, there was no address on it anywhere. Something slid around when he shook it, but he couldn't make out what it was. He grabbed his car key, slid it under the tape, and began opening it. The phone rang, and he jumped. "Damn landline." He huffed and put the box down.

It was his mother, calling to check on him, she said, but Bruce knew better than that. She was calling to make sure he was doing everything she asked him to do while they were away. He reminded her that he was seventeen years old and almost an adult and that he wouldn't forget to water her orchids, feed Muffy, or vacuum. When he heard her sharp inhale, he interrupted her before she could add anything else and promised he wouldn't get anything on her brand-new Natuzzi couches either. Bruce was still bitter that they hadn't invited him to join them overseas, but had instead enlisted him to babysit the damn cat. *God forbid the fuzzball was boarded*, he'd thought. "But they won't give Muffy her spray of whipped cream at night," his mother had pleaded.

Where is Muffy anyway? he thought as he looked around the room. He called for her and listened for the ting-a-ling of her collar, but she didn't come. "Stupid spoiled tub of lard … and I don't care what Mom says, I'm not giving you any damn whipped cream or combing the dingle berries out of your fluffy butthole," he grumbled, then sniffed his armpits. "Whew, might be time to take a shower."

Bruce hopped out of the shower when he heard a loud crash. He put his wet hair into a man bun, wrapped a towel around his waist, and headed into the living room. Nothing seemed out of place, so he tiptoed to the kitchen. His glass of orange juice and cereal bowl from breakfast were shattered on the floor. "God damn it, Muffy," he shouted, then walked out to look for her. "Come out, you fluff ass!" He froze when he heard growling coming from the guest bedroom. "Muffy? You in there?" He kicked himself for leaving the door open. The guest bed was significantly more comfortable than his own and he'd been sleeping in there until his parents got back.

He walked slowly to the door and peeked in. Muffy was hunkered down beside the bed, growling at something underneath. Her tail twitched angrily back and forth and her ears were flat against her head. "What is it, girl? What's under there? Is it another lizard … or maybe a frog?" Bruce clutched his towel and went in. *Fucking Florida and its goddamn lizards*, he thought. He hated the things. They left their disgusting little white-capped turds all over everything. "Get it, Muff! Get that lizard!"

Muffy's growls turned to a whine. She crawled under the bed and started hissing and carrying on so loudly that Bruce started to think it wasn't a lizard but something else. Maybe when he was carrying the boxes in, something ran into the house? He flipped on the light and closed the bedroom door, hoping to trap whatever it was inside. When he heard Muffy's urgent gurgling cries, he threw his towel down and bent to look under the bed. It was dark, but he could see Muffy rolling around erratically. Something was attached to her back, and it was pulling her collar against her throat. Alarm surged throughout Bruce's body and he reached under to try to grab her.

She clawed his forearms and bit his hand as he pulled her toward himself, but whatever had been on her back took off. He popped up and reeled around, but didn't see anything. Muffy panted and gripped the flesh of his damp chest. Carefully, he pulled her claws out of his skin and put her on top of the bed, then walked around to the other side. The cat's eyes grew wide with terror and her hair stood on end. As Bruce looked around the room, he sighed with relief when he saw the closet door was shut. If it was still in the bedroom, it could only have run under the dresser or nightstand.

He cursed himself for not bringing any of his own clothes into the bedroom. His penis dangled against the carpet as he got on all fours and bent forward with his ass in the air. He squinted under the dresser, but didn't see anything. Before he could get up, he felt a sharp stabbing pain impale his anus. "Gaaaah! Holy fuck," Bruce cried, then jumped up and clenched his ass cheeks together. Something was definitely sticking out of his butthole. He held his breath, reached around, and gently pulled the object free. He winced as he held up a blood-and-shit-streaked Bank of America pen. "What in the hell …" he whispered. "How'd that get in there?"

Bruce knew there was no way he could've sat on the pen. He also knew that no lizard, frog, or rodent could grab hold of a cat's collar and attempt to choke it to death. Whatever this thing was, it wanted to hurt them. *What could it possibly be?* he wondered. Florida was not just home to human oddities, but also all kinds of mutant creatures that defied explanation. He still had to find whatever it was, and he was afraid. *Maybe it's a mini trained assassin monkey? Or some kind of evil parrot … those things are pretty smart!* None of those things seemed logical, but something had been choking the cat and that something had also put a pen into his asshole.

A noise erupted from under the bed. Muffy was hissing and growling again from atop the comforter. Bruce wished he had a weapon, then remembered that his mom kept some beach umbrellas in the closet. He hopped over the bed and opened the closet door, doing his best not to take his eyes away from the area. He grabbed an umbrella and felt around a pile of folded clothes and pulled out what he hoped were a pair of pants. He looked down, *Oh, fuck.* They were pants alright, but they were his mother's and they were neon green yoga pants. *Well, at least they'll stretch*, he thought.

He didn't want his junk hanging free, not with that pen-raping monster still loose. It was a struggle, but he was able to pull them on. When he looked down at his crotch, his dick and balls were smashed and separated into what he'd call a mooseknuckle. With his hand wrapped tightly around the umbrella, he trudged toward the bed. When he got on all fours and lowered his head, he felt the skintight material split open. He cussed out loud when one of his balls popped free, but didn't take his eyes off the miniature figure staring out at him from the darkness.

"What the fuck are you?" Bruce asked, then he shoved the umbrella under the bed and tried to poke it, but it skittered out and went under the nightstand. "I got you now, you little bastard!" He laughed, and ran around to the nightstand, then he pushed the bed further away and rammed the tip of the umbrella under the stand. A shrill squeal stabbed his eardrums, but he kept stabbing. When the squeal stopped, he dropped the umbrella and pulled the stand away from the wall, but there was nothing underneath. "Oh, you've got to be kidding me!"

Bruce pulled open all the drawers, but other than the TV remote, nothing was in them. When the umbrella rustled, he turned and could see something moving around inside it. He grabbed it, hit the button on the handle, and it burst open. An olive-green and mottled-brown creature the size of a large rat hung from it and wildly kicked its legs as it screeched. When it opened its mouth, he could see all its tiny razor-sharp teeth. Bruce gulped and mouthed, *Holy hell.*

It held onto the metal framework of the umbrella as if it was a parachute. There were three long fingers with claws and scaly three-toed feet with dagger-like talons. Its face reminded Bruce of the chayote squashes his mom sometimes brought home from the farmer's market. What looked like thick brown snot hung from its gnarled blob of a nose and two pointy ears stuck out on the sides of its head. It swung its body and narrowed its beady black eyes as it continued to screech at him.

"Fucking A, you're an ugly little thing," Bruce spat, then he closed the umbrella on it and squeezed its squirming body in the exact manner that he did when he captured a palmetto bug in one of his socks. As it writhed under the pressure of his grip, he tried to decide what to do with it next, because after all, it was no palmetto bug and he couldn't just deposit it outside.

He opened the bedroom door with his free hand, and Muffy darted from the bed and ran out of sight. The bathroom, he decided, was a good place to deal with it. He shut the door and threw the umbrella into the bathtub like it was a bomb. The thing moved with lighting speed from underneath and looked up at him. Its talons scraped against the porcelain and it reached toward him with its grotesque fingers. It grunted, then sprang upward like a giant grasshopper and latched onto his free testicle, biting down with its needle-sharp teeth. Bruce shrieked in agony and battered his fists against it, but it held on, digging its claws and talons into the meat of his upper thigh.

The pain was excruciating and Bruce scrambled to find something, anything, to get it off. He stumbled into the bathtub and turned on the water. He turned it as hot as it would go and thrust his crotch under the steaming stream of the shower. The two of them squealed in harmony until it finally relented and let go. "You son of a bitch! I'm gonna fucking kill you," Bruce wailed.

The thing climbed the shower curtain and sat atop the rod, looking down at him.

"Oh, you want me to try to get you, don't you? I bet you'd like that, you ugly fucker! Not this time. I'll be back, and when I come back, you're fucking toast!" Bruce sneered at it, opened the door, and slammed it behind him. He tore the yoga pants off and looked down at his throbbing cherry-red crotch. Beads of blood poured out of all the tiny teeth marks on his battered testicle and the puncture wounds on his thighs. He hadn't cried since he was a young boy, but tears streamed down his face as he limped down the hall toward his bedroom.

Bruce's hands trembled as he pulled on a pair of sweatpants, then he paused and grabbed several balls of socks. He shuddered as he stuffed the socks down the front of his pants. He'd have to deal with his wounds later and hoped that whatever that thing was, it didn't carry rabies or something else. He worried about his dick and his testicle. What *if it damaged them for life? There's always the double-headed dildo, I guess.* He pushed the troubled thoughts away and waddled to his parent's bedroom.

His father's Glock was in the drawer. He knew it was loaded, because his pop told him it was. He took it out of the holster and when the cool steel hit his hand, he felt a little better. There was no way the thing would get away from a bullet, but just in case, he grabbed his father's signed David Ortiz baseball bat out of the closet. His pop would understand—he hoped.

Outside the bathroom, Bruce took a deep breath. His knuckles turned white while gripping the doorknob. He gave himself a pep talk. "You can do it, Brucey, boy. Just open the door and shoot it. But how'll I explain all this to Mom and Pop? And what if someone calls the cops when they hear the gunshot? I'll just tell them there was a wild animal in the house and I panicked. Well, what about all the stolen packages?" *Fuck ... yeah, what about all the stolen packages?* "I can't worry about those right now."

Bruce threw the door open and shut it behind him. He leaned the bat against the wall and looked all round, but didn't see it anywhere. Where the hell could it have gone? *He's probably clinging to the damn curtain.* He pulled the curtain back with force, but it wasn't on it or in the tub. "Oh, for fuck's sake! Where are you, you fucking monster?"

He opened all the bathroom cabinets, and still, nothing. *There's no way it opened the bathroom door. It couldn't have,* he thought, *could it?* Then he heard the splashing. A grin spread across Bruce's face and he shouted, "Got ya!"

He lifted the toilet seat, and it looked up at him, tilting its ugly face one way and then the other. Bruce pointed the gun at it. Before he could squeeze the trigger, it leapt out of the toilet. He tried to shield himself, but it was able to dig its claws into one of his eyes. The gun fell to the floor. With the thing still clinging to his face, he reached for the bat and squeezed its body as hard as he could. When it let go, he started swinging the bat in every direction, knocking holes in the walls and cracking the marble tiles.

The damage in the bathroom was bad, but in his rage, he wasn't sure if he even hit the thing. One hand covered his bleeding eye, but he was able to spot it atop the shower rod again. It held its arm as if it were wounded and joy filled Bruce's heart; he'd hit it after all. He picked up the gun, but decided it might not be the best choice. He'd already smashed the bathroom to smithereens. He didn't want to fire a gun too. He swung the bat at it and it hit the wall before it dropped down into the tub. "Gotcha," he said and fist pumped the air.

It lay on its back, barely moving, but Bruce was skeptical and poked at it. When it didn't flinch, he felt satisfied. He thought about pulverizing it in his mother's Margaritaville blender until it resembled nothing more than a guts-and-gore smoothie or cooking it in the microwave until it exploded, but then decided he might want to keep it intact. His mom and pop would already want to strangle him when they saw what he did, and he'd need proof. He used a towel to lift its grotesque, lifeless body. *Freezing it could work*, he thought, and shrugged.

He held it away from himself as he made his way to the kitchen. When he walked past the boxes, he stopped and turned back around. The red box he'd been opening before his mother called sat wide open on the floor, his car keys still next to it. Bruce's heart started clamoring around in his chest because, somehow, he was sure that the red box had something to do with the creature he held in his hand.

He walked over to the box and spotted a Christmas card inside. A picture of Santa, rosy-cheeked and jolly, was on the front of it. There were presents piled around him, and he held his list in one hand and a feather quill in the other. Bruce set the thing down next to the box and lifted the card out. His wounded eye pulsed and his stomach did somersaults. He opened the card and there was a message scrawled in black ink. He read it aloud, "Dear Porch Pirate, perhaps next time instead of being so naughty, you'll be nice, and before taking off with other's packages, you'll be much smarter and think twice."

There was no signature, and he frowned as he put the card back inside the box. Just then the thing started twitching, and without thinking, Bruce stomped on it several times and splattered the slimy brown contents of it across his mother's new cream-colored Natuzzi couches. The smell of it was putrid, a vile mixture of rancid blue cheese and an open sewer on a hot day. Vomit crowded his mouth as he lifted what was left of it up and put it back into the red box on top of the card. Bruce knew one thing for certain: he didn't care if it took all night—he was packing his car back up and delivering every single box back from where they came from.

OUT OF HER GOURD

Kendra was afraid of the dark. Not the actual darkness, but the darkness she felt worming around her innards, tickling her thoughts. Thoughts that were splinters, wedged beneath her flesh, waiting to fester and come to a head. They were a part of her now, and they always would be, but she had to pull herself together, because the aroma of ripe apples and fallen leaves were present in the crisp autumn air. Halloween was around the corner, and even though sorrow clung to Kendra like moss on a tree, she wouldn't want to miss her window of opportunity. The veil would be paper thin in the coming days, and the thinner the veil, the better the chance she'd have to speak with *him* again.

When Kendra and Vinny bought a house together, she was sure it would happen then. They'd made love when she was at her slickest, in every room and against every surface, but still each month the cramps raked her insides, followed by the bloat and shed lining of her unfit womb. What had she done wrong? Why did her body betray her again and again?

Vinny left the day she'd bought the crib. It took her most of the day to put it together and when he came home and saw it, he went nuts. He told her to take it back to the store along with the other items she'd gotten in recent months, but she'd screamed at him, and told him she wouldn't. She told him she only bought what was on sale, and that they might need it soon, but Vinny just shook his head and then packed his bags. Even after all the doctor's visits and their savings were spent, Kendra still couldn't accept the fact that her body might not be baby-making material. "Give it time," everyone always said. "Some women get pregnant when they least expect it."

Adoption was still an option, but it was proving to be harder than Kendra thought, and the waiting list for a baby was miles long. Not only did she feel punished for being a thirty-something single woman who lived alone, but she felt punished for being a woman without a child. Other women looked at her like she was some sort of child-eating mutant, and she couldn't blame them. She felt like one. All those years ago, when she had wished for someone like Vinny, she wondered if it had been a big mistake, that maybe she'd wished for the wrong thing. She couldn't help but feel that it was too late, and her fate to be a childless crone was sealed.

It had been Halloween night when she first tried it. Kendra wasn't one to dabble in black magic, but after handing out candy by the handful and drinking a bottle and a half of wine, she'd figured what the hell could it hurt. She was going on twenty-eight years old, and each night, as she sat alone in her apartment eating a Lean Cuisine while watching reruns of *Friends*, she pleaded for someone—anyone—to love her. She didn't do any research or look up specifics, she just went by the various movies she'd seen and stories she'd read. It wasn't like she expected it to actually work.

Kendra's heart pounded as she stumbled around her apartment, looking for items to use in the ritual. She giggled as she drew a pentagram on the middle of the living room floor using an entire tube of her favorite red lipstick. After placing various candles at the points of her drawing, she poured sea salt around the entire thing. She inspected her work before she turned the lights off, then carefully stepped over the salt ring and stood in the center of her lipstick pentagram. Kendra was pretty dang proud of herself, considering she was no expert on how to summon a demon.

It occurred to her after some time that she might have to say something to get the ball rolling, so she began to talk. "Oh, mighty fallen angels and people of Hell … denizens of the deep, dark pits of torture, might you show yourselves? Will you hear me now and come forth to shower me with your greatness and undivine presence? Might I ask of you a favor? I would be forever indebted to you." She felt like a fool and began to scold herself. *People of Hell?! Denizens of the deep dark pits … Are demons even considered people? It doesn't matter, they're not real, this's stupid. You're stupid! You were raised Catholic, for Christ's sake, Kendra! Get a fucking grip!*

Kendra stood in silence until she began to wobble with fatigue and as she lifted her foot to step out, all but one of the candles extinguished and she froze. The room turned into an igloo and the smell of rotting meat and sulfur singed her nasal passages. Her blood felt like it had been replaced with hot mud, and then she collapsed. When her eyes opened again, she thought, *Oh, fuck, Kendra. What've you done?*

Somehow, she'd managed to remain inside the circle. She sat up and looked around the dark. Her ears rang and she could feel a presence in the room with her. It was as if she'd hugged a giant plasma ball; every hair on her body stood on end. Then she heard his voice. It boomed around her like bass, rippling her flesh and making every cell in her body vibrate.

"What is it you want? I have many things to tend to, so make it worth my while," the voice roared.

"H-hello?" It was all Kendra could manage.

"I'm not here to go in circles, mortal. Tell me what it is you want!"

"Who are you?"

"I am Zepar, I am a duke of Hell." A figure stepped into the sparse candlelight and stopped short of the salt. Kendra gasped when she saw him. His head almost reached the ceiling and crimson armor shielded all of his body except for his large hooved feet. She couldn't see his face, because it was hidden behind a Barbuta style helmet, but she saw his eyes, and they bore into her like smoldering coals. She marveled over his beautiful red armor, but recoiled when she spotted his long forked tongue dart forth several times like a snake tasting the air. He tapped one of his hooved feet impatiently.

"I—I thought you weren't real …" Kendra murmured.

"Turns out I am. So, again, what is it you seek? I have many places to be. Halloween is a busy night for us demons and you're not the only one who calls."

"Love … I seek love."

"Don't we all—and what is it you offer in return, mortal?"

"I hadn't thought that part through …"

"You have little time before I lose interest—"

"I'm sure I have nothing to give someone like you."

"Oh, but you do. All mortals do."

"What is it?"

"I cannot tell you. You must offer it up on your own."

"My … my soul?" Kendra choked.

"Hardly. You always think we want your souls, but the truth is, we have so many of those ridiculous things already. In fact, we are overrun with them. I prefer to keep things interesting."

"But I have nothing to offer you. I'm sorry … I called you here for nothing."

"If I give you what you ask, would you be willing to offer me something in the future?"

"I don't know. I'm unsure what I'd be giving up."

"Nothing much. After all, you cannot miss what you never had to begin with."

Kendra's head began to ache and throb. Hot tendrils seemed to be weaving in and out of the coils of her brain. Everything went dark, and she saw nothing at first. She closed her eyes, and when she opened them again, she stood in the middle of a dry and cracked wasteland. The sun scorched her naked body and sweat poured off of her in sheets as she began to walk. She spotted a pitcher of water floating in midair just ahead.

Her mouth was drier than it had ever been in her life and the fat beads of condensation dripping down the glass pitcher made her long for it.

"Drink," a far-off voice said.

Kendra shook her head.

"Drink," the voice said again.

The water gleamed and her throat constricted so much so that she thought she'd suffocate. Her feet were moving before she even realized, and then she was running. She grabbed the pitcher with both hands and drank … and drank… and drank until it was empty. A feeling of fullness overwhelmed her, and then she crumpled to the ground.

Kendra opened her eyes and stared up at the demon. He spoke without speaking. "*Your family has not called since you moved over three thousand miles to get away from them. You have prayed to God for love, and he has yet to answer, so why not trust in the powers that be?*"

"All right … whatever you want. I give to you whatever it is you want."

He nodded, and then he was gone.

Vinny came into her life only a week later and he was everything Kendra had ever dreamed of in a man and they were happy for a while, but the demon lied. She did miss something she'd never had—a baby. She'd tried several times to call Zepar back, but he never came. When Vinny left her, she had nothing but her loneliness and it was eating her alive. With each passing day, she swore she could feel her uterus rotting from the inside out.

She had everything on hand this time, including a red silk robe she planned to wear just for him. The pentagram and circle were already drawn and the salt and candles laid out. Tomorrow was Halloween, and Kendra knew he'd be listening.

Her sleep had been disturbed all night, and at work she was in a haze. She was glad no one asked her what was wrong, because she might've confessed right then and there. Demon conjuring wasn't on the list of acceptable behavior for anyone, but especially not a teacher. When Kendra arrived home, she saw an enormous pumpkin sitting by the front door. She wondered who'd left it there? It was an odd thing to leave on a doorstep, but she did have students in the surrounding neighborhood, so perhaps one of them left it there as a sort of gift.

Even though the holiday fell on a Friday this year, she knew trick 'r treating would be over before nine, and then she could begin her summoning. She drew a face on a small pumpkin and placed it next to the one that had been left on her doorstep. Something about the gifted pumpkin made her uneasy, but she didn't know why. Other than its large, bulbous size, it looked like a perfectly ordinary gourd.

The knocks and doorbell rings slowed around 8:45 p.m. She waited until nine, then shut off the outside light, took off her clothes, and slipped into the robe. Once every light was turned off, she lit the candles. She stood in the center of her pentagram, closed her eyes, and chanted his name over and over, "Zepar, Zepar, Zepar, Zepar, Zepar …"

Kendra's eyes fluttered open when she heard the doorbell. "Who the hell could that be? I thought I shut the damn light off," she whispered. She pulled the belt to her robe tighter and walked to the door. The doorbell sounded again, and she nearly tripped over her own feet, but this time, whoever was ringing it, didn't stop. "Kids," she grumbled. When a sound similar to several pairs of knuckles started to pound her door, she shouted, "I'm all out of candy, guys! Go play your pranks on someone else!"

She peered through the peephole, but there was no one there. *I need to get one of those doorbell camera things*, she thought. *They're probably hiding in the bushes, the little shits.* As soon as she started to walk away, the ringing and knocking began again. Kendra stomped to the door and hollered, "If you're trying to scare me, it's not gonna work! Go home, it's late! I'll have to call the police if you continue—I mean it!"

With her hand on the doorknob, she looked through the peephole again, and this time she saw the gifted pumpkin sitting front and center. But someone had written a message on it in big dark red letters. She read it aloud, "For You." Kendra rolled her eyes. "Oh, how sweet. I better get that thing in here before they try something else."

Kendra opened the front door and a rush of cold air washed over her and made her shiver. There was no rustling in the bushes or movement by the trees as she suspected there'd be, but she figured they ran off when she shouted about the police. The pumpkin was heavy, and she had to tumble it forward like a bowling ball to get it inside. She inspected it for possible dog poop or whatever else until she was satisfied, then tumbled it into the kitchen.

The mood was ruined, and she thought she should wait before she tried calling to him again, if at all. She poured herself a glass of wine and, as she sipped it, she stared at the pumpkin and sighed. "What the fuck am I doing? I'm losing my mind, that's what." Then she heard muffled crying. It seemed to be coming from the pumpkin. "What in the hell …?"

She bent down next to it and let her hands glide over the cool orange skin, then she pressed her ear to it. There was no sound, of course, and she laughed out loud. "This's batshit crazy, Kendra. You know that, right?" But she heard it again. First a cooing and then a whimpering. She pressed her ear back and heard the faintest of noises. "It can't be …" she whispered. "Could it?" Against her better judgment, she went and got the biggest knife she could find.

Kendra held the gourd down with one hand and began to carefully carve into it with the other. With each cut she made, she felt a sharp pain claw at her insides, but she refused to stop. The deeper she cut, the worse the pain became. Tears flooded her eyes, and she had to keep wiping them away in order to see what she was doing. She wasn't sure why none of her cuts were making a difference; it was like the exterior was protecting whatever was inside. When the pain became too much, she clutched her lower abdomen and stopped to catch her breath.

She sat in front of the pumpkin and panted. A cold sweat covered her body. All the cuts she made seeped like wounds. Kendra touched the clear mucus and brought her fingers to her nose. It smelled faintly of blood. Her heart quickened, and she choked back a sob. The knife was slippery, so she wiped it on her robe, then she gripped the handle with both hands and plunged it deep into the thick orange flesh.

Kendra's screams erupted around her as she dragged the knife down over and over, and it wasn't until she collapsed from the pain that she stopped. When she was able to move, she wasted no time. She dug her hands through the pulp and guts, ignoring the blinding white-hot agony she felt as she did. Dark gobs of what looked like raw liver littered the floor around her. She wept with each handful, but continued to work her way through the carnage. When she noticed the blood start to gush from in between her own legs, she shrieked, "What have you done to me? What have you … no! No goddamn you, nooooo!"

CHRISTMAS COOKIES

Gunner insisted on leaving cookies out for Santa. He'd been doing it every year since he could remember. It didn't matter what kind, whether they were homemade or store bought, but they absolutely had to be placed on a plate next to a glass of cold milk before bedtime. His parents had been bickering off and on for days, but he knew he had to get their attention because today was Christmas Eve. He pulled down all the ingredients he'd seen his mother use on previous occasions and placed them on the counter in the hope she'd see and remember, but when she saw what he did, she began hollering instead.

"Gunner, why in the heck did you go and pull down all that stuff from the cabinets? You could've fallen off the dang chair! I've got so much to do already and you're making more of a mess for me to deal with. Sometimes, you're just like your father, you know that? Always thinking about yourself," his mother grumbled under her breath as she noisily put each item back.

"But Mama, it's Christmas Eve! What about Santa … and the cookies?" Gunner rubbed the tears from under his glasses. He hadn't wanted to cry, but once his nose got to burning, he couldn't stop it.

"I guess he'll have to go without this year, just like the rest of us. I'm not in the mood anyhow. I know, why don't you ask your daddy to make them?" she said, then smirked.

Gunner might've only been eight years old, but he knew by now when his mother was trying to poke fun at him or his daddy. He felt his anger well up like an overfilled water balloon from deep inside his gut. They'd already forgotten his birthday over the summer, only remembering when his grandma called. His parents had said they were sorry, that they'd take him out to pizza the next day and then to the store to pick out a toy, but when the next day came, they'd forgotten again. Gunner forgave them for that, but he wasn't going to let them get away with not giving Santa his cookies!

Gunner jumped when his daddy came into the kitchen. He was scratching his beard. A lit cigarette hung from his mouth, as he asked, "Make what?"

"Your son wants to make cookies for Santa. I told him to ask you to do it. We all know how good you are at doing stuff … or you could just run on over to the store and buy some pre-made ones. Isn't that girl working today, the one you seem to like to chat up every time we go in there?" His mother's face turned the shade of fruit punch.

"Oh, hell, c'mon now, Colleen. You're being ridiculous—how old's that girl anyhow? All of what, seventeen?"

"Oh, I bet you know her age! You're such a pig, Jimmy. I swear if I find out you've been sniffing around—"

"For crying out loud, I ain't fiddling with no grocery store teenager! Cool your horses and quit saying stuff like that in front of the kid. I'll go get the goddamn cookies. Christ almighty, can I get a cup of coffee first? I have to go in and work half a day today anyhow, so I'll pick them up on my way home."

"Forget it, Jimmy. I'll make the damn things myself. Gunner, quit standing there like a dolt watching us fuss. This was all your idea, so move your dang feet and help me." His mother opened the cabinets and began to slam each item back onto the counter.

"Okay, Mama!" Gunner tried not to run.

He did as his mother told him and kept quiet unless spoken to. She turned on the radio and sang along with some of the festive songs. Gunner beamed when she let him lick the raw dough from the spoon and then he used a cookie scooper to drop the balls of dough onto a slick sheet pan. Chocolate chip cookies were his favorite, but he wouldn't eat too many, because he knew they were Santa's favorite, too. One year he'd made oatmeal raisin and Santa hadn't touched a single one of them, so he knew not to make those ever again.

Gunner saw his mother pour something from a glass bottle into her coffee mug throughout the morning and, though he wanted to know what it was, he didn't dare ask. After she drank it, her breath smelled like peppermint mouthwash, but he didn't think she'd drink that. She told him she was going to sit down and rest her feet while the cookies baked, so he went into the living room to watch some cartoons. The aroma of the cookies baking filled the house—and Gunner—with joy. He sure hoped Santa knew how good he'd been this year.

When the timer beeped, Gunner shot up and ran to the kitchen. His mother was asleep at the table. Her head was slumped over to one side and her mouth hung open like a dead catfish. He tried to nudge her awake, but she moaned and moved her head to the other side. He saw the oven mitts on the counter, so he put them on. The heat blasted Gunner's face as he reached in to get the cookies and his thin arms shook as he removed the tray. He had to use his knee to close the oven door, which snapped shut and made a thunderous thud that woke his mother.

Gunner dropped the hot tray on his bare feet as his mother screeched, "Gunner! What're you doing? Are you out of your dang mind? You could've been burned!" Her eyes drifted to the floor then. "Look at the mess you made! What am I gonna do with you, huh? Get away from the oven and go get the broom. I'll save what I can, but you better hope we got enough left for one more batch."

Gunner ignored the searing pain on the tops of his feet as he went to retrieve the broom. His mother had already picked up the cookies that weren't broken and put them back onto the tray to cool. He didn't care that they'd hit the floor and ate the ones that were mutilated before he wiped up the gooey chocolate stuck to the tile and swept the crumbs. When the oven beeped a second time, his mother was thankfully awake, and he was grateful for that.

They made enough cookies to fill two plates, so they each had one with some cold milk. Then his daddy came home, and he ate one, too, smiling and saying how good it was. Everything was going well until his daddy looked in the trash can.

He pulled out the bottle his mother had been pouring from all morning and held it up like a trophy. "Colleen, what the hell's this?"

"It's what it is," his mother spat.

"Have you been drinking all morning? And while y'all were baking? You trying to burn the house down? The one that I work hard to keep over our heads?"

"Is the house burnt down, Jimmy? I wish it would burn. Maybe then I'd be free of this dilapidated shithole in the middle of nowhere! And I wouldn't need to drink if you didn't go sticking your thing in and out of every—" His mother whirled around then and shouted, "Gunner, go to your room, right now!"

Gunner pretended to go to his room, but he stayed flat against the wall that led to the kitchen and listened as best he could.

"Go on, then. Say what it is you have to say. You're just itchin' to say it, aren't you? Like you always do," his daddy said.

"If you could keep your hands to yourself and your grub in your pants—"

"Oh, there you go! It was only a handful of times. You ever gonna let it go? That was months ago—I ain't done nothing since!"

"Months … you say that like it's a glowing achievement that deserves a trophy. People go their whole damn marriage dedicated to one another, Jimmy! You're a pig! I should've never married you … I should've married your brother—at least he's a real man. And I know he don't raise his hands to a lady!"

Gunner heard his daddy snicker before he said, "I don't see no ladies round here. In fact, I don't see nothing but a cow in a gingerbread turtleneck."

The sound of chairs being shoved filled Gunner's ears. When the table squealed across the floor, he peeked around the wall and saw his daddy raising his hand to his mother.

"Daddy, no!" Gunner ran and yanked on the back of his daddy's pants. All of the sudden he felt the back of his daddy's hand strike his cheek, and his little body went flying in the other direction.

"Jimmy, you son of a bitch!" his mother wailed.

"That boy shouldn't be meddling. That'll teach him."

"You're a monster!"

"It's your fault. If you hadn't riled me up, none of this would've happened. See what your drinking causes? All of this is *your* doing. You're making that boy soft. He don't belong baking cookies anyhow, that's woman's work."

"Get out," his mother said.

"What'd you say?"

"I said, get out! I swear to Christ, Jimmy, get out of here now before I—"

"Before you what, Colleen? Huh? Before you what?"

Gunner was still cowering in the corner of the kitchen. He had to squint to see what was going on since his glasses had gone flying when he was pushed, and he wasn't about to try and find them right then. He saw his mother flinch when his daddy raised his hand again.

"That's what I thought. You're like every other dumb bitch, all bark and no bite. I think I just might go on down to the store after all. I like chocolate chip just fine, but I'd like some sugar—cookies, that is. Variety and all."

His mother slipped to the floor and cried as soon as his daddy slammed the front door. Then she got up, walked right past Gunner as if he wasn't there, and disappeared up the stairs without another word. Gunner's cheek throbbed along with the tops of his burnt feet, but he ignored both as he scrambled to find his glasses. When he did find them, he tried to put them on his face, but they were all twisted and the lenses were cracked. He wondered if it was too late to ask Santa for new ones.

It was getting dark and his mother still hadn't come back down, nor had his daddy come home. Gunner went into the kitchen and poured himself some cereal for dinner. When he was finished, he stood on a chair to rinse his bowl in the sink, and then he reached for the nicest glass he could find. He carried the two plates of cookies into the living room and set them on the coffee table. Then he went back and poured some milk all the way to the top of the glass, being careful not to trip and spill a single drop on his way back. He plugged the Christmas tree in and watched the blurry blinking lights until his eyes grew heavy with sleep. Even with everything that'd happened, he still held on to hope that Santa would come and make everything better.

Gunner woke when he heard his daddy come home. His heart thudded in time with the sound of his boots as they trudged up the stairs. He heard him stumble down the hall and stop right outside of his bedroom door. Then his daddy let loose an obnoxious, lengthy burp, followed by a wet hacking cough. Gunner pretended to be asleep in case he opened the door and breathed a sigh of relief when he heard him finally walk away. He waited for his parent's fussing to begin, but to his surprise, it didn't. Minutes later, he heard his daddy's hog like snores and drifted back to sleep himself.

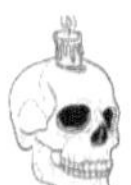

A thump on the roof lifted Gunner from his sleep. He shot up in his bed like a jack-in-the-box and murmured, "Santa?" Then he tiptoed to the window and looked out, but he couldn't see much. He grabbed his mangled glasses and pressed them against his eyes to try and get a better glimpse. Snow had fallen during the night and blanketed everything outside like pillows of marshmallow fluff. Gunner pressed a hand to the frosty glass and jumped back when he spotted the large metallic egg-shaped object hovering in the air. A red-and-green incandescent light radiated from the object's bottom and lit the snow underneath. "Santa, is that you?" Gunner whispered. "Where's your reindeer?"

Gunner's breath kept fogging the glass on the window and he had to wipe it again and again to see. He wondered if maybe Santa started using some sort of magical ship to save time. After all, it was an awful big world and he could understand if he needed to do that. The thumps on the roof were getting more frantic. Just then, Gunner remembered they had no chimney and thought, *Oh no! How'll Santa get in?* As quietly as he could, he raced down the stairs and opened the front door. A blast of snowflakes and frigid air flew in through the open door and caused Gunner to shiver as he squinted into the blue-black night and waited to see if Santa would appear.

Something fell from the roof and hit the snow with a formidable crunch. Gunner wasted no time; he ran and hid behind the couch in the living room. Was he really going to get to see Santa? Gunner couldn't believe his good fortune! A strange sound filled the room; a series of clicks and other noises he couldn't decipher. Gunner's ears started to feel like they once did when he went on an airplane ride, so he wiggled his fingers in them. When he poked his head up to take a peek, he yelped. A figure stood near the Christmas tree, then it turned toward him, and he thought his heart would stop ticking.

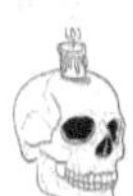

The only light was from the ones on the tree and Gunner wasn't sure what or who he was looking at. He'd forgotten his glasses upstairs and was squinting hard enough to make his eyes water. The figure was tall and thin, tall enough to hit its head on the ceiling. It was taller and thinner than Gunner ever imagined Santa would be, but more shocking was that it didn't seem to be wearing any sort of clothes, not even a coat. It moved closer and Gunner ducked. When he popped his head back up, two enormous black oval eyes stared back at him.

"Holy smokes," Gunner said, still crouched behind the couch. "You're not Santa … are you?" Gunner wasn't really sure. He only knew Santa from movies, books, and pictures. Maybe Santa didn't look anything like the Santa from those things, maybe he was from space. Was Santa an alien? That'd make sense, since he could travel the world in one night. Gunner tried to catch his breath and settle his heart, which was walloping hard enough to fill his ears.

The figure's head reminded Gunner of an octopus, except without the tentacles, and it tilted it one way and then the other as if to study him. As it inched closer, Gunner whimpered. He could now see that its lean body was muscular, with greenish grey skin that glistened just like the river frogs he liked to catch. There were two gaping holes where a nose should've been and it had a mouth like a rotten jack-o'-lantern grimace. Gunner mustered up the courage to stand so he could get a better look. On trembling legs, he looked to see if it had ears, because maybe the thing was a type of elf. But there were no ears that he saw.

Gunner gulped and said, "I don't know who or what you are, but if you try anything funny-like, I'll scream and get my daddy up. He's real mean, why just today he knocked me clear across the room and broke my glasses, so no telling what he might do to you."

The thing didn't answer Gunner, it just watched him with curiosity. Gunner came around from the side of the couch and went over to the plates of cookies. He picked one up and took a bite. Then he picked another one up and held it out toward the towering figure. It didn't move at first, but then it glided over until it stood directly in front of him. Gunner looked down at the thing's feet and thought they looked sort of human, except for their massive size and the sharp claws protruding from its long toes.

Gunner still held the cookie out. "I reckon the milk's probably not that cold anymore, but then maybe it's not so bad, seeing as it's cold in here with the door open and all. I'm probably gonna get in trouble if my parents wake up. They'll whip me good for having the door wide open with the heat on. Mama says we don't live in a barn."

The figure looked over its shoulder, held its hand up, and the door swung shut. Then it turned back toward him and reached out with its sticky looking elongated fingers. It took the cookie, then it used its free hand to cover the entirety of Gunner's face. Gunner tried to open his mouth to protest, but before he could get a word out, his eyes rolled back in his head and all of his memories from his short-lived life played in his mind like a movie in fast forward. When he finally came to, the figure removed its hand and stepped back.

"What'd you do to me?" Gunner whispered. He felt different. Not in a bad way, just different, lighter, like he didn't have a care in the world. The burns on the tops of his feet were gone and his sore cheek was no more. But the most astonishing thing of all, was that he could see! He didn't know how, but he could see just like if he had his glasses on, better even.

The figure ignored Gunner's questions and took a bite of the cookie. Somehow, its eyes grew larger than they already were and a sound similar to a purring cat erupted from its puffy throat before it devoured the remaining bit. Then it lifted its hand and the rest of the cookies floated up from the plates on the coffee table and sailed toward its gaping mouth. One by one, it demolished the cookies until there wasn't a crumb left. Gunner was in complete awe. He'd never seen anything like it. He picked the milk up and said, "You might need this. Sometimes the chocolate chips can stick to your teeth—"

The milk floated out of the glass in a white globule. The figure slurped it up. Not one drop touched the ground.

"Whoa, how'd you do that?" Gunner slapped his thigh and laughed. "That was so cool! Can you do anything else?"

A footstep creaked at the top of the stairs, and Gunner smelled cigarette smoke. *Daddy.* "Gunner, who the hell're you talking to down there? You woke me up, boy!"

"No one, Daddy! I'm just … I was just seeing if Santa came is all!"

"Well, he ain't gonna bring nothing now, is he? Not with you sniffing around like a damn hound dog! Get on up to bed before I come down there!"

Gunner heard his mother. "Jimmy? Who're you shouting at?"

"Your son is downstairs looking for Santa. Ain't got enough sense yet to figure out he ain't real."

"Jimmy, don't," his mother said.

"Well, he's almost nine years old, Colleen. Damn kid needs to grow up some time, believing in fairy tales and all that is for sissies! And no son of mine is gonna be a sissy if I have anything to say about it!"

Gunner heard his daddy slam the bedroom door and then he heard the arguing start. His heart crumpled in his little chest. "Sorry you had to hear that," he said, then he looked down at his feet and fought the urge to cry.

The figure purred, then moved with lightning speed across the living room and stopped at the foot of the stairs. It looked back at Gunner, then disappeared up the steps before Gunner could even flutter an eye. He heard his parent's bedroom door fly open, and he heard them scream. Their desperate cries for help echoed through the house as things crashed and broke above him, but even when his mother's blood-curdling cry pierced his eardrums, Gunner stayed superglued to the floor. The tree's lights flickered off for a few seconds and then everything went silent.

Gunner swallowed the sawdust lodged in his throat as he watched his daddy come floating down the stairs in nothing but his underwear; his hairy, beefy limbs dangling by his sides like a rag doll. His mother came next, and he winced at the blood that'd soaked through her nightgown and at the way her head looked, like it'd been twisted almost all the way around. The figure followed behind his parents' hovering bodies; its hand held up as if stopping traffic. Gunner wanted call out to them, but he didn't. Then the front door flew open, and he looked on and did nothing as his parents sailed right out of it.

When Gunner finally found his feet, he raced outside, but it was too late. A force shook the ground, and he fell backward into the snow, and by the time he scrambled to get back up, the egg-like ship launched upward like a bullet and disappeared among the stars.

It was morning when Gunner awoke on the floor next to the Christmas tree. He wiped the drool from his chin and looked around in a daze. *Where is everyone?* he wondered. As he scanned the empty room and realized how well he could see, he remembered and ran up the stairs in a hurry. He looked into his parent's bedroom first. The bedsheets were bloody and rumpled and the comforter lay in a heap on the carpet. He stepped around the shattered debris on the floor and looked in their closet, and then in their bathroom. They were gone. They were really, really gone. Next, he ran to his bedroom, then he ran all around the house, calling their names over and over. Still nothing. His body trembled as he began to cry, then a smile spread across his face so wide it hurt. Santa or no Santa, he'd gotten his Christmas wish after all.

LAKE SLUDGE

"How much longer 'fore we get to where we're goin', Robbie? I've got prickly heat somethin' fierce and these bugs're drivin' me crazy!" Peyton Dobeck swatted away the barrage of mosquitoes and gnats attacking his sweaty face and neck.

"We're almost there. Not much farther."

"Well, I don't see why we can't just eat our lunch any ol' where. Why's it gotta be a big deal? And anyhow, Mr. Mitchell—aka your daddy—said we weren't to stray from the trails."

"Since when do you care what our parents say?"

"Since our parents brought us to some raggity ol' woods to go campin' instead of the state park like we usually go to. There ain't even got proper bathrooms out here! I swear I'm gonna drop dead 'fore we get to where we're goin' if ain't comin' up soo—"

"We're there!" Robert moved some low-hanging branches out of the way and both boys came upon a small body of water. "This here is Lake Sludge."

"That ain't no lake. Looks more like a muck pond to me." Peyton plopped down in the sparse grass and pulled a wrapped sandwich from his paper bag.

"Well, it's called Lake Sludge. That's what I was told."

"I don't give a toad's tit what it's called, Robbie, that ain't no lake. Now, I'm hungry, so let's eat."

Robert and Peyton ate their lunch and discussed what they'd do when they were through. Peyton wanted to swim, and when Robert refused, he called him every name under the sun.

"I don't care how many more names you call me … I ain't going in that stank water!" Robert hollered.

"Well, you don't have to, but it's muggier than your grandma's gooch, and I don't see any other way of coolin' off." Peyton pulled his shirt over his head and threw it to the ground. "You're the one who wanted to come out here anyhow."

"Yeah, but not to swim."

Peyton rolled his eyes. "You practically pulled my arm when your mom gave us those paper bags filled with bologna sandwiches and chips and told us to go have a picnic. Which, by the way, a *picnic*? Boys don't have freakin' picnics, Robbie! We have lunch, like real men do."

"Don't be stupid. Boys do to have picnics, ain't no difference than girls doin' it."

"Whatever you say. Well, since we didn't grab no fishin' poles, what're we here for then if we ain't goin' swimmin'? Damn skeeters are suckin' all my blood!"

Robert shrugged. "I don't know. Explore a little, check it out, I guess. I ain't never seen Lake Sludge and wanted to see it for myself. See if it was as creepy as I've been told it was. I heard it used to be a small graveyard, but years ago, due to nearby urban development, it got flooded or somethin'." He noticed a Pepsi bottle and a plastic bag drifting on the water's dark oily surface. The bag's handles swayed in the hot breath of a breeze, as if beckoning him to come in. He shielded his eyes as best he could from the sun's blinding glare and looked around further. There was no hint of any animals that he could see; not a bird, a frog, or even the hiss if a cicada. The sight of a massive Eastern red cedar nudged a memory that made him uneasy, but he decided to shelve it for the moment.

"Urban, wha? What in the heck're you talkin' 'bout, Robbie?"

"De-vel-op-ment. Ya know, buildin' and stuff."

"Oh."

"Anyway, I also heard somethin' else … like that sometimes … it moans."

"Moans? You mean the lake?" Peyton raised his eyebrow.

"Yeah, it moans."

"Robbie, please tell me it wasn't Jodie who told you all this horse pucky?"

"It might've been him." Robert's cheeks reddened.

"Your brother also told us it was bigfoot who dropped a mondo fudge dragon in our tent last time we all went campin', and we both know whose turd that really was, don't we? This here ain't even a lake, it's just some dingy pond. Jodie's been tryin' to scare us since we were shittin' applesauce! You still believe what he says? If this here lake moans, it's prolly a bunch of horny ol' bullfrogs, or hell, maybe it's even Jodie and my sister doing the you-know-what!" Peyton humped the air then held onto his stomach as he laughed.

"Yeah, you're prolly right."

"Prolly? C'mon Robbie—we're almost teenagers! We can't go believin' in this kinda crap no more. This pond might look gross, but it's just water. Besides, we've swam in worse. Remember that ditch fulla tadpoles last summer? Plus, I ain't seen no signs tellin' us *not* to go in."

"It don't smell so good, though, smells like rotten eggs and roadkill." Robert held his nose.

"That's just the way some water smells. I ain't tryin' to pick at you, but the well water that comes out of your house faucet smells like my dog's farts and we drink that!"

"What about ditch lizards? You wanna risk that?"

"Yep, I do. Gators're everywhere, Robbie, it's Florida. But I ain't heard so much as a fish jump since we got here, so I'm guessin' this's just a giant muck puddle just waitin' for someone to dive on in. Look, I'm done tryin' to convince you otherwise. I walked my ass all the way out here and now I wanna go swimmin'. You comin' in or not?"

Robert sighed. "Alright, then. I'll go in up to my knees, but I ain't going no deeper than that!"

"That's the spirit!" Peyton tugged his camo Crocs from his sweaty feet, slid his shorts off, and ran into the water in his underwear. "See ya, wouldn't wanna be ya!"

"I'll be a minute," Robert called, then bent down to untie his hiking boots. His parents would give him a whipping if they knew what he was about to do. He'd already broke one rule by not sticking to the trails and wandering too far from the campsite, but swimming in an unmanned body of water in the middle of the woods? That was enough for him to be knocked into next week; he was cruisin' for a bruisin', as his father liked to say.

And what if Jodie wasn't making it up? What if it really was an old graveyard that'd been buried under water? Jodie seemed to be telling the truth when he told him the story. His eyes had been as big as moon pies, and he never once cracked a smile the entire time. He said he and his friends had come out to Lake Sludge a few months back to check it out, said they heard rumors of it being haunted or something. He said that while they were all out there, one of his friend's dogs chased after a stick they'd thrown in the water, and that when it went to get it, something had pulled the dog under. Robert asked why they didn't try and get the dog back, and Jodie said that when his friend ran toward the water, a series of gurgling moans echoed around them, so they ran off and never looked back.

Jodie said his friends and him later asked around about the lake and that's when they heard about the supposed small graveyard that used to be where the lake was now. Robert had full-on chills when he asked Jodie what he thought actually happened to his friend's dog and where he thought the moans came from. Jodie's face had paled, and then he'd whispered, "The lake, Robbie. It was Lake Sludge. Stay away from it."

Robert shivered as he folded his shirt and shorts and set them neatly atop his boots. Then he stood up and watched Peyton move around in the sketchy water. He kept slapping the surface of it.

"This water's weird—feels like I'm wadin' in warm Jell-O! You comin in' or what?"

"Yeah, I'm comin'. Hold your horses."

Robert's dread-weighted limbs caused him to move slower than normal toward the rank water's edge. The boughs of the massive Eastern red cedar creaked, heavy, warning. What had his ma said about them again? Tingles ran from his toes all the way up to his legs, then tap-danced along his spine and traveled to his scalp. It was like the roots of every hair on his body stood up in panic. He didn't want Peyton to see him shivering, so he bit down on his tongue and tried to ignore the fear that racked his innards. *Calm down*, he told himself.

It's just a little ol' lake, and nothing more! But he couldn't stop seeing the image of his brother's wide eyes and pale face when he'd told him that story. He couldn't stop hearing the fear in his voice. Jodie didn't ever get scared, but he'd been scared. That was a fact.

Peyton was now in up to his waist and was slapping the surface with both hands. "It's cool the way it kinda jiggles! Hurry up, Robbie, you gotta try it!"

Robert stood at the water's edge; his toes grazing the muck. He looked out at the trees and vegetation surrounding the lake and couldn't believe he hadn't noticed earlier. Everything was covered in what looked like black slime. It hung from the bushes, cypress, and oaks like thick snotty moss. The place was like a graveyard. Graveyard? It came back to him then, how his mother had told him Eastern red cedars were special, that they were known as graveyard trees.

It was just two years ago when his mother had told him that; they were visiting their grandmother at the town's cemetery. As their mother had placed fresh flowers in front of Grandma Minnie's headstone, she'd told them she was glad there were so many red cedars where Grandma Minnie was laid to rest. And when they asked why, she'd smiled and said, "Because these trees live very long lives, and they needle a perpetual evergreen foliage that symbolizes eternal life. It's even thought by some Native Americans that they hold the spirits of our ancestors. Isn't that something?"

At the time, Robert had thought it was something, but he'd also been a little scared too. To think that Eastern red cedars were really just trees full of ghosts was pretty dang creepy. As he continued to look at the foreboding tree, he thought it looked hungry. He was about to shout out to Peyton what he saw, but before he could form the words, several large ripples raced across the surface of the water and stopped directly behind his friend. His first thought was, *gators.*

"P-Peyton? There's somethin' behind you!"

"What'd you say? I can't hear you over all this fun I'm havin'!"

"I said, there's somethin'—

The water bubbled like a cauldron behind Peyton and waterlogged moans began to erupt from all around the lake in a terrifying unison. Peyton wailed for help as the water undulated around him and he paddled feverishly to get away and struggled to stay afloat. Robert watched as the water cut off Peyton's urgent pleas by heaving itself into his mouth over and over, and though his friend's strangled cries pierced his pulse filled ears, his feet didn't move an inch. He was glued to the ground. Fear had crippled him.

"H-help! I c-can't br-breathe! Robbie, h-help me," Peyton choked.

"I can't, I'm sorry," Robert muttered, fat tears spilling down his cheeks.

Dozens of arms and hands made of thick black slime reached up from beneath and began to wrap themselves around Peyton's upper body like serpents. They squeezed and squeezed around him until his eyes bulged from their sockets. One of the hands reached for his open mouth and forced its fingers in. It pulled down until his jaw unhinged, then reached down into his throat. Slime oozed from Peyton's eyes and nostrils and gushed from his ears.

Robert watched in horror as his friend's entire face and head became cocooned in thick black slime, and after one last strangled cry for help, Peyton slipped below the surface, his urgent grasping hand the last thing to go under.

Bile, mixed with his dad's famous campground breakfast of griddle-fried eggs and ham, crowded Robert's mouth. He let loose a torrent of hot vomit that splashed onto his bare legs and feet. With his head between his legs and his hands on his knees, he continued to puke until there was nothing but dry heaves. It was only when he felt something grab his foot that he was able to snap to.

A grotesque humanoid form moaned as it launched itself toward him from the water's edge. Robert screamed, then stumbled and fell backward. Tendrils of the black slime shot out from the thing's fingers and arms like sticky webs, then wrapped themselves around his feet before it crept up his legs. Robert flipped himself over and fought as hard as he could to escape the thing's slimy, sticky grasp, but it was too strong and dragged him to the water.

Before he was yanked under, the last thing he saw was a cracked slime-shrouded headstone sticking up out of the ground, wrapped in the roots of the red cedar.

WILD, WILD, WEST

Two men emerged from two different ships and both stood motionless as they observed one another. After nearly five minutes of standing and observing, one of the men began walking in the direction of the other man, who stood with his hands on his hips. The man stopped when he was a few feet away, then he raised his hand and gave a little wave.

"You walked over here to wave? You could've just done that from over there."

"My name is Dragomir Volkov." Dragomir dipped his head as a way of introducing himself.

"Oh, great. Another one of your kind, just what I needed. Out of all the ugly fucking rocks, you had to choose this one?" The man took one of his hands off his hips and pointed at Dragomir. "This one's ours, Spud."

"I see your manners have not changed."

"Say what? Your accent is thicker than a cow-shit milkshake."

"Forget it. I do my business and you do yours."

"But this here rock was already spoken for years ago by our government and you know as well as I do, Spud, that this here is grounds for me to kick your Cosmo ass!"

"Always the cowboys … listen, we both know that even with the Outer Space Treaty and all the foolish laws, none of it matters once we are up here. Our country never agreed to align with your ways. But something tells me you probably already know this."

"What I do know, is that you better get off this goddamn rock and go mine somewhere else, before you've got bigger problems. I was given strict orders to dispose of anyone who tried to mine without consent. Now, we've already been mining this rock for months, and I got partners that're on their way as we speak. Better get, Spud!"

"I take my chance. I have traveled some time to be here. Just like in the middle of ocean, you have no authority. This is space, Cowboy." Dragomir shrugged and began walking away, but when the other man's hand fell on his shoulder, he stopped.

"I don't want to do this, Spud." The man held a weapon in his free hand. "Just get back on your hunka' junk and get on. I won't even tell anyone you were here."

"You are willing to kill me? Over what? I am doing job, just like you. I have family. I have not threatened you, and yet, you are ready to kill. There are plenty materials here for all of us. It is one of the biggest asteroids and boasts some of the most valuable of materials. And we knew about it before you."

"That's not the point, Spud. And if you knew, then why didn't you come first, huh? We've been coming here for a while, and we haven't seen any of you 'til now."

"We wait until you leave to come, then we bring back goods. Is easier that way, no? No one gets hurt and we all get what we want."

"Sneaky, Spud, I see. Well, I'm here now, so get the hell outta here!"

"I cannot do that, Cowboy."

"And why the hell not?"

"I also have strict orders. I must wait until my comrades arrive. They know I am here and they will not be happy if they find me dead."

"Who the hell says they'd find you? Besides, my buddies'll probably arrive before yours."

Dragomir shrugged. "Maybe they do or maybe they don't."

"Well, we might have a real Mexican standoff shortly. Fucking A! I don't need this aggravation. I really don't. I got a family to get home to and a well-deserved vacation from this son of a bitch, giant, jagged piece of shit rock. I've been here for a month … a month! I saw you coming on my screen and got excited. Thought you were gonna be my replacement. Turns out, you're just another dirty space raider."

"I am no space raider. I am a miner, just like you. We all have to make living. I never caught your name, Cowboy?"

"I didn't throw it, Spud. You know what? This never would've happened if they didn't start letting any ol' body become a miner. I should've stayed where I belonged—but the damn money was so enticing! None of us are actual astronauts. Us miners? They look at us like the bottom-feeders of space! They laugh when they send us here. They trained us just enough to get us here and then to do what they needed us to do, but when something breaks, we gotta wait for someone to come get us … or die up here and become petrified space turds!"

"That is too bad. We are trained to fix ships. I am no bottom-feeder, but yes, I hear things about the way your country treats its miners. Very unfortunate, Cowboy."

"Stop with the Cowboy, will ya? Name's Huxley, Huxley Grant. I've been mining going on seven years. Takes its toll, Spud, takes its toll. Listen, I can't let you do this. I'll lose my job and possibly even serve time in the pokey. Give me a break, will ya?" Huxley put his weapon away and held out his hand, but Dragomir didn't take it.

"I cannot give break. I, too, will lose position If I go. I waited for this chance. Not only to bring back raw materials but also, our country is low on water reserves. This asteroid has plenty water. This is not just about money, Cowboy, it is about humanity, and I care deeply for my people. You Americans are greedy. Remember what the Romans said in their legal maxim? What concerns all, must be decided on by all. You cowboys never abided. We all, as whole world, suffer because of it. You blamed others, but it began with you. You think you are the only ones to lay claim on asteroids. You take, take, take!"

"Oh, here we go, the fucking political rigmarole. Blah, blah, fucking blah, Spud! Oh, woe is me, like every other country who dug its own hole and wants to use America as a scapegoat! You know what? Fucking stay here then! Just don't say I didn't warn you, you crooked, long-nosed bastard. When everyone shows up and it becomes a rootin' tootin' gun fight, it'll be too late! You think they'll talk it out? Nope. Ka-boom!" Huxley mimed an explosion with his hands, then he shook his head, turned around, and left Dragomir standing there.

Back at his ship, Huxley tried to think of a way to twist the situation in his favor. He knew that he'd be in deep shit if he didn't alert someone of the Russians' approach. "I knew this shit would happen one day, an all-out war," he said aloud as he pulled his helmet off and lay back his sweaty head, thinking of how to word his message. "Goddamn ugly rocks … just another modern-day gold rush with bigger and better weapons."

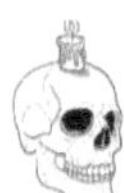

Dragomir watched the American walk back to his ship, then he walked back to his own. He, too, brooded over what to tell his comrades. They were headed to the asteroid, and fast. He was supposed to get rid of the American before they got there. But he signed up to be a miner, not an assassin. He'd purposely left his weapon on the ship, hoping to find a way to settle the matter without murder. Although he admitted to himself that murder seemed more and more appealing every time the Cowboy called him Spud. He thought to himself, *maybe the Cowboy will leave now that he knows more are coming?*

What both men did not know, was there were others watching them, others that were very displeased with their presence. They observed as countless humans plundered and polluted. They surveyed as they contaminated celestial bodies with their sordid foreign microbes and they were incensed.

"What right do these beings have here?" they asked one another. "As anticipated, they have broken their own treaties and laws and now they fight over what is not theirs in the first place. We will not permit them to ruin what is bigger than them. They milked their own resources, and now, like the vile parasites that they are, they think they will spread elsewhere to milk what is not theirs to milk. It is time." The beings nodded in union.

Hours passed and both Huxley and Dragomir contacted their parties. Soon, they'd have to face down the opposition. Locked inside their ships, they sat and waited until suddenly they felt a tremor. It started softly, but then became more intense. Both men pulled on their helmets and grabbed their weapons before exiting.

A large metallic cylinder had planted itself into the bed of the asteroid. The men looked at each other and shook their heads in confusion as they approached it. Without warning, the cylinder shot open, radiating a plume of green fog, and then a hologram materialized. Huxley had to shield his eyes from the hologram's glare. "What in the Devil?"

The hologram was an enormous white glove. The glove flickered for a moment, and then a message appeared in its center. Huxley read it out loud. "Greetings. You have been challenged to a galactic duel. If you should prevail, you will gain the sovereignty of space and be free to plunder to your heart's desire without interference from any other beings. Losers will be punished by death and it will be known that any who try to impose after their loss shall meet a very unfortunate end. We will meet here in twenty-four Earth hours." Then the message began to switch to multiple languages in quick succession.

"This's a joke, right?" Huxley grunted.

"I have no idea." Dragomir reread the message several times.

"A duel?" Huxley chuckled.

"Must be some kind of practical gag, no?"

"I asked you that, Spud. You trying to scare us off? Is that it? Trying to get me all ruffled up so that I'll get my men to retreat?"

"I could ask you same thing," Dragomir spat.

"Well, alright then. A duel, eh? This's the biggest pain in my ass. I'm not sure who's pulling whose leg here, but someone is getting their ass kicked."

"I do not recognize this contraption." Dragomir squinted as he touched the surface of the object. The cylinder abruptly snapped shut, causing Dragomir to stumble, then it shot back up and was gone before either man could blink.

"I don't like this, Spud. I don't like this at all," Huxley said.

"Well, is no dessert for me, Cowboy."

"You mean picnic?"

"Picnic, dessert, both good. This could be joke, no? But then maybe it is not."

"So, you're saying we're gonna have a duel … on a damn asteroid … nicknamed Big Bertha? Unreal! Someone's a real comedian, I tell ya. Look here, I'm gonna go and eat something, maybe, just maybe, rub one out, before this shit hits the fan."

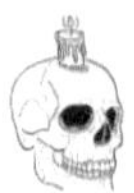

Dragomir and Huxley both returned to their ships. Time passed slowly as worry set in. Neither knew what they'd just witnessed, and they wondered who sent the message and was it serious? As the hours passed, they tried to come to terms with the fact that they might not make it off Big Bertha alive after all.

Several ships began to land. Huxley and Dragomir anxiously greeted their colleagues. Each side convened in private. Soon, most everyone could be seen walking around with a multitude of weapons. Huxley saw Dragomir holding something that made his throat constrict and his mouth go dry. Dragomir carried what looked like a heat blaster. Those things could melt off a man's suit and helmet in mere seconds, turning them into a human grilled cheese. Heat blasters were supposed to be forbidden due to the risks to themselves and their ships.

Huxley's hands shook, and his head hurt. It felt like someone was using his heart for a stress ball. This was not what he signed up for. Not at all.

In a very formal and uniform fashion, people from both sides began walking toward each other. No one smiled, no one waved, and no one lowered their weapons. They stood across from one another by the gaping crater the cylinder had left behind. Dragomir stepped forward first. He lowered his weapon, then he cleared his throat and spoke. "I have been asked to speak for my troop. We are giving you the option to leave now and not come back."

"No can do, Spud. We were here first," Huxley replied and stepped forward. The people behind him all aimed their weapons toward Dragomir.

"You got here first, but we knew about her first. You stole our intelligence. Your people have lots already," Dragomir said.

"Look, who do you think you all are? Huh? You had a lot, too, and you blew it! Every time you fuck up, you think we're supposed to wipe your asses? All of us fucked up one time or another, but at least we're trying to fix it!" Huxley shouted.

"Fix it?" Dragomir scoffed. "For yourselves, yes. You greedy cowboys have always taken what you wanted and never thought about the repercussions! You are mining several asteroids, reaping all the benefits … the rocks were never supposed to be owned. You bullied your way through everything on Earth, and now that it is on the verge of collapse, you have made gains to harness what we need to survive. You made sure to exclude us as part of the list of countries who could join you. You want to have most, so you can give least!"

"Oh, real nice speech, Spud. Now listen up, you all had your shot. Your leaders are no angels. They starved their own people and stepped all over their own. You think we don't remember that? I'm real sick of America getting the bad rap. I really am!"

"We are trying to do what is best right now. We learned from our past, but not you, no, you continue to repeat history. You want us under your proverbial thumb. Like ants, you are always gathering and gathering. When will it be enough? We just want what you do, a chance at another life on earth. Why do you think you can monopolize space?"

"Well, I guess it's like the Wild Wild West up here, isn't it, Spud? All this hateful rhetoric and hyper drama, I'm not so sure you aren't the ones who sent that message," Huxley said.

"And we are not sure you are not the ones who sent message!" Dragomir aimed his weapon toward Huxley's face.

"Us? Look at you! We're not the monsters, Spud. You've always been the monsters. You're the rats of the human race. Dirty rats, all of you!"

"Rats are smart. Rats learn and figure things out. You are like crocodiles, big and strong, but dumb with no logic. You are scum of the earth." Dragomir's nostrils flared behind his helmet.

"And you are all a bunch of backward crooked long-nosed savage bastards!"

Dragomir fired his blaster at Huxley, who ducked and hopped out of the way of the white-hot beam of heat. This action caused both sides to fire their weapons, and then chaos erupted as everyone began running, racing to dodge certain death. No fancy space suit or helmet with its thick faceplates could save them if they were hit.

As Huxley ran for cover, he gasped when he caught a glimpse of Dragomir melting the suit off one of his victims, caramelizing their flesh like burnt sugar on top of a crème brûlée. He was glad he couldn't smell anything and swallowed back the vomit that burned his throat. His own weapon slipped from his hand and he scrambled to pick it up before he continued running.

Huxley hid behind his ship, trying to catch his breath. He peeked around to see more people fall to their deaths amongst the rocky rubble. His heart was beating so fast he couldn't think straight. He squeezed his eyes shut, calmed himself as best he could, then peeked again. Dragomir was roaming around, heat blaster still in hand, and Huxley watched as he destroyed his colleague's ships. Huxley whimpered, then stopped breathing when Dragomir began walking toward his ship. *He's looking for me. He's gonna melt my flesh from atop my bones and I'll never see my wife or kids again … or my dog, Chopper. I hate this fucking rock. I hate it. I hate it. I—*

Huxley didn't wait for Dragomir to reach him. He stood up and came from behind his ship.

"Well, ain't this kinda funny? Just the two of us again, Spud. Some coincidence, huh?"

"Yes, is a bit of coincidence."

"So, you gonna try and leave, or are all the ships toast? I saw you aiming that damn torch gun at 'em."

"I'm not leaving, Cowboy. Come out now. Loser dies, remember? That is how this must end."

"Fucking Rat, Spud," Huxley rasped.

"Fucking Crocodile, Cowboy."

"You know what, Spud?"

"What?"

"I … I never thought it could get any uglier up here on these massive pieces of cold shit. All this goddamn darkness … I-I never thought I'd hate to look at the stars. You ever think that, Spud? That you'd hate lookin' at the stars?" Huxley leaned against his ship, his shoulders shaking. Fat tears slid down his cheeks. There was a time he would've been embarrassed to have anyone see him cry, but he didn't care anymore.

"You are stalling."

"I ain't!" Huxley coughed on his own snot.

"You are."

"Fine! If that's what you want, alright then … you wanna meet by the crater? But no melting me, alright? I-I don't want to go like that … please," Huxley pleaded.

"Was that in rules?"

"I don't know … but I ain't got one of them blasters and a duel should be fair."

"Okie dokie. I use gun, you use gun." Dragomir nodded.

"Fine, then. Step away and start heading off." Huxley was going to try and get into his ship, but Dragomir refused to move. *Shit!*

"One step ahead of you, Cowboy. We both go at same time."

Both men held guns pointed at one another and began the awkward walk around their dead. They reached the crater and then stood facing one another. Huxley sobbed openly. "Well, this is it," he choked.

"Yes. It is."

"Sh-shouldn't we be several p-paces back?"

"I have no idea. I never had duel."

"Well, I'm pretty sure you have to take several steps back before you take a shot." Huxley felt his stomach doing flips.

"Fine. We do that."

"Spud?"

"Yes?"

"I don't really think you're a rat. I just ... I just wanted to make some damn money."

"Perhaps you are no crocodile."

Both men took several steps back, each one slower than the next. When they finally stopped, they stood about twenty feet apart. Both realized they didn't want to do this, but also, both were sure that the other knew who sent the message. They raised their weapons, nodded, and then fired several shots. Both of them were hit several times. Faceplates shattered; they lay on the ground gasping for air that would never come. Their lungs struggled briefly, then collapsed as their blood boiled in their quickly expanding bodies. The spit on their tongues fizzled along with their spilled blood and sweat, which beaded up and evaporated. But before they could enter death's sweet void, their shriveling eyes saw one last horrifying thing.

The ground trembled around the dying foes as a large, luminescent diamond-shaped ship landed nearby. The ship's honeycombed bottom opened and several beings emerged. They floated toward the men, their elongated heads and limbs moving like jellyfish underwater. Eyes protruding like a crab, they looked down at both men, inspecting them as if they were unsure what they were looking at, but then gaping grins spread across the being's sallow faces and they began to laugh, gutturally. When the laughs petered out, they pointed with long spindly fingers and said, "It appears you've lost!"

ALL'S WELL THAT ENDS WELL

Madge was afraid of her refrigerator. It was just last night when she realized something wasn't right with it. She'd gone to get a bowl of Chunky Monkey ice cream and the bottom freezer wouldn't open no matter how hard she tried. She'd pulled and pulled, only giving up when she started to break a sweat. *What could possibly be the problem,* she'd wondered, then yelped and skidded backward when the ice maker began to snarl like a rabid dog. Once she had collected herself, she bent forward to inspect the ice chute.

She didn't see much of anything, but she continued inspecting the chute until a bevy of frozen shards came straight for her eyes. "Son of a bitch," she'd cried and once more skidded backward. It was then that Madge had decided to throw her Chunky Monkey towel in for the night and deal with the rabid appliance in the morning. *Maybe I'll call Rick. He knows how to repair almost anything,* she'd thought, then padded off to bed, rubbing her sore eyes.

When morning came, Madge shuffled groggily to her coffee maker. As soon as she opened the fridge's door and reached inside for the toasted marshmallow creamer, the snarling began. The fridge's door rattled and shook and if she hadn't of jumped out of the way, she might've lost her arm when it slammed itself shut. Despite the door's protest, she tried to pry it back open. "You've gotta be kidding me," she hollered at the fridge. "I just want some goddamn coffee creamer!"

Calling Rick would mean having to deal with his condescending remarks. That's why she'd broken up with him in the first place— well, that and the naked tits and ass of some whore on his phone— but still, she missed him. Plus, she couldn't afford a repairman, not since Rick's departure had left her with the entire amount of the rent and utilities. And the rent was already past due. She picked up her phone, put it back down, sighed, then picked it up again. A groan escaped her lips as she scrolled through her contacts. Her finger hovered over his name. *I really, really hate black coffee*, she thought, and finally allowed her finger to tap the name on the screen.

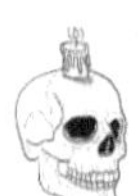

As expected, Rick was an asshole, but Madge sighed with relief when he said he'd come take a look. He showed up with a bag of tools thirty minutes later, looking something like a modern version of James Dean in blue jeans and a white tee that strained against his muscular chest. She kicked herself for not changing out of her sweats or making more of an effort with her bird's nest for hair. As much as she hated to admit it, she was still attracted to him. Over the phone she'd promised that if he could get the fridge to function, she'd cook him some breakfast, but now she wished she hadn't said that. If he stayed longer than he needed to, she was afraid she'd do something she'd regret. She averted looking at the bulge in his form fitting jeans, bit her lip, and willed herself to ignore the tingly feeling she was feeling below.

Almost an hour had already gone by, and Rick was on his second mug of black coffee. He leaned against the counter, bitching about money, his new apartment, and about the few dates he'd been on recently. When he proceeded to open old wounds and somehow blame her for everything going wrong in his life, Madge rolled her eyes. "I didn't ask you over to have you take a giant shit on me, Rick. Can you just look at the damn fridge already?"

"Jeesh. Alright. Can't wait to get in there and stuff your face, huh?" he asked, then chuckled. Rick walked over to the fridge, wiggled his eyebrows, and ran his hand along the door in a seductive manner. "Remember, I get this open and you make me breakfast. I want pancakes and bacon, woman," he jeered.

"Yeah, yeah. I know what I said." Madge nodded, almost thankful for his behavior. Her lust was waning.

"Okay, so you said the door won't open?"

"Yes, and it keeps making this god-awful sound … sorta like a big growling dog."

"Fridges don't growl, Madge. That was probably you when you realized you couldn't get to your precious ice cream! What was your fave again? Chunky Monkey?" He slapped his knees as he laughed.

"You're such an asshole, Rick," Madge spat.

"Damn, still haven't learned to take a joke, I see. You want me to help you or not?"

"Yeah, I do, sorry."

"That's more like it." Rick tried the freezer first and when it didn't open, he pulled on the door again. "Jesus H. Christ, did you super glue these fuckers shut as a new diet trick or something?" He tried again, his face turning red with the effort. "You used Gorilla Glue, didn't you?"

"Just forget it. I'll call Becker." Madge reached for her phone.

"Becker? As in Becker the Pecker? He doesn't know a damn thing about anything!"

"Yeah, well, he's the landlord and he's obligated to fix it."

"No, he's not. You bought this hunka'junk, remember? From that estate sale. Didn't you wonder why they wanted to get rid of a fancy brand-new refrigerator? I told you it was too good to be true. Should've just kept the one that was already in here, but no, you had to have a stainless steel one with a bottom freez—" The fridge growled and Rick wheeled around. "What the fuck was that?"

The door to the fridge flung open and a vile odor filled the kitchen. Rick and Madge covered their noses and stared open-mouthed at rows of dripping metallic fangs. Before anyone could move, a gray whip-like tongue darted forth from between the fridges fangs and wrapped itself around Rick's torso. He screamed as it dragged him toward its eager jaws. Madge struggled to move her feet, and by the time she did, it was too late. She had to let go of Rick's hands if she was to save herself. He was already halfway in. "You bitch, you knew this would happen! This's all your fault! H-help m-me," he cried. Rick's eyes bulged as the tongue squeezed the life from him.

Madge watched in horror as Rick's head disappeared into the orifice of her fridge. The door swung shut with a violent force and a noise resembling a burp vibrated the walls of her kitchen. Then the fridge rumbled and revved like an engine, before the bottom freezer spat out meaty bloody blobs of what she assumed had been her ex-lover. The blobs landed at her feet with a sickening wet plop. Stars danced in front of Madge's eyes, but a pounding on her front door jolted her back to the surface.

"Madge? Madge, you in there?" It was her nosy neighbor, Ms. Beaman. "Madge!"

The door must've been unlocked, because Ms. Beaman was soon standing beside a speechless Madge, patting her on the back. One of Ms. Beaman's pendulous veiny breasts hung free from her terry-cloth robe and she had a head full of pink rollers to match her fuzzy slippers. She rested a liver-spotted hand on Madge's shoulder and said, "I heard screaming and all kinds of carrying on. What happened over here, dear?"

Madge shook her head and shivered. "I-I'm not s-sure," she murmured.

Ms. Beaman wrinkled her nose. "What is that God awful smell?" she asked, then gasped when she finally spotted the mess on the floor. She clucked her tongue as she shuffled around the trail of gore that led to the fridge.

"Ms. Beaman, no! Don't get near it!" Madge managed to shout.

"Don't go near what, dear? What on earth happened—"

A piercing guttural howl frightened Ms. Beaman, causing her to stumble out of her slippers and fall to the floor. She looked up in shock as the fridge's door flung open, revealing its gnashing fangs still streaked with Rick's gristle and guts. Ms. Beaman managed to roll herself over and shrieked as she scrambled to reach for Madge's outstretched hands, but the fridge had already coiled its tongue around the old lady's legs, wrenching her into its ice-cold gullet. It squealed with what sounded like delight as it noisily ground her neighbor into a pulp, then spit her rollers out like pink missiles across the kitchen. Stars danced in front of Madge's eyes again, and this time, she hit the floor with a thud.

It occurred to Madge when she came to, that she needed to call the police. She peeled her face from the cool tile floor and stood up on wobbly legs. Her phone was still atop the counter. As soon as she picked it up, it rang. She yelped and almost dropped it, but caught it between her ribcage and forearm. It was Becker's name that appeared on the screen and tears of hope sprang to her eyes. She took a deep breath, steadied her hand, then swiped *accept call.* "H-hello? B-Becker? Something's happened and—"

"Don't play coy with me, girlie. You know good and well who this is. You owe me over fifteen hundred bucks! And no more sob stories. I want my freakin' money. To-day!"

Madge blinked her tears away and forced herself to smile before she answered. *Fake it till you make it, girlie.* "Today, absolutely. I have it now actually, if you wanna come on over and get it?"

"Great. I hope it's cash."

"Just so happens that it is. One more thing, Becker ..." Madge looked over at the refrigerator and felt only a single tinge of guilt. "Could you have a look at my fridge? I know it's not your problem, but it's acting up and I don't know what to do about it. I could really use your help."

"If you throw in an extra fifty bucks, but yeah, sure, whatever, I'll have a look. I'll be there in an hour."

"Perfect, see ya soon." Madge hung up with a real smile on her face this time, then went and grabbed a bottle of bleach along with a mop and a bucket.

ACKNOWLEDGEMENTS

I'd like to give great thanks to:

First and foremost, my husband, Chip, because without him, I'd have never taken the leap to do any of this. He is the most encouraging human I know, and his continuous enthusiasm for my work, along with his love and support, keeps me going.

My grandfather, the best grandpa and greatest storyteller that ever lived.

My mother for encouraging and nurturing my imagination and buying me so many books.

My late Aunt Maddie who also encouraged me to read and be creative.

Stephanie Ellis, a gifted writer, editor, friend, and mentor. This book literally would not exist without her!

Catherine McCarthy, a truly gifted writer and friend who wrote the fabulous introduction to this collection. She is always there when I need her and knows just when to tell me to stop being daft.

My big brothers, John and Matthew. Growing up wasn't always easy, but we made it. Thanks for being silly with me.

To my baby cousin, Steven, who has every single book I am a part of on his shelf.

To all at Brigids Gate Press, especially S.D. Vassallo and Heather Ventura, you are truly genuine human beings and I am very grateful that you gave my words a place to come alive and be read.

And I want to mention some people who have always said positive things to me, inspired me, or taught me something: Rhonda Jackson Garcia, Manny Torres, Kenzie Jennings, Brennan Lafaro, Candace Nola, Ronald Kelly, Ken Mckinley, Kev Harrison, Lauren Bolger, Laurel Hightower, Joe R. Lansdale, Mark Scioneaux, Lori Michelle Booth, S.A Cosby, SJ Townend, Kevin Kangas, Janine Pipe, Robert Essig, Joe Spagnola, S.C. Mendes, Chrystal Grundy, Rebecca Rowland, Shane Douglas Keene, Gabino Iglesias, Lindy Ryan, Josh Malerman, and also every editor I have ever worked with. Thank you, thank you, thank you. You are appreciated.

Lastly, a shout out to my haters and those who never believed in me. Thank you for being the gasoline to my internal fire.

ABOUT THE AUTHOR

Vivian Kasley hails from the land of the strange and unusual, Florida! She's a writer of short stories and poetry. Her words haunt places such as Written Backwards, Cemetery Gates Media, Brigids Gate Press, Vastarien, Ghost Orchid Press, Death's Head Press, October Nights Press, The Denver Horror Collective, and poetry in Black Spot Books inaugural women in horror poetry showcase: *Under Her Skin* and *Under Her Eye*. She definitely has more in the works, including her second collection *Room for Dessert*. When not writing or subbing at the local middle school, she spends time reading in bubble baths, walking through graveyards, snuggling her rescue animals, going on adventures with her partner, and searching for seashells and other treasure along the beach.

https://www.facebook.com/bizarrebabewhowrites/
amazon.com/author/viviankasley
https://twitter.com/VKasley

MORE FROM BRIGIDS GATE PRESS

LOVE THE SINNER

Mo Moshaty

According to Dante, a sin is the misdirection of love - the human will, or essentially, the direction of our beings. *Love the Sinner* is an examination of just how those sins can kaleidoscope into horrific consequences creating a distorted and deadly landscape. These stories stand stark before you in full glaring misstep and macabre to show the human psyche in all its twisted reality.

From grief and its rage to medical meddling to ensure a new world order to bloody revenge within a quantum leap, these stories seek to solidify one absolute truth: man is the scariest monster.

EXTINCTION HYMNS

Eric Raglin

A vengeful owl haunts the man who poached her. A desperate entrepreneur holds a ghost hostage for profit. An addict finds hope and terror in an imprisoned angel. A father and son search their dying world for something to eat other than human flesh. Eric Raglin, author of *Nightmare Yearnings*, returns with his second collection of horror and weird fiction. Strange, terrifying, and tender, these eighteen stories explore what happens when extinction comes for us all.

SICK GIRL SCREAMS

S.J. Townend

Woven together by the black ribbon of grief, with whispers of haunted children, feminism, and the unnerving concept of infinity, this inaugural collection of dark fiction by SJ Townend is an eclectic mixture of reprints and original material.

Prepare to unravel.

So Red and Other Tales of Madness

Mia Dalia

From Mia Dalia, the author of *Estate Sale*, *Haven*, and other **literary nightmares**, comes a uniquely **terrifying** collection of dark psychological fiction, featuring novelettes and short stories that range from **horror** to suspense to mystery to coming-of-age to thrillers.

SMILE SO RED - a man finds a strange graffitied house in the woods and a smiling darkness that follows him home.

SPINDEL - a twelve-year-old boy suspects that one of the neighbors on his paper route might be a local serial killer and sets off to investigate.

BLUES FOR THE SOUL - a library worker tries to help a troubled young boy and uncovers a terrible truth about his family.

DEVIL'S CHORD - return to the world of *Smile So Red* with a meta journey set to the earworm tune of your worst **nightmares**.

STUMP - a bullied young boy and a downtrodden family man from the same apartment complex unwittingly entrust their secrets to the same remnant of an old tree in the local woods.

FLAMINGOS - two sisters must confront their troubled past when a buried memory is triggered by the seemingly innocuous plastic lawn birds.

THE TRUNK - striving to achieve the American Dream, a first-generation immigrant from a war-torn country buys a new home and finds something in the basement that has other ideas for him.

REDDEST - another return to the world of *Smile So Red*, albeit from a very different perspective.

Go on. Turn the page. Pick a nightmare. I dare you.

Visit our website at: www.brigidsgatepress.com

www.ingramcontent.com/pod-product-compliance
Lightning Source LLC
Chambersburg PA
CBHW020801310726
48969CB00002B/648

* 9 7 8 1 9 6 3 3 5 5 3 7 6 *